Ashes to Ashes

Barbara Nadel

headline

First published in 2008
by HEADLINE PUBLISHING GROUP

First published in paperback in 2009
by HEADLINE PUBLISHING GROUP

1

Cataloguing in Publication Data is available from the British Library

Hardback ISBN 978 0 7553 7974 3

Typeset in Caslon by Avon DataSet Ltd,
Bidford-on-Avon, Warwickshire

Printed and bound in Great Britain by Clays Ltd, St Ives plc

Headline's policy is to use papers that are natural, renewable and recyclable products and made from wood grown in sustainable forests. The logging and manufacturing processes are expected to conform to the environmental regulations of the country of origin.

HEADLINE PUBLISHING GROUP
An Hachette Livre UK Company
338 Euston Road
London NW1 3BH

www.headline.co.uk
www.hachettelivre.co.uk

To my grandfather, who ran through the flames.

Resurgam

Acknowledgements

My thanks to the staff of St Paul's Chapterhouse for their assistance and for showing me around some of the areas not normally accessible to the public.

Prologue

The girl had already gone when I arrived. I don't remember seeing her. People described her to me; they described her to each other, too.

'Long blond hair down to her waist. Like an angel,' one bloke said.

'You think?' The speaker, a middle-aged woman who had just a hint of old Russia, via the Mile End Road, in her voice, looked a bit disgusted. 'You can't've heard the language she was using. A child like that!' She shrugged. 'Terrible!'

'Probably from the East End,' another, much younger and extremely posh-looking woman said.

The East End is my home, and so whatever was going on either inside or outside the great cathedral, I wasn't having that. We're not all toe-rags and shysters.

'I – er – I – um . . .' The stuttering that comes upon me when the bombs begin to fall drives me barmy. 'Just because she might be from the East End, d-don't m-mean the kid's a bad'un,' I blurted.

Something heavy and packed with high explosive detonated somewhere nearby and the whole building shook. Thin spirals of loose plaster threaded down from the ceiling of the crypt and on to our heads.

'Bleedin' 'ell!' the Russian-via-the-Mile-End-Road woman said. Then she said something I recognised, even if I didn't understand it, in Yiddish.

'Excuse me!' the posh woman responded. 'Madam, you are in a house of God, you know! I know it's not *your* house of God, but . . .'

From the look on the older woman's face, Jewish–Christian relations were about to take a turn for the worse. I would have intervened myself if I'd been able, but I had the pictures in my head by that time, of men and horses drowning in seas of mud, buried alive. The bombing happening these days makes me go back in my mind to the Great War. I went to that war a young man and came back a lunatic. While I whimpered at the images that terrify me, another bloke said, 'Look the important thing is that the little girl was in here when all of this bombing began and now she isn't!'

'Well, she must've gone outside or something then,' the posh woman said.

'Why would she do that?' the man who had described her as an angel – probably a volunteer fire watcher – said. 'It's hell out there!'

We all looked up towards the blackened ceiling of the crypt and I felt a shiver go down my back. The volunteer wasn't wrong. It was hell. I didn't know how long it had taken me to get to the cathedral through the fiery streets of London. The experience of so many attempts to pass this way or that only to be blocked by burning or collapsed buildings had shattered me and I was exhausted. I'd finally fetched up here because the cathedral was the only place I could see. The smoke was thick and the heat was so intense that lesser buildings were melting in it. I'm not religious, I hadn't come to the cathedral out of some sort of need to be closer to Jesus; I'd come because I was terrified. I'd have walked into the arms of the Devil if he'd have said he'd deliver me from the flames. As it was, I ran into something that had been built to last – or so I hoped.

'Anyway, why are we even talking about the whereabouts of a child none of us know?' another volunteer continued. 'She can't be outside, I can't believe that even a stupid kid would go out there. And if she's inside, then she's all right for now. What's important at the moment is that those of us who can, save the building.'

'You're saying that a place is more important than someone's life?' a smart man, a city type by the look of him, asked. Already shaking his head in disapproval he, like me, knew the answer anyway. Some volunteer fire watchers can get very funny about the buildings they're detailed off to protect – especially the blokes on the big, famous places.

'No,' the second volunteer said. But then he pulled a face. 'People are important, of course they are! Some more than others, but buildings are important too. This place is very important, as I think we all know.'

'That is appalling,' the city type said flatly. 'To even consider equating a human life with bricks and mortar! Appalling!'

'Listen, sir,' the volunteer said as he began to move towards the city bloke, 'this place is everything! The cathedral is the heart of this great capital!'

The city type cringed – which was not surprising, seeing as the volunteer was as keyed up and red in the face as he was.

'Calm down, Wally!' the first volunteer said, putting a hand on the second bloke's shoulder as he stood up and walked towards the stairs that led up out of the crypt. 'I'm going to have a look up top.'

Outside, the sound of ack-ack fire and the dull thud of landing incendiary devices joined the crackling of the fires that I knew were all around us.

'And anyway, you're not even supposed to be here!' Wally continued. 'No one from outside the cathedral is meant to be in here.'

One of the ladies, who was, apparently, part of the cathedral's little first-aid post, intervened. 'It's all right, Mr Smith,' she said to him. 'On a night like this, people must shelter where they can. It's our Christian duty to—'

'What's that to me? I care about the building!' Wally said. I could see that there were tears in his eyes now

– the tears of strain and of obsession. Men get like that in war, when their nerves have shredded to nothing. 'The child's gone, she—'

'Well, we can't just forget about her!' the city man said. 'She's a little girl.'

'With a dirty mouth,' the Jewish lady put in.

'Yes, well, with a dirty mouth and . . . Look, what are we going to do about her?'

Maybe if someone else had spoken, I would have kept schtum. But I didn't like the idea of a little kid being out and about on her own in the middle of what could be the biggest bombing raid on London in history. It was certainly the worst one I'd ever seen and I've seen a lot. 'I n-never saw her,' I stuttered. 'W-what did she l-look like? T-tell me again.'

'Blonde, dirty mouth,' the Jewish woman said.

'Dirty face too, as I recall,' the city bloke added. 'She came in with someone . . .'

'Mr Phillips,' Wally said. He was calm again now, no longer squaring up to the other gent.

'Mr Phillips?'

'He's another volunteer. Up in the Whispering Gallery now.'

'She's probably ten years old at the most,' the posh woman said to me. 'Very soiled clothes. *Very* dirty face, but quite pretty, I suppose, underneath it all.' She frowned. 'What exactly are you . . . Mr – er . . .'

I stood up. 'I – er – I'll go and l-look for her,' I said.

'Look for her?'

'Up in the er . . .' I pointed upwards to where small pieces of plaster still drifted down from the ceiling.

Mr Smith was not amused. 'Up in the cathedral?' he said. He moved towards me now in, I felt, a threatening sort of way. 'Don't you go getting in the way of the chaps protecting the building, will you? What they're doing, what we're all doing, is vital for the war effort! If Hitler and his *Luftwaffe* raze this place to the ground . . .'

Everyone knew how much Adolf wanted St Paul's Cathedral reduced to dust and ashes – even me. 'I won't m-make a b-bother,' I said. I couldn't say 'nuisance', which is what I'd wanted to say, it was just too hard. So many things are, when the bombs begin to fall.

Mr Smith, who was a short, stocky bloke, looked up at me with suspicion on his face. Obviously an educated man, I imagined that he was probably a city architect like most of the St Paul's fire watchers; it wasn't every day he met a tall, skinny bloke with skin as brown as a nut. It crossed my mind that he probably thought I was a Jew; a lot of people do. But I said nothing.

'Just you make sure that you don't get in the way, Mr – er . . .' he said as he watched me walk towards the stairs that led out of the crypt and up into the cathedral.

I stopped and turned. 'Name's H-Hancock,' I said. 'F-Francis H-Hancock.'

I don't know why I wanted to see the look on his face when I told him my very un-Jewish name, but I just did. As it happened, he didn't look surprised at all, but then who I was and what I was doing, didn't mean much to him – or anyone else, for that matter. London was burning and I was off to find a little girl with a nasty mouth. I, it was quite clear, wasn't quite right.

Chapter One

29 December 1940, 18.08, Public Warning

What follows here is a mixture of what is known by everyone and what is secret. Whether the full facts of that terrible night as I experienced it will ever truly be revealed, I do not know. This is a tale told by a madman, which doesn't mean that it doesn't signify anything. Quite the opposite.

I heard the air raid sirens whine into life at around ten past six. I was just about to leave my great aunt Annie's flat in Clerkenwell when both of us heard it go. Annie, who is my late father's aunt, is nearly a hundred years old and, as a consequence, isn't too bothered about sheltering or any of that nonsense. She also knows me better than to suggest that I do something like that too.

'You'd best get going, Frank,' she said as she pushed herself out of her battered old button-back chair. 'Get out while all the silly buggers are getting in to their horrible dingy old shelters.'

I smiled. For some reason Annie seemed to understand my need to be out and running the streets every time the bombing started better than most. A lot of people know why I do it, but not many of them sympathise with me. My mum, for instance. I know she feels it's selfish and in a way it is; I could very easily be killed out on the street. I can't help doing it, though. It's not an excuse, but I'm not what anyone would call sane.

Francis Thomas Hancock, that's me. Undertaker, old soldier and lunatic. On and off I spent four years fighting for king and country in the Great War of 1914–18. Unlike most of my mates who also went, I got out of it with my life – or, rather, a life of sorts. Everything frightens me – dark places, confined spaces, losing those I love, falling bombs and the potential they have for bursting bodies open, for vaporising people, for burying men and women alive. I've never been 'right' ever since the trenches, but I was better than this. Now, ever since all of this bombing started back in September, I haven't been sure about anything. Horror is an everyday, or night-time, thing. I conduct a funeral at any of the graveyards in my home manor of West Ham, and I'm not sure that any of the stranger things I'm seeing are real or not. Burying a coffin full of something that once lived down by our great Royal Docks, I look about me and I see a human bone in a tree, a bit of a rank shroud hanging off a bush or a flower. Our graveyards as well as our homes and businesses are bombed on a nightly basis. But is the bone really there? Is the shroud? Is what I'm seeing 'now' or maybe bits of 'back then' when all of my young life was given over to the ripping apart of human bodies and the indignities of their so-called burials? My father was an undertaker, and his father before him, and so giving the dead a decent send-off is in my blood. The Great War denied our poor servicemen that, our stupid generals threw them away like worn-out tea leaves.

'It was good of you to come over and see me,' Annie

said as she walked with me towards her front door. 'Give my best to your mother and the girls.'

We, my mother, my sisters and myself, live above our undertaking business which is in the middle of the borough, in Plaistow. My mother, a Christian Indian lady from Calcutta, is largely responsible for the colour of my skin and that of my older sister Nancy. Aggie, my younger sister, takes after our late father. Just as Annie once was, Aggie is a true blonde, a Hancock girl and it's Aggie who married and has kids. Not that her husband proved to be any good. He hopped off with another woman years ago, leaving my sister with two nippers, who have, of course, been evacuated to the country. I'm the only man in our house now, God help me.

'Goodbye, A-Annie,' I said as I reached the door and the reality behind the drone of this particular group of bombers from above hit me for the first time. 'What will you, er . . . Are you going to the s-shelter this time?'

I don't know why I asked. I knew she always just sat by her range and drank tea when the raids were on. Perhaps I had a premonition of what was about to happen. Perhaps because of it I needed some sort of assurance that Annie was going to be safe.

'Frank Hancock, when did you ever see me go into any shelter? No, no, no!' Annie waved a tiny, blue-veined hand at me and said, 'Can't stand either the company or the smell!'

As well as, for me, the problem of being buried alive in a shelter, there are other worries, too. Sometimes whoever you are sitting with isn't very nice; some people do some very strange things in shelters – it isn't all knitting and playing games of Monopoly! Babies are conceived in shelters, believe you me; men and women burp and break wind and die in them every day. And as for the toilets, where there are toilets . . .

'It was good of you to come, Frank,' she said as she opened the door and let me out into the gloomy, blacked-out street. Annie lives almost in Finsbury, just to the north of Mount Pleasant Sorting Office on Wilmington Square. We'd been visiting Annie all my life, but in spite of knowing her for forty-eight years, I realised that evening, as I began to run away from her flat as if the Devil was on my heels, that she was actually quite a mystery to me. She'd never married or, in my lifetime at least, had a job, and yet she owned her flat outright. There was a rumour in the family that

Annie had once had some sort of career on the stage, scandalous when she'd been young. But she'd never said anything about that to me and I wasn't about to ask. I might be nearly fifty, but even at my great age you don't ask about old people's private business. It's not done.

I don't know where the first bomb landed, but it felt as if it wasn't very far away. Usually if I'm away from home during a raid, I try to move myself in the general direction of Plaistow. In the blackout it's never easy to see where you're going and quite often I lose my way in the panic of the moment, but I remember thinking that what I should be doing was going south on the Farringdon Road. I also remember, because I looked up and saw it hanging in the sky like a huge silver rivet, that there was a full moon. Whether or not I thought at the time this was a bad sign, given what was to come, I don't now recall. Our own guns started up then, ack-ack fire lighting up the sky and those great fat-bellied barrage balloons. But none of that made any difference to what was coming down from the bombers up above. Our shells were bursting without apparently making contact with anything. I looked up at one point and saw against the light from the guns and the radiance from the moon what looked like great bundles of sticks falling down on London. Incendiaries.

Incendiary bombs are small. They don't make much noise when they hit the ground. In fact, to my way of thinking, they sound rather gentle. After the initial metallic clunk on the pavement their cases sound a bit like leaves scuttling across the ground, when they land. But then they burst into flame and some of them don't stop there. Some of them catch fire and then they explode. Within seconds, or so it seemed, there were hundreds of them, all around me. As they fell, I danced to avoid them, skipping and hopping along the pavement like a crazed ballerina. Windows behind, to the side and in front of me burst as the heat from the incendiaries melted them. As well as skipping I also threw both my arms across my eyes so I didn't get blinded by flying glass.

I don't remember doing it, but I came off the Farringdon Road at some point. I remember Smithfield meat market because there were a few people around and about and in the City at this time of night, on a Sunday, that was unusual. But, as I and millions of other Londoners were soon to learn, that emptiness was the whole point behind this raid. The City was quiet and vulnerable just the way Adolf and his mates knew it would be.

Around the market the incendiaries appeared to thin out. Such an enormous number of them wasn't what we were used to. Normally if they hit the ground a bucketful of sand thrown over the top of each one will finish the little blighter off. But hundreds all falling at once meant that, especially in a thinly populated area, those not put out immediately, continued to burn and then set fire to whatever was around them. Caught on top of roofs or in gutters the buggers are nearly always lethal. Getting up there to hook one or more down is very dangerous. Buildings were beginning to catch fire around me and although I could see and hear fire fighters and others doing their best to put them out, there was a sense that something unstoppable was beginning to take hold even at that early stage.

From what I later learned from the people in St Paul's crypt, the girl with the long blond hair and the not so savoury mouth arrived shortly after the bombing raid began. She came in at the same time as a Mr Phillips, one of the architects who acted as fire watchers to the cathedral. They used architects because the building is complex – lots of hidden corridors, an inner 'skin' beneath the famous dome, and lots of very flammable material. Mr Phillips, it was said, went off about his business fairly quickly. People thought the girl had just happened to come in with the man at the same time. The young posh lady, however, begged to differ. She saw, so she claimed, something in the child's eyes that seemed to find the architect familiar. The others disagreed.

'"Effin' 'ot" is what I heard her say,' the Jewish woman said. '"Effin' 'ot!" Blimey, we was all horrified at that! The man with her just turned tail and went! Disgusted, if you ask me!'

The child, whose name no one had bothered to find out, had made quite an impression. She was rude and coarse but with a face and colouring that most people seemed to think belied her behaviour. Like me she'd come in to the cathedral to shelter from the fires that were beginning to melt London's streets. Not many people, let alone children, actually live in the Square Mile or City of London, so where she'd come from was anybody's guess. After all, as I later pointed out to my fellow shelterers, it's not just East Enders who swear. And it isn't just little girls who don't necessarily want to talk about their experiences when they've just come through something that looks like the fires of hell.

It was after Smithfield, as I headed east, that things started to go really wrong for me. London is still, in the way it's laid out, a medieval city. There are big roads like Gracechurch Street and Leadenhall Street, where Lloyds of London has its elegant offices. But much of the City consists of little roads, courts and lanes that date from God alone knows when. They have some strange and clearly very ancient names. 'Stew Lane' down by Southwark Bridge is one; 'Bleeding Heart Yard' off the jewellery quarter at Hatton Garden is another. As someone who was brought up a Catholic, even if I haven't been to Mass since well before the Great War, I recognise 'Bleeding Heart' as a name that must have come from before the Reformation. The Sacred and usually Bleeding Heart of Jesus is an image that I don't see every day in this mainly Protestant

England of ours. But on Sundays, when I was a child, there it was, in a side chapel of our church; Jesus pointing to his exposed red and bleeding heart, frightening kids like me rigid. I don't believe in him any more than I believe in Father Christmas, but I called out to Jesus and the Virgin Mary as I ran from one dead-end court or alleyway to the next. I say 'dead end', but they weren't always blocked by actual buildings; sometimes where a house or a pub had been there was just a fire, huge white-hot flames lapping up into a sky filled with ack-ack noise and drowning in an ever widening sea of smoke. Everything looked the same after a bit. I ran from one tiny lane to the next identical, melting and disintegrating place. The bloody incendiaries had come down in such numbers that everything was burning. In my head the voices left over from the Great War told me I was sure to die. Sometimes when I'm in trouble and they do this, I get angry. But not this time. This time I believed every word they said. This time I invited the buggers to come and get me if they wanted to! When a window exploded almost in my face I fancied that it was some sort of devilish answer and I screamed.

Whether I was actually on Ludgate Hill or in some tiny, disintegrating court just off it, I don't know, but at some point I saw the cathedral from the front. Because St Paul's is at the top of Ludgate Hill, I must have been near it because when the smoke around me cleared for a moment, I saw the whole of the western façade with its two great towers shining down at me. It was the only thing, the *only* thing that wasn't crashing down or melting around me.

Two blokes, firemen holding on for dear life to a dirty great hose they had trained on what had once been a warehouse, saw where I was looking and one of them shouted, 'Get up there, mate! It's your only hope!'

I looked again, through eyelashes caked with soot and air flooded with smoke and what little water the firemen were hurling into the fire. White, in spite of everything against the blackened screaming sky, St Paul's was all I could see, all I felt even a papist like me could trust. I began to make my way towards it as the paving stones fractured and went liquid beneath my feet. I thought I would be safe in the cathedral. I was right in a way, but I was also more wrong than I could ever have imagined.

Chapter Two

So once I was, as I thought, safe inside St Paul's, why did I volunteer to go off and look for a child I hadn't even seen? I'd only been in that crypt for fifteen minutes at the most, I was exhausted, and getting in there in the first place hadn't been any sort of picnic.

Once I'd decided to head for the cathedral, that was it. Wheezing like a pair of broken old bellows, I'd stumbled up to that great double door at the front and I'd hammered and screamed for what seemed like hours. No one came. Some 'sanctuary' this was, I thought! Typical bloody religion, all show and no do! I didn't, to be truthful, think I would die at that point. Behind those enormous columns in front of the entrance you can get a feeling of solidity and even safety. That the screams and curses from the Somme were jabbering in my head was nothing new, and I just kept on fighting to get into the building in spite of them. It was, however, still a shock when something tapped me on the shoulder. Turning, I saw what I thought was a skeleton looking at me. I did, I will own up, scream.

'What are you doing? Who are you?' the skeleton said. It was, I could now see, wearing a long black cassock and its face, though moulded closely on a skull, was covered with skin.

I opened my mouth, but nothing came out. The stuttering when the bombing starts is bad enough on its own, but my lungs were full of smoke and soot too, and so I was completely speechless.

'Well, you can't come in here!' the skeleton said. 'We've a job to do and we've enough people to look after here already!'

I could just make out where he'd come from so quickly. On each side of that entrance, the Great West Door, are two smaller entrances. The one on the left was, I could now make out, open. The skeletal priest, or whatever he was, wasn't alone either. A bloke, little more than a boy, in a tin hat – which looked comical along with his cassock – was behind him.

'Oh, we can't turn people away, Mr Andrews!' the young lad said. 'Wouldn't be Christian.' He then leaned in towards me to get a better look at my face. 'Looks like one of those poor refugees. You know, from Czechoslovakia and Poland.'

'George, my dear boy, we can't have all and sundry—'

A whole canister of incendiaries burst on to the ground about halfway down Ludgate Hill. We all turned to look at the soft, almost silent bouncing of the things as they split up to do their evil business. I'd been where they were only minutes before. Nothing but silence and darkness at first and then, as we all knew they would, they began to burn brightly with that greenish glow they have and with the menacing promise of what we all knew was to come. The men fighting the fires that were already raging down there screamed at each other to 'put them bastards out!'.

In the breathless semi-darkness the young lad George looked at the older man and said, '"Behold, I stand at the door and knock; if any man hear my voice, and open the door, I will come and sup with him . . ."'

'George, we can't just have any old Tom, Dick and—'

'". . . and he with me." Revelations, Chapter Three, Verse Twenty, Mr Andrews,' George said as he looked down at me now. 'Jesus would let this man—'

And then the first fire from that canister of incendiaries began. It must have landed on something that was very easy to burn. Halfway up a building, on a ledge of some sort, a fire began. The flames must have reached a good eighteen feet or so as we looked on. It took only seconds. There were screams.

'Bloody hell!' young George said.

The frightening-looking Mr Andrews began to tell him off but when the whole street in front of us disappeared, or, rather, was eaten by the hungriest flames even I had seen so far, he helped the boy pull me inside the building. As the door slammed behind us the screams from the street had solidified into one terrifying howl. Exhausted, I hit the floor. God, but it was dark in that cathedral! Of course once I looked up I could see light from both the fires outside and the traces from our guns shining through some of the windows up in the dome. But down in the cathedral it was black save for a dim red lamp that glowed beneath the dome on the floor. I could still feel young George's hands on my jacket once the door to that hell outside had closed behind us. As I lay on the floor I also felt the swish of a cassock against my face as Mr Andrews disappeared off somewhere or other. I heard him speak just once as he went. 'Take him down to the crypt with the other waifs and strays,' he said as the cathedral echoed emptily behind him.

'He – er – h-he s-sounds cross,' I said once I'd managed to get my wits together enough to speak.

'Oh, you're English,' George said. He was shining a dim torch into my face now which also meant that I could see him too. His cheeks were chubby, and he looked more like a cherub than a young lad.

'Y-yes . . .'

'I'm sorry, I thought you might be a refugee,' he said as he pulled me up to my feet. 'There are so many about nowadays. I feel so sorry for them, don't you? There are some other people sheltering in the crypt. I'll take you down to them.'

Something fell down from somewhere and hit the

cathedral floor with a crash. George tugged on my arm and so I followed him down to where the small group of other shelterers from outside the cathedral were sitting with the ladies who provided first-aid support to the Watch – wives of those who worked in the church. There were also, the vocal Mr Smith included, members of the Watch itself taking rest breaks down there too.

St Paul's Fire Watch is mainly made up of men from the Royal Institute of British Architects. It was formed originally in the Great War to protect the cathedral from Zeppelins. But in 1939 it was reformed to deal with this latest bloody madness. Mr Smith, Mr Neeson and two others were resting on cots when I entered the crypt. One or two of them looked at me and I think the other shelterers, too, with not very well disguised contempt. What they thought we might be able to do out amongst the fires I couldn't even imagine. But then for me personally being in the crypt, though safe from the flames for the time being, quickly proved to not be a good idea. I don't know what, even now, St Paul's Cathedral weighs, but it's heavy, there's a lot of it, and in my head all I could hear was the sound of it caving in and crushing me. Burying me alive, just like the mud of Flanders had buried so many of my mates, smothering the last bit of life out of them. I knew as soon as I sat down next to the Jewish lady that I couldn't be there for very long. As the young lad George left, so the noises in my head grew louder, voices describing how it would be to drown in dust and mud and rubbish. After Mr Neeson had said hello and I'd exchanged a few words with him, I began to hum, tunelessly. I sometimes do this particularly if I'm with other people I don't know. It stops me answering the voices back. But the lady by my side didn't like my humming.

'Can you stop that, please, sir,' she said. In her eyes, I could see her disapproval of me quite apart from the humming. She was Jewish, but I was a 'darkie' and I noticed that she shuffled just slightly away from me as I sat down. I shut up. Words kept on wanting to burst out of my mouth, especially when there were very big explosions outside, but I held them in. I held them in until the subject of that young girl came up. I'll be honest, the disappearance of the girl with the blond hair and the dirty mouth was the perfect excuse for me to get out of there and up above ground once again. So I volunteered for it. I would have crawled across glass and fought anyone else who might have wanted to do it instead of me, and so what happened afterwards was in a way, my own fault. I have only myself to blame for young Milly and the story of her, me and the night of 29 December 1940.

As soon as I got to the top of the stairs up into the body of the cathedral I knew I was going to have my work cut out for me. From the sound of it incendiaries were falling in their hundreds, on to the roof. There was noise, if not light, everywhere.

A bloke's voice said, 'The dry riser's packed up! Dean, we've got no water!'

'Thank the good Lord that we have reserves!' a flustered but nevertheless posh voice replied. 'We will have to use the stirrup pumps, sand bags . . .'

There was water, but apparently the main supply had failed. The Dean, the man in charge of the cathedral, had sounded to me confident of what he called his reserves, but in the meantime, men were running in the direction of the cathedral's many roofs.

Every part of the building has its own roof – the nave, the dome, the Great West Door. So many places for incendiary devices to lodge their evil selves!

I'd been told that Mr Phillips, the watchman who had apparently brought the little blonde girl into the cathedral, was up in the Whispering Gallery. Unless I came across the child by chance in the church itself, it seemed to me a good first step in locating her was to talk to Mr Phillips. But then a lot of other people, if the sound of the boots on the stairs to the upper parts of building were anything to go by, were going up there too, the Whispering Gallery being a first step, as it were, to getting out on to the cathedral roof tops above. If I joined their ranks, I'd probably be in the way.

'What are you doing?'

I looked around and saw, through the gloom, a familiar tin hat above a cherub's face. It was not, however, a face at rest. It was strained, older-looking than it really was and the eyes were shining with something I must admit I found alarming.

'Er . . .'

'Listen, Mr . . .' George said. 'There are hundreds

of these fire bombs hitting our roof, we've no actual water supply, and so the Watch are having to soak the dreadful things using stirrup pumps. We're being attacked, Mr . . .'

'H-Hancock.'

'Mr Hancock, I think that Hitler wants us this night!' George said. 'I think he wants the cathedral!' One of his arms shot out towards me and briefly grabbed my shoulder. 'We have to stop him! We *are* stopping him!'

And then as quickly as he'd arrived, he left, running towards the stairs I felt I should be going up. George, whatever his position in the cathedral, was going to go and do his bit to protect it. I was, if I were honest, just getting away from the crypt and my own fear of being buried alive. Christ Almighty, I didn't even have a torch to help me look for this little girl! I stood by the red lamp underneath the dome, stock still as if I were waiting for a bus.

But then what was I supposed to do? What could someone like me even think about doing? I bury the dead. Sometimes, these days, I don't even do that properly, by which I mean that I don't always tell the truth as I once did back in the good old days. I lie to relatives. I say things like, 'Here in this coffin, love, is the body of your old dad. Peaceful and at rest he is, dressed him to meet his maker myself, sweetheart.' I know there's only a hand, a burst torso and nothing to even tell me whether the stuff the rescue lads pulled out of the rubble is male or female. All I know is that the woman's father is dead and that his family need a funeral. They need the dignity the *Luftwaffe* took away from their father when their bombs reduced him to atoms. Not all the victims of the bombing can be found and so people like me tell lies. We tell lies for the best of reasons, but we still tell them and, barmy or not, that doesn't sit right with me. I've done a lot of bad things in my life, I even killed back in the Great War, the First Lot as us old soldiers like to call it. But mad and bloodstained as I might be, I was never a liar before now. As I stood there next to that dim red lamp, with the sounds of brave men putting out fires all around me, I could have wept if I hadn't known it was only self pity. What a sad sight I would have made – had he really seen me – for the screaming man who rushed past me and up the stairs to the Whispering Gallery now. As it was he just glanced at me and shouted as he went. 'It's the dome!' he yelled. 'We've had a telephone message telling us the dome is on fire!'

Sometimes you don't think, you just do whatever it is that needs doing – even if you can't really know what that is. I followed the shouting man up the stairs – he was running, and I ran for a bit until my lungs gave out. I'm not a lover of spiral staircases anyway, and the one up to the Whispering Gallery is narrow, like a corkscrew. Dark at the best of times, the few windows in the stairwell were blacked out. I groped my way forwards, chest bursting from lack of air, stumbling on every other stair as my legs began to give up. I counted the steps to distract myself, not that it helped in reality, nothing would have done.

I'd been up to the Whispering Gallery once before, as a child, and had no memory of it being as bad as all that. In fact, my recollection of the stairwell had been of something quite wide. But then I'd probably been about seven years old at the time and so it had seemed wide to me then. I'm a good six foot tall now and so the narrowness of the stairwell, together with the lack of height underneath each spiral, made me feel as if I was being crushed. Shaking with fear, I knew that once I'd counted a hundred steps I had to be at least near to the top. But I'd really underestimated the climb and I'd reckoned without the passageway. Just underneath the Whispering Gallery there is a passageway of such claustrophobic narrowness it really does make you wonder about just how small people must have been in the old days. Christ knows why it's there! But as I shuffled, whimpering, along its length, my head scraping against the ceiling, I felt as if I were in some sort of mausoleum. When the stairs up to the actual gallery at the end began, I was almost relieved. By the time I got to the top, a combination of lack of air, exhaustion and fear about how I was going to get down a pitch-dark spiral staircase once I'd finished whatever I was doing, made me incapable of speech. Standing in the doorway at the top of the staircase, I shook and sweated and wondered whether my heart would stop. The Whispering Gallery, even in darkness, is awe inspiring. It runs around the base of the great dome on the inside and is, like the rest of the cathedral, made of stone. Or rather, it is mostly made of stone. As I leaned forward to look as far as I dared at the vast space in front of and below me, I saw that just underneath the railings around the inside of the gallery is a wide wooden platform. Logically, if wood is cared for properly, it's as safe as stone to step upon. But my barmy mind reeled away from this wooden part of the gallery in horror.

All around me men were passing buckets, running and shouting in what was, to me, such a dodgy and dangerous place. It seemed that an incendiary bomb had become lodged in the fabric of the dome and was starting to burn a hole. Because the Watch were mainly architects they spoke about what was happening in terms of how it was affecting the structure.

One said to another, 'If those timbers inside the dome are already alight, the air cavity underneath will turn that into an inferno. The dome will be completely kaput! It'll drop down into the cathedral like a ruddy stone!'

I didn't know at the time, but St Paul's dome is actually two domes, an inner one that you see from inside the cathedral, very ornate and decorative, and an outer one, seen from the street, made of wood and lead. Between the two is a brick funnel construction with air spaces all around it. So if the outer dome burned strongly enough to release the air from the cavity the whole thing would go up and, in the worst possible case, send the lantern and the Golden Ball and Cross on top of the dome crashing down into the cathedral. I was to learn a lot about architects and architecture that night.

'Get up to the Stone Gallery!' I heard someone shout as I stood at the top of the stairs, my heart still banging like a steam hammer.

The Stone Gallery is on the outside of the cathedral, about a hundred more stairs above the Whispering Gallery. I may have been away from the crypt, but I was quickly realising that being above ground in the cathedral came at a price to someone as unfit as I was. How could these blokes even think about going up to the Stone Gallery just after they'd climbed up so high already? I lit a fag to help calm myself down. It helped a bit.

'What are you doing up here?'

Mr Andrews was obviously someone who had the knack of appearing and disappearing at will. Looking as he did – and not in the slightest bit out of breath either – was unnerving.

I don't know whether it was because I couldn't hear any actual bombing then or because for some reason I'd lost my fear all of a sudden, but my words didn't stumble this time.

'I'm looking for Mr Phillips,' I said. 'He's a watchman.'

'Phillips?' Mr Andrews frowned. 'What do *you* want with Mr Phillips? The watchmen are trying to save the cathedral, he—'

'Mr Phillips brought in a little girl, to the crypt,' I said. 'Now she's missing.'

'Mr Phillips wouldn't have had anything to do with anything improper!' Mr Andrews said. 'Our own true watchmen are good men! No one is or will go missing. No one will be sacrificed!'

What he'd said was odd even though it didn't strike me so at the time. I said, 'Mr Andrews, the little girl is only about ten. She could've easily wandered off on her own. Mr Phillips won't have had anything to do with her taking off, I don't suppose. It's just that he brought her in, so it's said, and so he might know her name. I can't even call for her if I don't know her name, can I?'

A flash of red flame from outside illuminated his face for just a second. It showed me that thin skull shadowed by suspicion.

'Mr Andrews—'

'Mr Phillips is out on the Stone Gallery, I believe,' Mr Andrews said. 'Some of the watchmen are actually inside the dome. There's a fire bomb, stuck—'

'Yes, I know.'

'Then you'll also know that no one involved with it is going to have time to answer any sort of questions until that fire is seen to.'

'No . . .'

'Dean! Dean!'

Down in the cathedral, doors from the outside were flung wide open and men came streaming in from the west. I couldn't see how many there were but I heard their voices clearly.

'We came as soon as we heard!'

'Dean, we've got to save the cathedral, we—'

'Thank you, thank you so much!' a posh voice said. 'We've only stirrup pumps, but . . .'

Unlike me, this new group of watchmen thundered up the spiral stairs. When they finally passed me, breathless and sweating, it was as if I wasn't even there. They didn't so much as tip their tin hats in my direction.

'You're not doing any good here,' Mr Andrews said. 'It would be better if you went back down.'

'I'm not going back to the crypt!' As soon as I said it I knew that I'd betrayed far too much fear in my voice. What would this man, what would any normal man, make of such a silly fear, especially under these circumstances?

'Go back down into the cathedral,' Andrews said calmly. 'I'll come and see you once I've spoken to Mr Phillips.'

'Or send him to me?' I asked. 'What does he look—'

'I will take care of it.' He put one thin, almost weightless hand on my arm. 'Go back down.'

As I knew that it would be, the descent to the ground was a nightmare for me. In the dark I had to feel my way along the outside walls where the spiral stairs are at their widest. Although there's just enough room for your feet on each stair, you have to feel the edge with your toes before you go down to the next one each time you move. The stairs feel even steeper going down than they do coming up and so each one pulls the muscles at the front of your thigh something rotten. And if you don't like heights, as I don't, you feel unsafe all the time. It was cold but I was sweating again, especially when I had to pass through that blessed passageway. I also had the feeling, quite without any proof for it, that there was somebody following me down for some reason. It couldn't have been Mr Andrews because when I left him, he went off towards the Stone Gallery. But someone was there and it wasn't a person I felt had good intent towards me. In fact, although I couldn't see anything much, I kept stopping and listening and staring into the blackness behind me. But not once did I see or hear anything. What I had was a feeling which I expected to disappear once I reached the ground. But it didn't. As the shouting and the panic from the levels above my head increased, I became even more afraid than I had been on the spiral staircase. I stood by the red lantern underneath the dome, my legs shaking, my thighs in particular aching like hell. Above me brave men conquered their fears and ran with stirrup pumps up steep, blacked-out staircases, swung about on roof tops, and fought with every ounce of their strength to save this place Herr Hitler was showing such an interest in. Mr Smith had been right in his belief that the cathedral meant something. Some buildings are more than just bricks, some buildings mean something or represent an idea that can stand for a whole country. I know that for us, by which I mean Londoners, if not all English people, that building is St Paul's. I also believed then, as I do now, that the feelings we all have for it don't necessarily have anything to do with religion. What we all experience, that cold shiver down the spine when we think about the place, is far, far older than anything Christian. Underneath that dome, where I stood, something made me uneasy. I wasn't alone . . .

'Little girl?' I called out. I don't know why I thought it was her who had been following me, it just came out. But I still didn't know her name and so what could I call? 'Little girl, just let us know you're safe! People are worrying . . .'

There was no answer. In spite of all the noise and even a few splashes of water from above, the silence in the cathedral remained. It washed around me, stranded as I was by the little red lamp, like a vast, black sea. Then I heard the sound of an evil laugh somewhere about. It could have been in my own head, I know, that. But in view of what was to happen later, I still don't know to this day whether or not it was only in my mind.

No little girl came walking out of the blackness that was all around me. The noise up above of men's feet and voices and the crackle of incendiaries burning God knows what, was terrible. But in a way I was glad of it, I must be honest. Lamp or no lamp, I was now rooted to the floor by my fear as the darkness of the grave seemed to reach out towards me from all sides. My breathing became shallow and shaky and, although I knew absolutely that the thickness around me wasn't earth or anything like it, I heard myself whimper with the strain my mind and my body were both under. This is how I am if I go into a shelter. It's why I can't go into the Anderson with my mother and sisters and let them see it. The stuttering's bad enough without the mad look I know comes on to my face, and the horrible grey pallor my skin takes on.

Over in some distant corner of the building there was a scuttling noise.

'L-little g-girl?'

Nothing save a bit more scuttling just after I'd stuttered. Mice. So many people had their cats put down at the beginning of the war, fearing the poor things might suffer during the bombing, it's like a bloody dance hall for mice in some parts of London now. I don't mind them. I've eaten a fair few in my time, back in the trenches. Rats too, or rather a rat; I only ate one of those blighters once. The look of a rat puts you off, the sharp teeth, the tail you know has probably just brushed against the corpse of one of your comrades. I felt tears begin to trickle down my face as I remembered my old mates yet again. They were dead and I was in a church being pounded into the ground and I was so, so frightened of joining them. I was so scared!

For a long time the noises from the roof and dome above got louder. The running, the spraying of water, the clanking of metal buckets and the shouting voices all mixed up so you couldn't make out any human sense in any of it. Fighting up there, battling with an enemy using fire as a weapon, those watchmen weren't facing anything that could be controlled in the way that a man's hands and actions can be held or directed. Fire will, like water, do as it wants and so whether it is beaten, whether those fighting it live or die, is largely up to how it, and any wind behind it, might behave. I knew then that I should move. If the fire really did take a hold up above, the whole dome, as I'd heard one of the watchmen say earlier, could crash down into the cathedral. Everyone in the cathedral would die. People ask me sometimes whether being an undertaker makes you less frightened of death than the average person. It doesn't. Of course my thoughts on death are coloured by my memories of the Great War, but I fear death nevertheless. I fear the unknown that faces every unbeliever in religion, I fear the darkness and the grief of others I've seen so many, many times in my forty-eight years on this earth. My mother, the Duchess as we all call her on account of her bearing and good manners, would be so sad. To lose my old dad was bad enough and then to have her only son return from the last war just a ghost of what he had been had nearly killed her. But if I died? And what of my sisters, Nancy and Aggie, my lady friend, Hannah . . .

The noises from above had decreased. I knew this because I could actually hear my panicky breathing. If the noises had stopped, did it mean that the watchmen had given up their battle against the fire in the dome? Had I been able to move my rigid neck to look upwards, I would have done so, but my muscles were like wood. From where I knew the high altar was, I heard the sound of running feet. I don't know how I knew it, but I was just certain that the sound was that of a child.

'The incendiary bomb that was burning the dome fell out into the Stone Gallery. Just fell out and a chap extinguished it immediately! Just like that!' Mr Andrews said. He had a genuine look of wonder on his thin, old face. 'It was a miracle. God has not deserted His children yet.'

Where the bloody hell he'd come from so quickly and quietly, I didn't know. He must have just come down the stairs from the Whispering Gallery, but he was neither sweating nor shaking which, to me, was decidedly odd. But then suddenly there was a massive thud followed by screams from what sounded like the crypt. The sound of childish footsteps running flew past me and Mr Andrews on the smallest gust of wind.

Chapter Three

A huge explosion nearby, possibly in Paternoster Row, knocked out all the lights in the underground chamber. The watchmen in charge of what they called the Occurrence Book, or book of incidents for the crypt, said, too, that the whole cathedral was now ringed with fire.

'Off-duty watchmen will come from all over now, you'll see,' Mr Smith said as I helped him and a couple of the other blokes light small lamps in and around the crypt. 'We'll save this place. We have to.'

I'd come back down with Mr Andrews just after all the lights went out. The dome was safe for the time being and I wasn't doing any good just standing in the middle of the cathedral floor, imagining – as I thought – running children. Mr Andrews hadn't seen or heard anything.

'If there is a child running and hiding inside the cathedral then I haven't seen it,' he'd said when I tried to explain what I'd felt and heard. I asked him if he'd spoken to Mr Phillips, but he told me that he hadn't. He told me he hadn't seen him. They must have missed each other by seconds.

Mr Smith had a different view of the little girl problem. 'If you didn't see her anywhere in the cathedral, then she must have gone outside. Seems ridiculous, I know, but that has to be the way of it,' he said. 'Mr Phillips would never have taken her up to the Whispering Gallery with him anyway. It's not safe for children up there, not now.'

I lit another lamp whilst thinking that the Whispering Gallery wasn't, in my opinion, safe for any bleeder.

I said, 'B-but d-don't you think s-she, the girl, she could be h-hiding or—'

'Mr Hancock,' Mr Smith said patiently, 'you have to know this building to know where to hide, especially in the dark.'

'Y-yes but kids—'

'She's gone outside and that's that!' the posh young

woman said with no patience in her voice at all. Like all of us, she didn't like being plunged into darkness and was ratty as Gawd knows what until all the lamps really got going. Her sort weren't used to waiting, I thought. 'Good heavens, isn't there enough to worry about without going on about an unpleasant little girl!'

'Here! Here!' the Jewish woman put in her twopenn'orth.

'But—'

'Unpleasant or not, if a kid's missing, we should pull together to find her,' a woman I hadn't seen before said. 'Mr Churchill says we have to pull together to defeat Adolf.'

I looked at her and smiled. It didn't mean anything apart from the fact that I was pleased that someone was agreeing with me. But she avoided my eyes by looking down at the floor. I reckoned she was about thirty – it's not always easy to tell by lamplight – a little, mousy woman wearing a large and very misshapen hat. Poor and honest, as my Hannah would say.

Mr Smith looked at me, shook his head, and then sighed. 'Look,' he said, 'we can't have people running around the cathedral in a raid in the dark. Even you, Mr Hancock, have to agree that that's just silly.'

Of course it was and I said as much. But I also reminded him that someone needed to speak to Mr Phillips. It was then that the bloke in charge of the Occurrence Book looked up and said, 'Mr Harold Phillips? From Phillips, Steadman and Rolls?'

'Yes,' Mr Smith said. 'There's only one Phillips on the Watch as far as I'm aware, Mr Ronson.'

Mr Ronson, 'on the Book', said, 'Well, I haven't seen him tonight, have you?'

'He came in with this little girl we've been talking about,' Mr Smith said. 'You were here when she came in, Mr Ronson. I remember you being here distinctly.'

Even through the floor of the cathedral we could hear the thick drone of yet another wave of German bombers. This lot it would seem were dropping bombs as opposed to incendiaries. The bombs were just making the fires get even bigger which was of course, all part of Herr Hitler's plan. We all looked up, just for a second, all at the same time.

'I'm not doubting your word, Mr Smith. I must've

missed Mr Phillips,' Mr Ronson said as he wiped his eyes with the back of his hand. 'I remember the little girl. Blonde and noisy.'

'Mr Phillips went straight up to the Whispering Gallery,' Mr Smith explained. 'Then, a little later, the girl went missing. You were busy, Mr Ronson. I know you didn't speak to Mr Phillips.'

Underneath his tin hat, Mr Ronson's dirt-smutted face frowned. 'I know Harold Phillips quite well,' he said. 'As you know, Mr Smith, I worked for him before I started my own firm. I think I would've noticed if he was in or not, even if I didn't speak to him.'

'He didn't say much himself and, as I said before, Mr Ronson, you were busy,' Mr Smith replied.

'Mmm.' It was said doubtfully, I felt.

Mr Andrews hadn't been able to find Mr Phillips in the Whispering Gallery. I told this to Mr Smith and Mr Ronson. If anything it made Mr Ronson doubt whether Mr Phillips was in the building even more. Everyone else, the other shelterers as well as the cathedral first-aid ladies had gone off about their own affairs just after our conversation started. No one, it seemed, except me actually wanted to find this kid.

Even the poor but honest woman had buried her head in a magazine of some sort by this time, although what she could see in the dim light from the lamps was hard to imagine. In truth they were all only doing in their way what I was trying to do in mine – take their minds off the bombing. I said something about wanting to go and look for the girl again then.

'You mustn't go outside the cathedral,' Mr Ronson said. 'Everything's on fire out there. Guy's Hospital is burning to the ground, Lombard Street has taken a massive hit.' He shook his head in what was not defeat, but was a measure of his own tiredness, I felt. 'We're in contact with centres all over the city. This place is a target for the *Luftwaffe*, we all know that, but we're still here. It's safer in here than it is outside. If we manage to avoid taking a direct hit or having an incendiary set the dome on fire, we'll be all right. I know this building, it's very resilient.'

'Would any of you gentlemen like a cup of hot Bovril?'

The lady who was asking, clearly a cathedral first aider, was elderly with fluffy, thinning grey hair underneath her felt beret.

'Oh, no thank you very much, Mrs Andrews,' Mr Smith replied.

Mr Ronson turned her offer down as well. Once she'd gone, I asked the others who she was. I assumed she was connected to the Mr Andrews who was some sort of priest.

'Andrews is a chaplain,' Mr Ronson said. 'The lady who offered us the Bovril is his wife.'

'W-what's a c-chaplain?' I knew about army chaplains, but what they did in civvy street I didn't know. 'W-what's that mean here?'

'I really don't know,' Mr Ronson said. 'I'm Jewish.'

Mr Smith was talking to another man now and so I sat down in the chair next to where Mr Ronson was sitting at his desk. Like me he was a dark, rather thin man, although very much younger. Mr Ronson was, I thought, about thirty-five years of age.

'So why do you, er, why if you're J-Jewish . . .'

'Why do I come and watch over the cathedral?' He smiled and offered me a Passing Cloud fag which I took very gratefully. 'Because as an architect, I know that St Paul's is the heart of the City,' he said. 'A St Paul's of one sort or another has stood here since

Saxon times. Fires and wars, and God alone knows what other disasters, have overtaken this place, but it's always gone on and it must continue to do so.'

I said I thought that even if St Paul's was destroyed, we, the people of Britain, would build it up again as our ancestors had done before us. I believed that then and I believe it now.

Mr Ronson frowned. 'Mr Hancock,' he said, 'do you believe in evil?'

I did and do. I may not believe in God, but the Great War acquainted me very closely with the evil, some would say the devil, that lives in people's hearts. How else would you explain how our generals and the generals of France, Germany and Russia allowed so many of us to die? Whatever side they were on, they were all as wicked as each other.

'Hitler is evil,' Mr Ronson said. 'What he's doing, what it is said he is doing to Jews in Czechoslovakia, Poland, well it's . . . I hope it is beyond belief, Mr Hancock, but I really do fear that it is not.'

Hannah, my lady friend, is Jewish and she's told me some things about Hitler. There's nothing much in the papers of course, but word amongst the Jews is that

Hitler is killing them in their thousands. For some reason he hates certain types of people; Jews and Gypsies, mainly. Some folk even go so far as to say he wants to completely do away with such people, so there are no more Jews and Gypsies. That's far more frightening than the destruction of just one building . . .

'Mr Hancock, this cathedral was built by a very great architect,' Mr Ronson continued. 'Sir Christopher Wren built this place on the ashes of the old Gothic cathedral that burnt down in the Great Fire of London. He built it as a symbol of survival. Yes, I agree with you that if St Paul's is destroyed tonight, we, or people like us, can build a new cathedral on this spot yet again. But if we can protect it, if we can ensure this place survives . . .' He stopped for a moment, turned away, and, I think, wiped some tears from his eyes. 'Christian or not, a Londoner is a Londoner and this great big dome we're sitting under is our mascot.' He turned back towards me and smiled. 'It's sticking two fingers up at Adolf – you understand?'

I did. But then he said something that I didn't understand.

'Sir Christopher's true men are here tonight, Mr Hancock, we're fighting the enemy both outside and in.'

'Outside and—'

The ringing of the Watch telephone meant that Mr Ronson had to go and find out what was happening. The Watch are very well organised with telephones in the crypt and up in the Whispering Gallery. These instruments are connected to each other and to control rooms across the City. The message this time was about another incendiary on the roof. It seemed to me, ear-wigging as I knew I really shouldn't to Mr Ronson's conversation, that on this occasion the Watch had failed to control the flames.

'Call the Fire Brigade,' I heard Mr Ronson say to Mr Smith. 'I'm going up top to see what I can do.'

'All right.'

Together with Mr Smith, I watched Mr Ronson go. By 'up top' he'd meant the Whispering Gallery. As far as I could see he went on his own.

I've always found the idea of the Whispering Gallery to be a little bit disturbing. Like most London schoolchildren I was taken to visit St Paul's when I was a nipper and, as boys will, I mucked around. I ran about in the cathedral, took the mickey out of the staff who patrolled the place and I was very uncomplimentary about a couple of the choristers I saw walking up the front steps. Maybe it was the long climb up to the Gallery that silenced me, but I do recall being far more sombre up there. I was also, so an old mate told me, struck dumb by it. But then that would make sense given my reaction to the Gallery now. To hear something whispered by a person to someone else can be exciting, but to have your own whisperings listened to, isn't. It is or has the potential to be very frightening indeed. After all, if you whisper something to somebody, you only mean for them to hear, no one else. The whole place breaks your confidences and sometimes more than that, too, as we were all soon to learn. I was glad, at the time, that it wasn't me going back up there again. I hoped at that point, to never have to face the Whispering Gallery's cruel stairs or the potential its walls hold for treachery ever again.

Once Mr Ronson had gone, Mrs Andrews came over and spoke to me.

'You're the gentleman who was looking for that little girl, aren't you?' she said.

'Yes, madam.' I put my hand up to my head in order to raise my top hat to her, then realised that I wasn't wearing any sort of head-gear. I hadn't worked that day and so I'd been in 'civvies' over at my great aunt Annie's. I'd had a hat, a flat cap, but that was long gone. It had blown or fallen off my head somewhere after Smithfield Market.

She put a hand, old and heavily veined, on my arm. 'I shouldn't worry too much if I were you,' she said. 'The cathedral is packed, what with the clergy and the watchmen. They'll find her. My husband's looking.'

I wasn't so sure about that. I know I'd asked Mr Andrews to do so, but I was also very aware of the fact that the clerics and the watchmen had a lot of other things on their minds too. Even down in the crypt I could hear yet another wave of bombers come over. The ack-ack was furious, loud as I didn't recall ever hearing the like of it before. I could, I was sorry to admit to myself, imagine what it was like up on the roof for the lads fighting the fire. Most old Great War soldiers have fought against fierce enemies with only very minimal equipment at one time or another. The Fire Brigade had been called for a very good reason. The dry riser still wasn't working and the water the cathedral staff had hoarded for just such an eventuality as this, was running out. There was so much activity in the skies above us that it had to be only a question of time before we suffered a direct hit and I didn't want to be in the crypt when that happened. I didn't want to be in the cathedral at all.

'You know that if I thought that death was actually the end, I couldn't be here?' Mrs Andrews said. 'I'd be a coward and get out of the cathedral now.'

Were I the fanciful sort, I might have wondered whether she could read my mind.

'No one is comfortable here,' she said. 'The Nazis are bombing us now, fanning the flames of the incendiaries. But we must put our trust in God and hope that He will bring us through this terrible ordeal. If not religion, then some faith in the skill of Sir Christopher Wren would probably not go amiss.'

Now that I was up close to her, I could see that she was livelier – her eyes positively twinkled with something or other – than her husband. She was also considerably older than he was. Mrs Andrews could be, I realised, as much as eighty.

'He, Wren, was not only an architect you know,' Mrs Andrews said. 'He was also a man of God. He was a Freemason . . .'

'The er, the Pope d-doesn't hold with Masonry,' I said. I didn't say it in a way that was judging it. I suppose I was making a comment more than anything. The fact that the Pope doesn't hold with it is about, or was, the most I knew about the Masons.

'Ah, you are a Catholic,' Mrs Andrews said.

'Well . . . yes, I suppose so.'

'Well, Masonry and the Catholic Church, they don't exactly go, do they?' She shrugged. 'But you know, Mr, um . . .'

'Hancock.'

'Mr Hancock, there are two sides to Masonry. There are two sides to most things, it's the natural order as it were. Male and female, day and night, et cetera. But Masonry definitely has its light as well as its dark aspects. Sir Christopher and those who appreciate his true legacy were and are good men, men of faith and of morality. Men of the light.'

I didn't know anything about what she was saying. I'm Catholic, and so as soon as the Masons were mentioned we cease to understand each other. I had thought that women were ignorant of the Brotherhood, but apparently not this woman. Talk of light and dark with regard to things way above my head was pointless also. Mrs Andrews either knew or sensed this and so she changed the subject. She asked me what I did for a living and I had just told her I was an undertaker – and clocked the usual frown this provoked – when young George came down the stairs and walked towards us. Mr Smith, who was sitting at Mr Ronson's desk behind us, stood up. He did this, I realised later, because the boy looked funny – pale and almost in another world.

'The fire's under control now, Mr Smith,' George said. 'You can tell the Fire Brigade that they don't need to come.'

Mr Smith got on to it right away. All around us people who'd heard him cheered and smiled because, yet again, St Paul's had made it through another crisis. The celebrations made what George was doing now even more peculiar. His face suddenly reddened and he gulped. I thought he might be about to have a fit.

'Oh, Mrs Andrews!' he said as his big young eyes filled up with tears. 'Mrs Andrews!'

As she had done with me, the elderly chaplain's wife put a hand on to the boy's arm.

'George Watkins, what is the matter?' she asked. 'Good heavens, lad, the cathedral roof is spared, what can the problem be?'

George just simply shook his head and then buried his face in his hands.

'All the excitement can do it,' Mrs Andrews said as she looked at the boy who was now almost bent over double at the waist. 'The older choristers, like George, want to do their bit but they're very inexperienced in the ways of the world. It can all be a tad . . . overwhelming.'

'Mr Ronson is dead!' George was upright again, tears streaming down his face.

Save for the sound of the bombers up above and Mr Smith on the telephone, the whole crypt fell silent.

'He fell,' George said after what seemed like a very long time indeed. 'The floor was wet, he fell from the Whispering Gallery on to the cathedral floor. That wasn't meant to happen! He . . .' Then he looked around at all the people in the crypt and said, 'Didn't you hear him? Didn't you hear his body hit the floor just above your heads?'

When you actually fight a war as a soldier you get used to, if not comfortable with, the idea of blokes being here today and gone tomorrow. Civvy street, even in the middle of bombing raids, doesn't quite get a handle on this. There was shock, which I didn't share. Why shouldn't Mr Ronson, nice though he was, die in the middle of a bombing raid? What I overheard a few minutes later was, however, another matter. While everybody talked and sobbed over someone who to most of them was a perfect stranger, Mr Andrews came in and took his wife to one side. Whether he just had no idea that I was so close to them or whether he actually wanted me to hear what came next at that point, I did not know. But as plain as day I heard him say to his wife, 'Sidney Ronson was murdered.'

They exchanged a look that seemed to tell me that this was not a surprise to either of them.

I didn't know what to do or say and so I just stood

there, pretending I hadn't heard anything, sweating, my head pounding with fear. But then as I stood there thinking, I wondered whether I had heard what Mr Andrews had said or whether it was just another example of my madness. The things I hear and see that others do not are always of this sort, always frightening and sinister. Events in the mad side of my world are never innocent or benign. Men die because they are murdered not because they fall because a floor is wet or greasy.

'What's the matter? What's going on?' It was Mr Smith, just off the phone to the fire brigade. His face was drained of all colour and was more lined than I'd noticed before.

'Mr Ronson has had an accident,' Mr Andrews said. 'It's wet up in the Whispering Gallery, and he fell. Unfortunately he's dead.'

No murder now. Not even a suggestion of it.

'I see.' If someone that I knew or had worked with had had such an accident, if accident it was, I would have wanted to know the hows and whys of the affair. But Mr Smith on this occasion did not give in to any further curiosity he might have had.

He said, 'The Fire Brigade film unit want to come and film from the Stone Gallery. What's happening must be recorded. They won't stay long, they won't be able to. The heat and . . . I said they could come.' He walked away then, his head down, Mr Andrews's sharp gaze following him for a moment until he returned it back to his wife.

'I'll have to go . . .' he began.

'Do you want me to come with you?' I asked. Fidgety as I get sometimes, I had to do something. I was also in one of those short phases that happen to me sometimes during a raid, periods when I can speak without stuttering.

Mr Andrews looked at me with what seemed to be contempt. 'Why?'

It was a fair question but it wasn't one I had a real answer for and so I said, 'I'm an undertaker, in Plaistow. Can't help the poor fellow if he's passed on, but I'm accustomed to the dead if you need to do anything or . . .'

'I think we can do without the advertisement for your business,' he said with even more contempt, and made as if to go right then.

I thought that was the end of it. But then Mrs Andrews took her husband to one side for a few seconds and whispered something to him. When she had finished he came back over to me and said, 'But if you think you can help . . .'

I followed him up into the cathedral. He was a miserable old sod to my way of thinking, but I wasn't doing what I was doing for him.

It would have been strange in peace time to see a dead body lying, as this one was, alone, either inside or outside a building. Although people might not want to touch a corpse there is often a feeling of not being comfortable leaving the dead alone. But war takes even that away. There are so many of them, the shattered dead, how can it be otherwise? They lie and wait for us to 'deal' with them, and no one gives them so much as a second look. The dead have, after all, gone.

Mr Ronson had fallen on to his front, narrowly missing the red lamp underneath the dome. Wetness covered the floor. In the gloom, fortunately, it wasn't possible to make out what it was even though I knew only too well. The impact of a body on a hard floor from that sort of height would cause the body to burst, which was what had happened here. The stomach, well it splits apart and throws everything inside, out. There are no 'good' ways to die but falling forwards from a great height is particularly ugly. There's a smell of undigested food, of the last evacuation from the bowels.

Although we could both hear the sounds and voices of the blokes both overhead in the dome and down below us in the crypt, there was no one actually about and so I told Mr Andrews what I'd heard. I had to know if that sentence he'd spoken to his wife was real or not. I said, 'I heard you say that Mr Ronson was murdered. You told your wife.'

Mr Andrews didn't even flinch. 'We'll have to do something with him,' he said. 'We can't leave him here like this. I'll have to get our biggest watchman, Mr Bartholomew, Welsh, a rugby player in his youth, to—'

'Mr Andrews, if you think that Mr Ronson has been murdered . . .'

He looked up at me with a steady, inscrutable gaze. 'Mr . . . whatever your name is . . .'

'Hancock. F-Francis H-Hancock,' I said as the nervous stuttering came upon me once again.

'Mr Hancock, if you think that you can help, that is in your professional capacity . . .'

'Y-you said m-murder . . .'

His face changed not a bit but he moved in close and then pulled my head down roughly, and suddenly, in front of his face. 'Forget what I said,' he hissed. 'It was nothing! I saw nothing, nobody did! It was an expression of fear only. Not something for you to be worrying about, not something for you to be listening to!'

He then let me go as quickly and as sharply as he had grabbed me. As he moved away I saw that there were tears in his eyes; whether they were tears for Mr Ronson or just a result of his own frustration, I didn't know. But what I was certain of now was that what I'd heard wasn't just the madness in my head. Mr Andrews had said he believed that Mr Ronson had been murdered. In one way it was a relief, but in another way it wasn't. If Mr Andrews believed that Mr Ronson had been murdered that meant we had to have a killer in the cathedral. And even to me, that was much more frightening than anything that might or might not be going on in my head.

'C-cover him,' I said as soon as I could speak again.

'No, we have to get him out of the way! We—'

This time I pulled his face close up to mine. 'I – if he was, er, if he was killed, w-we must leave him,' I said. 'F-for the – the coppers.'

He gave me that furious, blank look I was beginning to know so well. Mr Andrews hadn't liked me from the start. I'd been a nuisance, an inconvenient 'refugee', unwelcome in his cathedral. Time passed and then he said, 'The police won't come, not with all this going on! But . . .' He knew that what I was saying about the coppers was true. He knew also, and more significantly to me, that they would need to view Mr Ronson's body at some time. I had not misheard what he had said to his wife and I was not about to forget that whatever he might think. 'I'll find some canvas or something to cover him with.'

'Yes, that will, er, that . . .'

'I'll do it,' he said as he headed off up towards the altar. 'I don't need an undertaker to advise me about that.' And then as soon as he was almost invisible to me he turned and said, 'Are you really a papist? I thought you were a Jew. You have the look of a Jew.'

'I-I am a Catholic,' I said. 'I d-don't follow it though.'

'But you are one, a born one, I understand, and maybe . . .' He didn't finish that sentence but instead he said, 'You were looking for that little girl, weren't you?' Before I could reply he continued, 'I suggest you find her.'

And then he was swallowed by the gloom.

Maybe I would have thought more about why Mr Andrews was suddenly so interested in the little missing girl no one but me seemed to want to find, but I was distracted by what sounded like an army of watchmen running on to the Whispering Gallery.

'What happened?' I heard one bloke say to the chap who had charge of the telephone up there.

'I don't know,' the other one replied. 'One minute he was up here, the next . . . It's said he slipped on the water on the floor.'

'He was looking for Harold Phillips. I heard him myself. He said he was looking for Harold.'

My ears pricked up at this. Once again, Mr Phillips

was being talked about. I still hadn't seen him even though I'd been up to the Whispering Gallery once myself.

'Well, he didn't find Harold,' the bloke on the telephone said. 'Don't know why he was looking for him at all.'

'Why's that?' some other chap asked.

'Because I've not seen Harold and if I haven't, I can't see how he can be up here,' the telephone man said. 'Harold, of everyone, is . . . well, Harold is distinctive, isn't he?'

There were some murmurs of agreement from the Whispering Gallery. Down below I wondered what they meant by 'distinctive'. I stamped my feet a little to get some life back in them but then I realised that what I was actually doing was kicking blood up into the air and so I stopped.

Chapter Four

As well as the London Fire Brigade film unit, who went straight up to the Stone Gallery to film and record the events unfolding up there, more watchmen turned up over the next half-hour. Their faces blackened by what they described as the inferno outside, they talked of the fires that surrounded the cathedral as if they were living, intelligent things.

'They're getting closer all the time,' one chap said. 'Hitchcock Williams looks as if it could catch at any minute! Bloody fires! It's as if they're seeking buildings out to burn!'

'The bombs are just feeding the flames, that's what's happening,' another bloke said.

Hitchcock, Williams and Co., the famous textile

wholesaler, was very near to the cathedral, in St Paul's Churchyard. If they were in danger from the fires, then we had to be in almost as much peril. I had no idea what the time was by then. It was one of those moments when it feels as if you've been in a place for ever and, at the same time, just for a few minutes.

'You didn't see anyone, er, o-outside?' I asked a man whose clothes were so hot they were smoking.

'Outside?' he shook his head. 'No. Poor bloody LFB engaged in battles with these endless fires is all I saw. There're no civvies left out there – at least, I hope that there aren't!'

The little girl would have come back in to the cathedral. Whatever people might have said to her, the fires were now so fierce that she would have been left with no choice. Even inside a great cathedral made of thick stone, we were beginning to feel the heat. She was either somewhere in the building or she was probably already dead.

'What's that?' one of the new watchmen asked me as he pointed towards Mr Ronson's body. Now covered with a canvas tarpaulin, which Mr Andrews had found to cover him, Mr Ronson's dead body was just a thing as opposed to a person in the middle of the cathedral.

'He, er, he fell . . .'

'It's Sidney Ronson!' I heard someone call down from up above.

'Blimey!'

'He's dead!'

'What?'

'Dead. He's dead.'

The bloke in front of me, the one with the smoking clothes, made as if to go towards the canvas, but I stopped him.

'It's er, he's very . . . unrecognisable,' I said.

'Is he? Is he just . . .' He was holding what he felt inside, as we all do, or at least try to. Then, as if suddenly coming to himself and remembering where he was, he said, 'Who are you? You're not a watchman, are you?'

I told him, faltering as usual as I did so, but he stood patiently listening to my story until I'd finished. 'So this little kid . . .'

'Is not your concern, Mr Steadman.' Mr Andrews was once again at my elbow. The man was like bloody

Dracula! 'Mr Hancock is looking for the child. It's better that way.'

Mr Steadman, whose name I recognised as being the same as that of one of the partners in Phillips, Steadman and Rolls, looked as confused as I felt. What could possibly be 'better' about a man like me, as opposed to anyone else, looking for the child, I did not know.

'M-Mr Steadman,' I said, 'you, you work with Mr Harold Phillips?'

'Yes, I do.' Mr Steadman pushed his tin hat back a bit on his head. His fire-smutted face was thin and, although it was impossible to tell his age accurately underneath all that, I reckoned that he was about fifty. 'We're partners, Mr Phillips, Mr Rolls and myself. Poor Mr Ronson, he – well, he worked with us for a number of years. He was a good lad.' He swallowed hard, pushing his feelings right down deep into his body. 'Very conscientious. A good man.'

'Mr Ronson was going to see Mr Phillips for me when he, um, he fell,' I said.

'He fell.'

'He fell,' Mr Andrews moved just slightly in front of me. 'The floor up in the gallery was wet.'

'Did Harold, er, Mr Phillips, did he see it happen?' Mr Steadman asked. 'God, Harold's always on watch he'll be, he'll . . . He always had a lot of time for Sidney Ronson. A lot of time – in the past, you know.'

'We don't really know precisely what happened,' Mr Andrews said as he effectively ignored Mr Steadman's thinly disguised grief. 'No one saw it happen. He went to another emergency "up top" and also, as Mr Hancock here has said, to see Mr Phillips too.'

'Harold is here?' Mr Steadman asked.

'He is believed to be.'

They looked at each other for a while, Mr Steadman and Mr Andrews. God alone knew what was going through their heads, but then Mr Steadman upped and headed off towards the stairs to the Whispering Gallery. I had meant to ask him, he being a fellow worker, so to speak, what was so very 'distinctive' about Mr Phillips. But then he was gone and once again I was left with Mr Andrews. We were not, however, alone. As well as a couple more soot-stained watchmen who were catching their breath before they went about their business, young George the chorister had reappeared.

'Have you found that little girl yet?' he said to me.

'No, he hasn't,' Mr Andrews answered for me.

I hadn't moved from Mr Ronson's side. I hadn't known where to start. St Paul's is huge and it's difficult enough in the daylight to get into all its nooks and crannies, but in the dark, as I well knew from my little adventure up in the Whispering Gallery, it's terrifying as well as huge.

'Everywhere is open to you, Mr Hancock,' Mr Andrews said. 'Every room in the building. Do you have a torch?'

'N-no.'

'George, give Mr Hancock yours and then get another one from my office,' Mr Andrews said.

The boy passed his torch over to me without a word. Now with a light in my hand I just stood there, until Mr Andrews said to me, 'Then go about your business.'

Unlike Mr Smith, who had been of the opinion that a child would have to know its way around the cathedral in order to hide, Mr Andrews obviously felt that anything was possible. But then so did I. What Mr

Smith had said was nonsense and I couldn't at the time make out either why he'd said it or why I'd bothered to listen. But Mr Andrews was waving me away now and so I began to move eastwards towards the high altar. I had wanted to ask him not only where I might begin my search but how I might recognise Mr Phillips, should I come upon him, too. But my voice wasn't really working at all now and I could see something thick and black dripping down the walls of the great building. Blood from the First Lot, blood of my comrades. I stopped and closed my eyes and listened as Mr Andrews and young George argued about something behind me. I didn't know what it was, but George sounded very upset. The ack-ack barrage had intensified over the course of the last hour and that, combined with the pictures in my head and in front of my eyes, was beginning to drive me out of my mind. I would never save or even find the little girl, if she even existed. I wasn't even going to be able to save myself. But then suddenly, as I stood in the middle of what was an even darker, more blood-covered part of the building, the guns stopped.

* * *

I wasn't expecting to fall over. I was using my torch and, once the ack-ack had stopped and my mind had a few seconds to actually sort itself out, I came back to the real world again and knew where I was. The quire is where the choristers sit in normal, sane times. It's made up of dark wooden pews on either side of the nave, just in front of the high altar. Like the rest of the cathedral it was undamaged so far, or so I thought. My foot went in to some sort of hole that shouldn't have been there and I ended up hitting the deck and landing on my back. It wasn't what could have been called a proper accident, but it was unexpected, it hurt, and it caused me to swear. Not that anyone except God and the angels heard me. George and Mr Andrews had gone and I was a long way away from all the other blokes now. I picked up my torch and looked at the floor which was in a very sorry way indeed. There was a lot of damage in actual fact and I was just beginning to wonder what might have happened when a sound started that froze my marrow. Machine-gun fire! Christ, the bloody *Luftwaffe* were shooting at people on the ground! God Almighty, when were they going to stop? *Were* they going to stop?

'What you doin' down on the floor, mister? You have an accident, did you?'

I couldn't see her face or even her body, just her hair. Long and blond and shiny, it danced about in front of my face – in front of the altar – like a puppet.

'Blimey, little er . . . I've been looking all over for you!' I said.

'Why's that?' East End or no East End, this little'un was certainly no child from anywhere posh. This kid's voice was husky as if she smoked Woodbines and the bolshie cheek behind it wasn't difficult to find either. No wonder those ladies down in the crypt hadn't taken to her.

'What's your name, love?' I asked as I pushed myself up off the floor and tried to stand up.

The answer was not one I had expected. 'Me boyfriends call me Milly,' she said.

'Oh, is that—'

'Why? Want to talk when you fuck me, do you?' Milly said and then she laughed. 'You'll have to wait your turn, you know, like a good boy!'

I've seen and done a lot in my forty-eight years, but I was shocked by this. If Milly was, as everyone said, ten years old at the most, what was she doing talking like this? Was it just devilment on her part or was she, poor kid, one of those little girls who did indeed earn money by immoral means? My lady friend, Hannah, provides for herself in that way. We met because I was lonely and ill and I couldn't get the confidence to meet ladies in the usual fashion. Years on now, I care for Hannah and I think she cares for me. I've learned much about her life and the lives of others who live by that trade. Little girls are used more than people know or want to know. Now I could see her, just a little bit. Not her face, but her short thin body as she stood, laughing still, in front of me.

'Milly,' I said, 'why don't you . . .'

My words were drowned out by the sound of machine-gun fire from outside the building. Bloody bastard Jerries! Weren't we suffering enough for them? I suppose I looked away from her for a second at the most, but it was enough time for the kid to hop it.

'Milly?'

But she'd gone – if she'd even been there in the first place. But then although I see things that aren't there probably more than anyone else I know, even I only tend to see certain things. Like the phantom voices in my head, the pictures are sinister. Blood and screaming men's faces and mud are what generally push themselves unbidden in front of my eyes. Bits of body turn up, too, from time to time, but little girls especially with long golden hair are unheard of. I don't and never have had any thoughts about little girls. Milly, or whatever her name was, had been there and she'd been as coarse as the shelterers in the crypt had said she was. What she was doing now and where she'd gone to, I didn't know. I was cross at myself at the time for not managing to grab a hold of her and take her to safety. Loose in the cathedral at night, even without all the bombing, she was liable to have an accident or get into mischief of some sort.

My feet wobbled on the uneven floor as I went further on towards the high altar. It was only then that I thought, suddenly, how strange it was of Mr Andrews to think that Mr Ronson had been murdered. For Mr Ronson to have an accident was very possible, but murder . . . to my way of thinking murder under circumstances such as we were experiencing was very unlikely indeed. By his own admission, Mr Andrews had seen nothing, if he was in fact telling the truth. Also why, suddenly, did he want me to find the little girl? Not that I – stupid beggar – had managed to hang on to Milly. She'd gone somewhere and, apart from the gunfire up above, I was in an area of the cathedral that was very, very quiet. Maybe she had just been inside my head? Maybe just the wanting to find her had made her happen?

'You mustn't tell anyone, about the damage.' It was young George who now, it seemed, had finished arguing with Mr Andrews and had a new torch in his hand which he shone up into his face so that I could see him. He said, 'It happened before Christmas. A bomb landed on the high altar. It didn't go off, thank God. But no one outside the cathedral is supposed to know. Mr Andrews shouldn't have sent you up here.'

'He said I could go wherever I wanted. He sent me to find the little girl who's missing,' I said. 'And, and . . . George, I saw her!'

He frowned. 'Here?'

'A m-minute ago, at the m-most.'

George looked around, flashing his torch into corners that I could now see were splintered and damaged. Bad for morale, are scenes like that, which was why I supposed I wasn't meant to tell anyone about what I'd seen.

'Mr Hancock,' George said, 'the guns you can hear outside are not the Germans, they're our RAF boys taking on the *Luftwaffe* over the city.' His eyes filled with tears. 'We're fighting for our lives! Tonight it could all be over, unless . . . Mr Hancock, we are in the hands of the Divine and we must trust that power to protect us. But we must also, all of us, do what we can for each other. You were right to go looking for this poor child. We have a duty to her, to everyone in the care of the cathedral tonight.'

'S-she's g-gone.'

'You don't know where?'

I shook my head. Outside, something, probably some previously untouched building close by, burst into flames which then roared up the side of the cathedral, the brightness of it even shining through the huge blackout curtains at the stained-glass windows.

I watched George sigh and then he said something that reminded me of that strange little conversation I'd had with Mr Andrews's wife. 'Sir Christopher's building cannot fall, Mr Hancock,' he said. 'If it did, that would send the wrong message.'

Even through the gloom he could make out the confused look on my face.

'To Hitler,' George said. 'Sir Christopher was a master. Hitler is nothing. Hitler must be shown his place.' And then I saw him smile. 'But maybe our RAF boys are doing that for us now. Let's go and find the little girl, shall we?'

I don't know how long young George and myself looked around the altar, treading lightly on that delicate, shattered floor. But we didn't find Milly. With the fires from the incendiaries crackling around the building as well as the great clatters of machine-gun fire from the battling air crews overhead, it was like being in what I was told hell was like when I was a kid. Now, of course, I know that there is no hell beyond the one we've created here for ourselves on earth. That's where I was.

George, I imagined, from what he'd said before, was only really concerned about the cathedral. He most probably had friends and family somewhere, but maybe that wasn't in London. He didn't in any case talk about people or places outside of St Paul's. But his silence on these matters didn't stop me from thinking. If the bombing was bad here, what was it like at home?

Plaistow, where I live, is just about bang in the middle of the borough of West Ham. To the north there's Forest Gate and Stratford, but to the south we have the docks and the settlements around them – Custom House, Silvertown and Canning Town. Ever since the bombing began back in September, the *Luftwaffe* have been after the docks. Most nights have brought bombs and fire and death to the docklands. For us in Plaistow – my mother, my sisters and myself – it's bad enough, but where my lady friend Hannah lives, in Canning Town, it beggars belief. When I go and see her, which isn't as often as I'd like these days, I have to climb over piles of rubble so big they make me sweat. Piles which were once people's houses, flats and shops, now collapsed and blasted under Hitler's determination to destroy us. For me, who has to look smart and who has to dress in black, dealing with all the dust and rubble just in terms of clothing is difficult. People expect a certain standard from men in the undertaking profession. A level of cleanliness is required and is in fact a sign of respect. But it isn't easy and, I have to admit, one of the reasons I don't see so much of Hannah now is because I want to keep the one decent suit I do have, reasonably clean. There is also what she does for a living to deal with, too, and that doesn't get any easier. I've offered to marry her, in spite of the differences in our religions – Hannah is Jewish – but she wants to keep herself, so she says. Something in her wants to keep on selling itself on the streets to drunken sailors and men who beat their wives. But whatever she was doing and whoever she was doing it with, I thought of Hannah on this night of fire. I wondered how she was. Was she all right? How were my mother, my sisters, my poor old horses stabled at the back of the yard? Sometimes the raids can nearly drive the horses mad. They neigh and rear and get very distressed indeed. What was happening in West Ham now?

I'd told George that the little girl was called Milly and so now, as I heard him move away from the high altar and make his way into the left-hand aisle, called the quire aisle, as I was told later, I heard him call her name. I was calling her name myself, but I wondered what, if any, good it would do. There are kids like Milly all over the place. Kids who swear and cheek their elders and who, for lots of different reasons, muck around and range about with no control from any grown-ups. Sometimes the parents of such children are drinkers, or the mothers are poor and alone and have to sell their bodies to support their kids. In Milly's case, or so it seemed, she was giving herself to men either for money or for some other reason. All that, sadly, I could understand. Things just like it, and worse, happen all the time. What was strange was what this little kid was doing around St Paul's Cathedral when the bombing began. Not many people live in the City, as in the actual Square Mile, and those who do, are not generally of Milly's kind. Children of honest and respectable tradespeople live in the City, as do the offspring of clergymen, caretakers of firms of brokers, and book-keepers' kids. Milly, if I was right about her, was little more than a beggar. This Mr Phillips people kept talking about, the architect who was supposed to have brought Milly in, must have found her outside the cathedral somewhere and taken pity on her. But until I got to speak to Mr Phillips, I couldn't know what Milly had been about. He seemed to be very elusive. And so it was lucky, I felt, when shortly afterwards I came across his partner, Mr Steadman, sitting on one of the quire pews. He'd just come down from Watch duty up on the roof and was taking a break to rest what he called his 'gammy' leg.

'Got shot in the damn thing,' he told me as he lifted his bad leg to cross it over the good one. 'Gallipoli.'

'I w-was in Flanders,' I said. 'Gallipoli was—'

'Madness,' Mr Steadman said. 'Running up beaches into the Turkish guns! I was only a lad at the time.' He looked at me. 'Much as I suppose you must have been.'

'Yes.'

'Leg's never been quite right since. Gets tired,' Mr Steadman said. I could've said the same for my mind, but I didn't. People don't want to know about things like that, with good reason. Given the problem with his leg it was marvellous to me that Mr Steadman made the terrible trip up to the Whispering Gallery and maybe even beyond so willingly. My legs were as stiff as boards from my one trip 'up top'.

I asked him about Mr Phillips who, I discovered, was about the same age as Mr Steadman and myself. 'I think Harold, Mr Phillips, was in Flanders,' Mr Steadman said. 'Lost his face.'

For a moment I thought I'd misheard him, then Mr Steadman, seeing my confusion said, 'You were in the trenches, Mr Hancock, you must have seen what happened to chaps who put their heads above the parapet?'

I had, and usually they died. If they didn't, the mess a bullet or a piece of shrapnel made of their faces generally meant that they wished that they had bought it. I've a mate like that myself. He only goes out at night or when the smog's really thick over the city.

'Harold Phillips lost his nose and most of his mouth,' Mr Steadman said. 'Not that you'd necessarily know. Mr Phillips wouldn't mind my telling you that he wears a mask. A very good one, made by an artist. Very good it is. All you can see is a slight lopsidedness to his face, but apart from that there's nothing.'

I'd heard of such things, although I'd never actually

seen one. I imagined, maybe stupidly, that those masks were only available for the rich. The fact that Mr Phillips, an architect, had one of them, and my mate, who is unemployed, didn't, seemed to bear this out. This had to be what people meant when they said that Mr Phillips was 'distinctive' in looks.

'D-did you see M-Mr Phillips up in the Whispering Gallery?' I asked.

'No.' Mr Steadman shook his head. 'But then it's chaos up there. No one can do more than twenty minutes on dome watch. Swinging about up there, running across rooftops and such like, it's so dangerous it makes your head spin.'

Nobody had told me that before. No one had mentioned how disorientated a person could become that high up in the dark. I knew that it happened to me, but I wasn't normal. Apparently others, who were sane, could feel that way too.

'But I understand people have seen Harold and so I've no doubt he's somewhere about,' Mr Steadman continued. 'He's the most enthusiastic watchman I think there is. He's always here.'

And yet, so far as I was concerned, he was always

somewhere else. If only briefly, I'd seen little Milly, but Phillips was still a mystery. And that bothered me. I didn't know why at the time. Maybe like my search for Milly, my search for Phillips was just an example of my mind wanting to have something to distract itself with.

Chapter Five

I don't know now whether I took my next trip up into the dome because I wanted to find Mr Phillips, or whether Mr Steadman's words about blokes only being able to stand twenty minutes up there made me feel guilty. Not that I was about to 'do my bit'; I knew that wasn't my place. But I went. And given the state of my legs, it wasn't lightly done. It hurt, and the claustrophobic feeling I got when I did it was as bad as the first time I climbed up there. But if Mr Steadman could do it with his bad leg, then I had no excuse. In fact, I could go on further than I ever had before. First to the Whispering Gallery and then up a further 119 steps, which brought me outside, to the Stone Gallery. I took it slowly, very slowly. But I did it and I was, I admit, a little proud of myself for it. I was just about ready to die, but I arrived in one piece, which was good enough for me.

From the Stone Gallery you can see the whole city and if the smog's not settled over London, even the fields of Middlesex and Essex beyond. As I came out into the burning air, I didn't even know whether there were any other blokes out there with me the air was so thick. Everything was being incinerated – wood, cloth, and, I've no doubt, people. The smell, though slightly sweet, it has to be said, was enough to make you heave. The drone of the bombers up above rattled and reverberated in my chest like a dickey ticker. Down below, everything was on fire. Everything: churches, warehouses, shops, graveyards. I couldn't see one patch of ground that wasn't burning and the smoke notwithstanding, my eyes wept tears. Bloody hell, this was my home they were destroying here! My mind had gone a long time ago and now my city was going with it!

I just stood and looked and looked and said, 'Christ!'

Back in the trenches, blokes used to call where we were 'hell' – as in endless torment – just like the place the priest had said we'd all go to if we were bad, when I was a kid. But what I was looking at from the Stone

Gallery as my city burned below my feet, that was real Bible-bashing hell. The Devil himself could be ranging around in such huge red and golden flames. In fact, atheist as I am, I felt that if I just reached a hand out into the conflagration, maybe I could touch his evil, pointed chin. Maybe it was just lack of oxygen to my brain, who knows, but that image was very real to me at that moment.

'Excuse me, but who are you?' A posh voice I had heard before said. 'Are you with the LFB film unit?'

The group of firemen I'd seen earlier were filming all of this for posterity. I turned away from them and looked at my interrogator.

'N-No. I'm um, er, F-Francis H-Hancock.'

With the flames hurtling up into the sky from the burning buildings below it was all too easy to see the bombers overhead – great black masses of them. My stomach lurched and I was grateful, not for the first time, that I hadn't eaten and that the ruddy thing was empty.

'I'm the Dean,' the posh man, the Very Reverend W. R. Matthews, said.

'Yes, I er . . .'

'That chap's all right. I saw him advising Mr Andrews about Mr Ronson, Dean,' a man I recognised as being one of those who had come in with Mr Steadman said. 'He's looking for that young girl Mr Phillips is supposed to have brought in with him.'

'Oh?' Revd Matthews put his head on one side, making the left-hand part of his face disappear into an eerie darkness.

A blithering idiot as usual, I just stared. Luckily the other chap was much more chatty. 'I heard you found the kid and then you lost her again,' he said.

'Y-yes,' I said. 'S-she's called M-M-Milly.'

'Milly,' Revd Matthews frowned. 'We will all keep an eye out for Milly then, Mr Hancock. People other than cathedral staff watchmen, and the fire service shouldn't be anywhere outside the crypt. It's far too dangerous. However . . .' He moved his head and his face came into the full glare of the fires once again. 'With Mr Ronson and his er, his accident, plus this child . . . Mr Hancock, we have much to contend with here, as you can see, but I am also aware that things are happening in my cathedral that are additional to the bombing.' He smiled just slightly. 'Opponents inside and out, as it were.'

What he seemed to be saying was very close to something that Mr Ronson had said to me earlier, about fighting enemies both outside and inside the cathedral. We shared a look of what I supposed was understanding. I knew something was up and so, I thought, did he, and then he said, as if to confirm this, 'I haven't seen Mr Phillips myself, although I am told that he signed in downstairs.'

I wanted to tell him what I'd heard Mr Andrews say to his wife about Mr Ronson's death, but I had the feeling the Dean knew about this already.

'The Devil has many faces and they do not all wear Nazi uniforms,' he said. In spite of the heat from the fires I felt cold. If anything, this confirmed what Mr Ronson had said. Dean Matthews leaned in towards me and said, 'When you find young Milly, bring her to me, won't you? She needs looking after.'

Terrified, although exactly what of I didn't know, I nodded my head. While London was being destroyed, with St Paul's clearly the Nazis' main target on this occasion, something extra, something disturbing, was happening inside the cathedral. Somehow Mr Ronson's death and the sinister appearance of what was not a nice little girl were connected – or so I felt at the time. I was also not at all comfortable about the elusive Mr Phillips either. Was he, in fact, still about or even still alive? He'd come in with Milly, and then he'd vanished. Everyone had been so caught up with where the child had gone, that Mr Phillips had been almost overlooked. Was he, maybe, lying dead or injured somewhere in the vastness of the cathedral? The strange Mr Andrews, whose position in the cathedral I didn't understand, had said that I could go and look for Milly anywhere I wanted. The whole place was open, was what he had said.

Now the Dean, too, was asking me to continue to look for the girl. He seemed to be placing some trust in me, although I couldn't for the life of me think why. Neither the Dean nor Mr Andrews knew me from Adam. Mr Andrews hadn't wanted me here at all when I'd first fetched up at the cathedral doors. Now it seemed that I was important in some way, and this was peculiar. I have never been, nor wanted to be, important. Important people, in my experience, do far too much harm to others.

* * *

I went back to the crypt. I didn't want to look for kids or have anyone ask me to do anything. I wanted to be what I usually am, nothing special to anyone except my own family and friends. It wasn't like me to want to be under the ground but at that moment I just needed to be with people. Anonymous, but amongst people. When I arrived I found that there were a lot more of them in the crypt than there had been before. Some of them were even trying to get some kip amongst the monuments.

Hitchcock, Williams and Co., the textile wholesalers in St Paul's churchyard, was now burning furiously and all the fire watchers and employees from the shelters over there now decamped to the crypt. They came with as much as they could carry in the way of records and ledgers. Would I be that conscientious if my shop was on fire? I don't know. But my office girl Doris probably would be. These women who keep companies running to a large part these days are marvellous. Doris Rosen is a young widow with a sad past and an uncertain future, but in spite of all that she's always there for Hancock and Co. Maybe our little firm is what helps to keep her going? Maybe these ladies from Hitchcock's with their arms full of hot, smoking ledgers were of the same type?

The wives of the cathedral staff gave the newcomers, and me, cups of cocoa. It was actually Mrs Andrews who handed my cup to me and I caught her eye, but she said nothing even though I tried, and failed, to speak to her. Up above, on the cathedral floor, Mr Ronson's body lay hidden underneath a tarpaulin and I wondered as yet more men, women and children came in from other shelters nearby that were no longer safe, whether any of them wondered what was covered up underneath the dome as they passed. I decided that they probably didn't, and I knew that the shelterers who did know had been asked by Mr Andrews not to talk about it. People in general do as they're told in situations like this. The newcomers were just grateful to be safe and, as they all took their cocoa and sat down wherever they could, I listened to some of their conversations.

'It's creepy, isn't it?' one very young, very smart-suited clerical sort of bloke said. 'Down here with all the dead!'

The girl he was sitting next to on the floor, a pleasant dark-haired little thing answered. 'Well, I think it's quite a privilege to be sheltering with the likes of the Duke of Wellington and Lord Nelson.'

'Yes, but Mabel,' her companion continued, 'they're dead. Their bodies are underneath the floor right here!' He pointed to a place just in front of him. 'Just here!'

'Lord Nelson, so they say,' an old bloke with old-fashioned mutton chops who settled down slowly beside the couple said, 'had to be carried home from the Battle of Trafalgar in a huge barrel of brandy.'

Mabel put her cocoa cup down and said, 'You what?'

'To preserve the body so it could lie in state when they got it home,' the old chap said. 'Alcohol stops things from decaying.'

I didn't involve myself in their conversation, even though I particularly, out of everyone there, could have spoken with authority on this subject. I know about alcohol and its properties. Formaldehyde is what embalmers use to preserve corpses and, although people in our poor manor of West Ham don't have the money for such luxuries, I've met embalmers and I know what they do. Lord Nelson was an early and very primitive example of embalming, as the old man now told the horrified youngsters.

'Keeps a body fresh, alcohol does,' he said. 'Mind you, it's said that some of the men transporting Lord Nelson did have the odd nip from the barrel from time to time!'

The girl put her hand up to her mouth and squeaked.

The young man put a protective arm around her shoulders and said to the old bloke, 'Mr Wilkins! I do think that was a bit strong!'

'You'll have to get used to a lot stronger than that when you're in the army, Ted!' the old man said. 'Can't be too squeamish when you're fighting the Hun.'

A couple of families came over then; two women, one bloke with a wooden leg, and five children – three girls and two little boys. They were neighbours, I heard them say, and they came from the Friday Street shelter in Blackfriars. The bloke had apparently decided to move to the cathedral because he felt it was probably safer than the shelter. Not many families actually live in the square mile but the few that do are generally business people, like one of these women, who had a florist shop. Her friend and neighbour, by the look of her, was that rare type you occasionally find who live right in the City, the very poor person. The man with the wooden leg was, I gathered, her husband. Whether either of them worked, I didn't know, but their thin, patched-up clothes seemed to suggest that they didn't. The bloke's trilby hat had a hole in the crown that hadn't just been made by the fires – it had been there for years. One of the girls and both of the little boys belonged to this couple. The two other girls, who had ribbons in their hair and warm gloves on their hands, were the florist lady's daughters.

At first the children whined a bit as their parents made them sit down and behave themselves. But once they'd got their drinks from the cathedral ladies they spread their dolls and blankets out in front of them and began to settle. The bloke with the wooden leg offered me a fag, which I took gratefully, and he told me that his name was Mr Webb. I introduced myself to him and then we all, the families, the office workers and myself, sat in silence for a while. I was wondering what to do next. Young George, Mr Andrews and, I was led to believe by the Dean, the watchmen were all looking for Mr Phillips and young Milly now. Although I had been specifically asked to help, quite what I could do that would be of any good. I didn't know. After all, I was no expert on the building as all the others had to be. And yet these people, as well as the Dean himself, had seemed to want me to continue looking. I would, of course; I'd recovered a bit from my second climb now and felt a little less unhappy about what I'd been asked to do. But I'd finish my cocoa and my fag first. I didn't have any idea of what the time was but I knew that this fire bombing we were suffering had been going on for hours. I also knew that I wasn't going to get home that night, if at all. I didn't know if I, or any of us in that cathedral, would survive. The bombing never stopped, the fires, emptying shelters as they went, moved ever closer to us. I shut my eyes and listened to the sound of the little children's talk.

'Why's your baby got no coat on her, Ruby?' I heard one of the little girls say.

'Baby dollies don't have ordinary coats, they have matinee coats,' another, rougher-voiced girl said.

'All right, matinee coat,' the first girl said. 'Why hasn't your baby dolly got its matinee coat, Ruby?'

There was a pause then, during which I think I may have very briefly nodded off. When I woke the first girl was saying, '. . . took it. She's a horrible girl!'

'Well, if you will play with her!' the smarter women said. 'She's too old for you! I've told you and told you!'

'I know you don't remember her, Mrs Hughes, but the girl's mother was just the same,' the other woman said. 'My husband and me knew all that family. Butter wouldn't melt in that mother's mouth but what she got up to . . . well!'

'All the same, them Chiverses,' I heard the crippled bloke say. 'I pity the day we moved into their flippin' building! The old man'd sell his own mother for tuppence! That Milly, young as she is, ain't no exception.'

My eyes flew open and I chucked what was left of my fag on the floor. 'Milly?' I moved over towards the bloke and the women and looked into their faces. 'What does she look like, this Milly?'

It could've been some other kid called Milly, although it wasn't very likely. Milly Chivers from Blackfriars was ten years old, blonde and pretty, and had the mouth of a navvy. She was also local, which meant that her coming into St Paul's for shelter did make some sense. The crippled bloke, Mr Webb, and his family lived in the same building as the Chivers 'tribe' as he called them.

'Nine kids and no mother to care for 'em,' he said.

I explained as best I could why I was interested in Milly, but the women looked at me strangely anyway. I could understand that if the kid was on the game as it were, they would look on me with suspicion. After a bit, Mr Webb asked me to help him stand up and then moved me away from his party. I gave him a fag this time and we both lit up.

'Listen, mate,' he said as we sat down, 'it's like this. Milly Chivers's mum was . . . well, she was on the game, like . . .'

'Oh.' This wasn't unexpected. A lot of kids follow their mothers on to the streets. A prostitute, just like my Hannah. Poor woman.

'But she died,' Mr Webb said. 'Five years ago. Some say it was George Chivers, her old man, what done her.'

I frowned.

'Not actually, you understand,' Webb said, 'but 'cause she had to do what she done to keep him in drink! He's a boozer, George Chivers. His missus, Milly's mum – not a bad girl in spite of what the women say – she was always out getting money for him.' He lowered his voice. 'Would go with anyone, it was said. Then one night one of 'em, a bloke, like, beat her to death, poor cow – or so it's said. It was rumoured that perhaps old George had done it. You say Milly is here, in the cathedral like?'

'Y-yes.' I said. 'But now she's missing and—'

'Probably with someone, if you take my meaning,' Mr Webb said.

I did. Ten she might be, but just Milly's way of talking had made me think she had been making her living out of men. Hannah knows plenty of grown women on the game who started their trade as kids. It's always gone on, and it always will, especially around and about hard drinkers.

'B-but her father . . .'

'George Chivers, so it's said, had a good trade before the drink took him,' Mr Webb continued. 'Speaks nice, he does, educated. But he's been on the drink for fifteen years to my knowledge. Come from out Stoke Newington way, people said. Moved in to our building because it was all he could afford.' He smiled and shook his head grimly. 'People think it's all bowler hats and bookkeepers in the City, but there're some right places, I can tell you! Rooms left over from when poor people lived in Rookeries, you know? Ain't the Ritz where we live. It is a Rookery to be truthful. Only Mrs Herbert over there, the florist lady, only she's got a proper flat on our street.'

If indeed this Milly was 'my' Milly, then her prostitute mother had died when the child was five. She had one older sister, who also worked the streets, five brothers and two younger sisters. All but one of the brothers had, apparently, left home years ago. Milly and her older sister, it seemed, kept the younger children and their alcoholic father with the sale of their bodies. Once apparently a man of some substance, Mr Chivers's drinking had reduced his family to living in a bloody rookery, a collection of filth- and crime-ridden rooms that had been standard City accommodation for the poor in Victorian times. I had in my ignorance thought they'd all disappeared years ago. Thinking about what a grown man like Mr Phillips might have been doing with this girl from a rookery when the raid began and he brought her into the cathedral, made me feel a bit sick. But then maybe a man without a face does things that men with faces can't understand. Speaking as a man without a mind, I can see that. Not that that's an excuse for doing things with a child; there's never any excuse for that in my opinion.

'The Guildhall's on fire! Took a hit!' I turned away from Mr Webb and saw young George the chorister flop down beside me. 'Looks like it's had it!' He coughed on the smoke from the hundreds of fags people were puffing as well as that from the fires that burned outside. Although I didn't know it at the time, I later found out that getting water to put the fires out was becoming a problem all over the City. There just wasn't enough of it and high tide on the Thames was still hours away. It wasn't just the ancient Guildhall that was going to 'have it' this night. Monuments were, to me, the least of it, really. People's homes and businesses were already in ruins, and although there wasn't a lot of crying in the crypt that night, there were a lot of worried and just plain sad-looking faces.

Not that ordinary homes and businesses were on the mind of our Prime Minister, Mr Churchill, according to George. 'Mr Churchill telephoned Mr Matthews our Dean,' he said breathlessly. 'Mr Churchill has told the LFB to save the cathedral at all costs. Nothing else matters, not even to Mr Churchill!'

'Mr Churchill himself spoke to the Dean?'

'On the telephone, yes!'

Mr Smith, who I hadn't seen for some while and who looked as if he'd spent some considerable time fighting fires, had followed George in and now sat down beside him. His face was blackened and he gasped for breath over the top of his cocoa cup. 'Mr Churchill . . . gives us a few more firemen . . .' He sounded a bit contemptuous, but I said nothing. It wasn't my place. 'That little, er, the girl . . .' he started to ask me.

'I'm going to go and have another look around in a bit,' I said. 'I've seen her and we've spoken. She's called Milly, but she's not in here.'

'Probably nicking the silver candlesticks!' Mr Webb said. 'If I know Milly! I'd forget her, if I was you, mate. She'll be all right.'

Mr Smith gave me what I thought was a confused look.

I attempted to explain. 'M-Mr Webb here lives near to a g-girl we think might be the same M-Milly as—'

'I see,' Mr Smith said cutting me off as a lot of people do when the stutter begins to get on their nerves. 'Well, there's every watchman here tonight from all points north, south, east and west. One of us is bound to find her eventually.' He looked at me closely. 'You look all done in.'

I told him I always do, which is the truth. I told him where I was from and Mr Smith frowned. 'You East End boys have been taking it for a long time.' He then looked first at Mr Webb and then at me again and said, 'You should do as this chap says. Leave it. Rest up now. Who knows what we all may have to do in the next few hours? This church, believe me, is no easy lady to protect!'

I was exhausted – not that that was anything new. Young George had talked about how Hitler was targeting St Paul's and all the time I was thinking about how he was battering the docks. Mr Churchill wasn't apparently too worried about them at that moment. I could understand it. To destroy St Paul's would wound the soul of every Londoner alive. But still, killing the docks cuts us off from the world and the food it still manages to give us. The docks are our legs, if you like; take them away and we can't move. What Hitler was doing to the docks had kept me awake for months and, to be truthful, I was noticeably tired at this point. It wasn't like me. Maybe it was being around so many people hunkering down on cots and on the floor for the night? In spite of myself, for the first time in a long time, I felt quite peaceful. Were I a religious man, I might say that it was something to do with being in a church. But I'm not religious and so there had to be some other cause. Whatever the reason I went, very briefly, to sleep. When I woke up it was to find George, Mr Webb and Mr Smith gone and Mr Andrews standing over me.

'Mr Hancock, we have to talk,' he said.

Chapter Six

Mr Andrews led me out of the crypt and back into the nave of the cathedral. I'll be honest, I *was* done in. I hadn't slept in any real sense for months and as usual with me, every little bit of sleep that I did get was so precious, my waking from it was always a shock. As I climbed back up the stairs, my heart pounding in my chest, I felt sick and really quite unwilling to hear Mr Andrews out. But he gave me no choice which, as it turned out, was just as well.

Once into the nave, we made our way through the darkness, underneath the dome to the place where Mr Ronson's body had been. As I shone my torch at the pool of blood and offal that remained, Mr Andrews stopped and whispered, 'I'll explain in a moment. We'll sit in the quire stalls.'

I was horrified. I'd told him, and he should have known, not to move Mr Ronson's body until a copper could be found to take charge of it. If Mr Andrews suspected that Mr Ronson had been murdered, that was the right thing to do, even in very difficult conditions. The German raids are all too often used as cover for people wanting to knock off their relatives or rivals or both. It's so easy to miss clues in all the stink and destruction of the bombing. Now the coppers would never be able to tell from where, exactly, Mr Ronson had fallen – if he'd fallen.

Mr Andrews brushed something off the first row of quire stalls and sat down. He motioned with his torch for me to join him, which I did.

'M-Mr Andrews—'

'Mr Hancock,' he said, 'my wife tells me that you are a follower of the Catholic faith. Is that true?'

'Yes,' I said, 'I t-told you. I was born and brought up in it and . . . but I don't believe it any more, Mr Andrews. I'm afraid that me and God sort of parted from each other on the Somme.'

I expected to see an expression of disapproval, if not downright horror, on his skeleton face, but I didn't. By the light of my torch I could see that he was grave and drawn, but he wasn't disapproving in any way.

'Yes, well, I was . . . I was there too.' He swallowed hard. 'I served my country in the Great War.'

He said nothing more, but I felt that what he had said was enough. If I read him right he understood, even if he didn't approve, of my opinion about God. After all, I wasn't the first to lose my faith in the First Lot and I doubt very much that I was the last.

Mr Andrews moved his head closer to mine and said, 'Mr Hancock, whether you practise your Catholicism or not is of no interest to me. That you are a follower of Rome in any way, is.'

I frowned.

'Mr Hancock, strange as this may sound, now that Mr Ronson is no longer with us, you are the only man apart from the Dean that I feel I can completely trust.'

I was so shocked that I stopped stuttering completely. Or rather, I thought at the time that was the reason.

'Mr Andrews,' I said, 'you don't know me from a hole in the road.'

'Mr Hancock,' he replied, 'you have a friend, an Ernest Sutton, he is a vicar.'

Ernie Sutton was a bloke I'd been to school with. Vicar, Church of England of course, at our local church in Plaistow. We've stayed friends all these years, and we still share the odd pint from time to time.

'Ernest is a friend, of sorts,' Mr Andrews said. 'He has talked of you and so I recognised your name as soon as you mentioned your profession. You have been tenacious in looking for this missing child. Revd Sutton says that you have a skill and compassion with the dead, an abhorrence for the killing of the living.'

I would hope that most people would have an abhorrence for killing! And anyway, what did he mean about Ernie being a friend 'of sorts'? Did he perhaps mean that because they were both in the church they knew each other? Why didn't he just say that? I was just beginning to get exasperated when Mr Andrews explained.

'Mr Hancock, Revd Sutton, myself and an unspecified number of the men in the Watch are Freemasons.' He paused, letting me absorb his words which were really no great news to me. I'd known

Ernie was a Mason for years, I'd laughed at him for it! Like a lot of blokes, secret rituals and the wearing of funny aprons are not things I find myself attracted to. I found it, I must admit, a bit silly. Then when Mrs Andrews had just thrown the Masons into our conversation earlier I had thought, idly, that her husband was probably one of their number.

'I say unspecified because our watchmen come from many different lodges,' Mr Andrews said. 'I do not know them all by any means. However, you must know that the Freemasons of England are wholly opposed to Hitler and all his works.'

'I should hope so!' I said.

Mr Andrews shook his head as if throwing my comment away from him. 'But within the Brotherhood, opinions upon how this should be done, differ,' he said. 'The majority of us believe we must support Mr Churchill, his guns, his planes and the men who operate them. Tonight our leader has given us more firemen. We must also pray.'

The sound of boots and men's voices up in the Whispering Gallery briefly took our attention, but then Mr Andrews said, 'However, there are other brothers who believe that a more primitive solution is the way that we must pursue.' He looked down and the light, such as it was, shining up into his face made him look as if he had a face without eyes. 'There are brothers in the Craft who believe in dangerous things.' He looked up suddenly and almost pleaded with me. 'Not necessarily bad people, or, at least, I thought they were not until now . . . Mr Hancock, some of our brethren have been led to believe that the ways of our ancestors are our salvation. Alchemy, the science of the magician, is an element of their study. Also ancient rites created in former times by our predecessors . . . These were designed to appease . . . entities – devils, some would call them.'

For someone who had been brought up by Catholic parents, this was not news either. My old dad had always said that the Masons were rotten. Mum still didn't know that my 'nice friend Ernie' was a Mason and I had no intention of telling her. But it was our old parish priest, Fr Burton, I'd heard call them all 'Devil worshippers' – not that I'd believed that was in any way the truth. Now here was Mr Andrews, himself a Mason, telling me that there were 'some' brothers who were 'appeasing' devils. I didn't understand how this was anything to do with what we were all going through now and I told him so.

'With respect,' I said, 'none of us could be here tomorrow! This cathedral could be dust!'

'Which is precisely what these misguided brothers are trying to prevent!' Mr Andrews said, lowering his voice as he did so. 'This sorcery they practise is meant to save this place, don't you understand?'

'No.' If the magic these 'brothers' were practising was meant to be for the good of the cathedral, how could that be a bad thing?

Mr Andrews looked back into the thick gloom behind him and then leaned towards me. 'Mr Ronson went up on to the roof to help deal with the incendiary to which we initially called the fire service,' he said. 'On his way up, I met him and he said he had something to tell me. Mr Ronson was of the Brotherhood, but as a Jew, he was not sadly always approved of by everyone in it. Also he, like me, did not hold with what some of his brothers proposed even though he was initially privy to it. Some in the Craft are influenced by the Beast.' He suddenly looked very, very frightened.

'Maybe it was because as a Jew it wasn't strictly in Mr Ronson's tradition, although the Jews of course did practise it long ago . . .'

I didn't know what he was talking about and I said so. This sounded like a load of tommyrot to me and I was beginning to think that maybe Mr Andrews was barmier than I was.

'Sacrifice,' Mr Andrews interrupted me. 'Our ancestors practised it. Houses, great and sometimes small, too, were consecrated with human blood. There are churches where, it is said, bodies – particularly those of children – were buried underneath the foundations. It was by way of an offering to spirits and forces that pre-date Christianity. Such barbarism still survives. One does not walk under ladders for fear of tempting fate, for instance. But sometimes barbarity is inculcated, encouraged by those of evil intent.'

I must have looked like a codfish with my mouth open in shock.

Mr Andrews gestured towards the space underneath the dome and said, 'I believe Mr Ronson was sacrificed. He was pushed.'

'But you said that you didn't see . . .'

'I didn't see who did it, but I saw a watchman push him!' He wiped a thin, pale hand across his mouth and then said, 'There were only watchmen up there! I was down here, waiting for Ronson to come and tell me this thing he said was so important. Since November, when he first came to me with his fears, when we began discussing our brothers' association with the Beast, we had been conversing thus. I think he was about to tell me it was tonight. That tonight was to be the night of sacrifice. Something had alerted him and he was afraid, so afraid! Now—'

'Get the coppers!' I said. Why was he telling me? What the blazes could I do?

'The police are brothers, too, what will they do?' he said. 'And besides, you've seen how it is outside! You know what's happening to the City! Everyone is fighting fires, the police included. There is just fire now, just that!'

It was only then that I realised that something was missing. Sitting there in that hideous darkness, talking without stuttering in, I thought, some sort of shocked state I hadn't ever felt before, I hadn't noticed what had gone. But unless I looked outside, listened without great slabs of marble in the way, I would never know. I got up and, using my little torch to light me past the lake of blood underneath the dome, I headed towards the Great West Door.

Mr Andrews, hot on my heels said anxiously, 'What are you doing? Mr—'

I found the small door to the left-hand side of the great ceremonial entrance and I flung it open. The heat, the glare, the smell and the noise of Ludgate Hill melting into the stones of London flung me back into Mr Andrews's bony arms.

'Christ!'

'For the love of God, man!' Mr Andrews said. 'What do you think you're doing? Shut the door!'

'No! Not until I'm sure!'

'Sure? Sure of what?'

God it was hot! I could feel the skin burning on my face just as certainly as if I'd been blasted by flames from a forge. The noise of wood and plaster breaking down in the blinding flames was deafening. There were human voices too – the sound of firemen and coppers and wardens all calling out to each other, warning of the imminent collapse of buildings, of the danger from gas pipes, electric cables and deep, lethal cellars. There was a lot of noise, but none of it was anything like the drone of hundreds of *Luftwaffe* bombers overhead. No wonder I'd been able to speak like a normal human being!

'Sure that they've gone!' I said to Mr Andrews. Almost laughing now with the relief of it. 'The Jerries, they've gone!'

He looked at me with an expression that I just couldn't fathom on his face. I think that for a moment he might have felt that I believed that what he'd told me had been done to Mr Ronson had worked in some kind of magical way. I didn't. At that point I didn't believe anything except what I couldn't mercifully hear with my own ears. The bombers had gone!

'I don't know who it was that pushed Mr Ronson to his death,' Mr Andrews said. 'All I know is that it was a member of the Watch. I am sure of that.'

I looked at him again. He made me shudder and yet the fact that the bombers had gone was filling me with something that just might have been hope.

I'm not what you'd call an educated bloke. I went to

the local grammar school, so I was never any sort of dunce. I did well at my English, Latin and history learning, but science wasn't something I paid too much heed to. So I was surprised when my happiness at the absence of Jerry bombers overhead was cut so very short. Now I know, of course, that with so many fires raging through the City, Hitler didn't need to send any more of his Luftwaffe boys to possibly get shot down by our ack-ack. The firestorm that was just gathering its strength as I stood at that wide, open door was going to finish the job for him. I felt it as a swirling sensation around my feet. Mr Andrews, feeling it at exactly the same moment, screamed, 'Shut the door!'

I'm sure that, hot though my skin felt at that moment, I was white. I felt the blood drain at the same time as my feet began to lift up of their own accord.

'Bloody hell!'

It took both of us and all of our strength to get that door shut. Up above in the Whispering Gallery one of the watchmen called down and said, 'What's going on out there?'

Once he had managed to catch his breath, Mr

Andrews called back up, 'It's a firestorm! So much is burning, it's created a firestorm!'

I didn't hear what the watchman said in reply, but he ran towards the doorway that led to the stairs up top.

Mr Andrews turned to me and said, 'Listen, there isn't much time. Mr Ronson was aware that he was being watched by his brothers and that they knew he had passed certain details on to me. He had something more to tell, but whether they know if he had passed that on to me yet or not, I do not know.'

'The City's burning!' I said. 'Bloody hell, Mr Andrews, the City's burning and you're talking about bloody magic and alchemy and all sorts of rubbish!'

'Listen to me!' He grabbed me hard by the collar with his fierce, skeleton's hands and hissed into my face. 'You don't believe me? They will kill again in order to protect themselves because they know that I know something! It is tonight! It's *the* night! They will kill me!'

I gasped, catching my breath like a codfish yet again.

'Not that I am important!' Mr Andrews continued. 'But the cathedral must be protected, my wife must be protected, as must the Dean. I have Mr Ronson's body.

It is behind the quire stalls, where we were sitting. They must not have that either!'

'What?'

He'd moved a body he thought was a victim of murder to a place the coppers, should they ever be free, able and interested in anything apart from this fire ever again, would know was not where it was meant to be! Under the dome there was just that great pool of blood and offal. Mr Andrews couldn't be right in the head!

Mr Andrews whispered, saliva dripping into my ear from his mouth, 'They will defile it! It is what the acolytes of the Beast do!' I cringed, trying to pull back from this madman. 'There is a firestorm, the cathedral is not safe, their sorcery has not worked! More flesh, more blood will be required. I will die, I know that I will! They will not stop!'

'But Mr Churchill's told the fire service to save the cathedral! It'll be all right it—'

'They don't care about Mr Churchill! Their beliefs are driving them onwards! Tonight! I believe now they chose tonight! They will not stop!'

He pushed me away then and, crouching now beside

me, he began to weep. The poor fellow was quite obviously deranged. There was of course some truth in what he was saying as there nearly always is with people whose minds have gone. None of the blokes who lost it in the trenches did so because they believed that something that was unreal was happening. They were in danger and it was an evil, reeking hell. Mr Andrews was obviously exhausted from his fears for the cathedral and that had made him like he was. Probably, I thought, he had some sort of problem with some of the watchmen. Like him, most of them were educated people and, being architects, they possibly had ideas about how the building should be protected which he didn't agree with. In my head I talked myself into this way of thinking and as Mr Andrews slunk away from me into the darkness of the quire, I felt very sorry for him indeed. Freemasons were a bit odd and it was probably not a good thing that so many of them were in the police – them always being on the side of their own, as it were – but they weren't wicked. To think that a group of them might kill to gain protection from something far from Christian, the Devil – or the Beast as he would have it – was ridiculous.

But I didn't want Mr Andrews to think that I was ignoring him. 'I'm going to have a look for the little girl, Milly, Mr Andrews,' I said into the solid darkness of the quire.

'You do as you wish,' the bony man's voice replied bitterly. I had rejected his ideas and now he hated me. 'I will be here, you know who I will be with.'

Mr Ronson's poor dead body. I thought about going to get Mr Andrews's wife. I thought about telling her he'd lost his poor, battered mind. But then I remembered that she had gone on about all that Masonic stuff too when I'd spoken to her. Neither of them were right, poor souls.

'Oh, and when you find the child, make her safe, won't you?' Mr Andrews said. 'Children are especially valuable to the Beast.'

'Mr Andrews . . .' I was about to protest, but then my voice was literally drowned out by sound.

A noise like the hollow howl of an animal ran around the outside of the cathedral with the speed of a sprint runner. I spun as if trying to catch it, knowing that I couldn't. No one could. The winds of the firestorm were gathering strength.

Chapter Seven

Even though I'd met her, I didn't want to find Milly out of any sort of heroism on my part. I was sorry for her, especially in view of what Mr Webb had told me about her family. But I didn't care about her as such. I was still distracting myself from what was happening around me, and I was not thinking about Mr Andrews and his Beast, or whatever, at all. But calling 'Milly!' into the darkness of a building surrounded by a firestorm and possibly being laughed at and told to 'fuck off' as a result of that, was better than doing nothing. Milly was useful to me as a distraction.

'Have you seen Mr Andrews?'

It was George, the young choir boy. I was on the stairs going up to the Whispering Gallery yet again.

Not knowing the cathedral, I couldn't think of anywhere except 'up top' or on the stairs that the child could be. God knows I didn't want to go, although aside from the pains in my legs, I had to admit that the climbing was getting easier. I was still gasping for air, but by that time some of the panic over the smallness and darkness of the staircase had eased. I'm not what I used to be physically. Back in the old days, in my youth, I could run up flights of stairs and have breath left in my body at the top. Now I go up five steps and I feel as if I'm about to collapse. It's been like that for many years.

'I'm sorry, Mr Hancock,' George said as he watched my feeble struggles to talk. 'I'll let you catch your breath, shall I?'

'Mmm.'

'I don't suppose you've found that little girl yet, have you?'

Stupid boy had only just said he'd let me catch my breath! Christ! 'No . . .' I gasped.

We stood there, the boy and I, torches in our hands, almost nose to nose on that narrow staircase, until I'd recovered sufficiently to speak. I was a hundred and four steps up; I'd counted every one as I looked into every nook and cranny with my torch. Milly, given her obvious character and mischievousness, could, after all, be anywhere. I had been thinking that looking for her was not unlike how it must be chasing some little demon, when the thought of Mr Andrews and his barminess made me turn my mind away from all that and got me counting stairs again instead.

'I last saw Mr Andrews in the cathedral,' I said once my heart had stopped pounding so hard in my throat. I didn't tell him where exactly. If he was, as I suspected, back in the quire with Mr Ronson's body, it wasn't something a youngster like George needed to see. But could I tell the boy I thought that the chaplain had gone mad? Would George believe me? I doubted it. 'Why do you want Mr Andrews, George?' I said.

'I don't,' he said. 'But the Dean's still up top and' – he looked down at his hands – 'he told me to go down. There's a storm now . . .' He looked up suddenly. 'The Dean told me to go down and send Mr Andrews up. He, the Dean, said it isn't safe for me out there, on the roof any more.' He looked as if he was about to cry.

'The Dean's right, George,' I said. 'The wind's right

up now and it's whipping the flames really high. Where Mr Andrews is now, I don't know. But I'd get yourself straight down to the crypt if I were you, son. Let the ladies down there make you a nice cuppa.'

He smiled.

'Go on,' I said. 'You're a good boy, you've been all over the place tonight, looking out for people. Your mum and dad'll be proud of you when you go home.'

George looked at me strangely for a few seconds and then he flew down that staircase. But then he was only a youngster and he was familiar with the place. I, on the other hand, was so stiff from all the climbing that I felt almost broken. Still breathless, I could feel every second of my forty-eight years. I looked into corners of those stairs as if I were looking for rats or mice, peering into the tiniest crevices. I don't know why Mr Andrews's talk about the Beast and demons had got under my skin. I certainly wasn't going to find Milly, small as she was, in any of those places.

The Whispering Gallery, just like the crypt, has always got a watchman on the 'book' or recording the incidences of bombing, fires, etc. So I was expecting to see at least one bloke up there. But there didn't appear to be anyone about. I shone my weak little torch all around what I could see of the gallery, but I saw no one and nothing. There was just that great space beyond the precarious wooden floorboards and over the flimsy-looking railings. Down, down on to the cathedral floor below – where Mr Ronson had met his death – at the end of a fall I dared not even imagine.

There's a bench that runs around the inside walls of the Whispering Gallery and so because I was exhausted, I sat down on it. Panting and sweating, I rested my head back against the wall and it passed through my mind that I might hear some sort of whispering from somewhere, but I didn't. In fact, I didn't hear anything for about a minute, which was strange, given what was happening in the galleries and on the roofs above where I was. And even when the smallest noise that can be imagined, a slight scraping or brushing of the gallery floor, broke the silence I felt it rather than actually heard it. In fact, even that is not quite true because even before I felt it, I had that sensation of all the hairs standing up on the back of my neck. My eyes flew open and, just for a second, I thought I saw something, or some things, move over by the door to the stairs. Not that *I* could move to go over and have a butcher's. As well as being physically shattered, I was losing control again! I know the signs. Soon the blood of the battlefield would be pouring down the walls and then I'd be no use to anyone, least of all myself. My heart pounded and I began to sweat really heavily. Then I heard the things over by the door to the stairs breathe, huskily and with throats that rasped. Oh, God! Oh, Christ!

And just as the silence had been shocking, so was the noise that followed it. From there being no watchmen, there were now hundreds of them in less than a minute. Every trace of the fear I had felt only moments before, left, and I even managed a smile as a line of tired and blackened faces passed before me. Even the Dean had come in and, on seeing me, he sat down for a moment and asked me how I was.

'Can't be up there any longer,' he said as he took his tin hat off and then rubbed his forehead with the back of his soot-stained hand. 'Leave it to the other chaps for a bit. Any news about the little girl?'

'No.'

The Dean shook his head sadly and then, suddenly

remembering something he said, 'Oh, Mr Phillips is on the roof now! We're all on about fifteen minutes at the moment, so if you stay here you should see him in a bit.'

'Mr Phillips came to relieve you?' I asked – just to be sure.

'Yes, but only just,' Dean Matthews laughed as he said it. It was as if suddenly all of his earlier tension had left him. Maybe actually seeing Mr Phillips alive had helped to put his mind at rest. After all, Phillips was one of his watchmen, a person for whom he had some responsibility. 'Mr Phillips, Mr Smith and, I think, a new chap, a Mr Potter, I believe he's called, came in late. I'll be honest, I don't always know chaps' names unless I know people very well. But anyway, they'd run all the way up from the ground and were a bit puffed, I can tell you!'

Maybe it had been them I had heard over by the stairs, breathing heavily? Mr Phillips, Mr Smith and Mr Potter! But then, if that was the case, Mr Smith, at least, knew me and Mr Phillips had to know by this time that some foreign-looking bloke was searching for him. Why, if they were on the gallery at the same time as I was, hadn't they spoken up? Sometimes I get taken by this fear that people are trying to make me even more mad than I already am. Mr Andrews and his stories about the Masons had struck me like that. Not that I thought that he had been doing it deliberately. I just sometimes get the feeling that being around other mad people is bad for me and that had been one of those times. If things in my head had been different, I would have told the Dean about Mr Andrews's fears regarding the watchmen then. But I didn't. Instead, I watched the Dean and all the blokes with him go back down on to the ground once again and I waited for Mr Phillips, Mr Smith and Mr Potter.

The Dean had said that Phillips, Smith and Potter had run all the way up from the ground to help relieve the others on the roof, but I couldn't remember hearing any feet on the stairs breaking that silence I'd found myself in on the Whispering Gallery. How could anyone apart from a child run up such a flight? There'd just been some scraping then breathing, but not of a running or laboured kind. Now I thought about it, it was more like a suppressed laugh.

I sat by the stairs, out of the way of the bloke on the

book and the few others who were now on the gallery with him. From time to time they looked over at me and I thought I saw a couple of them exchange knowing looks. I'm used to this. I know that much of the time I come over as an odd character. I know I'm not right and especially when I'm frightened, as I always am on these bomb-filled nights, I have everything that a madman in an asylum has. I hear things, see things, and I don't behave as a man who is in control of himself should. But then I thought that maybe the blokes in the gallery were looking at me because of my colour. I'd lost my cap out amongst the fires hours before and I know that without any sort of hat I look about as oriental as it's possible to be. As an old teacher of mine used to say years ago, 'There's more than just a touch of the tar-brush about you, Hancock!' Yes, there's my Indian mother, and one of my sisters who is so dark she hardly leaves the house . . . Not that I've ever felt the colour thing badly myself and, in truth, I did feel that the men in the gallery had to be looking at me because I was odd rather than because I was foreign. I suddenly realised that I was muttering to myself. I stopped doing it immediately and then went out on to the stairs to wait for the blokes coming back down from the roof.

It smelt of smoke and melted metal out there, but I made myself stand and wait until I heard the tired footsteps of the men coming down as well as the more lively ones of those relieving them coming up. Pressed against the warm stone wall, so I didn't get in the way of the passing human traffic, I waited until I saw Mr Smith come down and then I button-holed him.

'Where's Mr Phillips?' I asked.

He laughed, which struck me as an odd thing to do. 'He went down below ages ago,' he said, 'with Potter. Didn't you see them?'

'No.' Nobody, as far as I could tell, had come down from the roof after Mr Smith and everyone else had gone up to relieve the Dean.

'Went down early, they did,' he said. 'Potter felt a bit dodgy.' His face dropped into an expression of sadness. 'It's nightmarish up there. Hot and . . . The London we know is going.' His smoke-ringed eyes filled with tears and so I didn't detain him any longer. I had no reason to embarrass him by watching him cry. I also knew how he felt. That was my city down there burning, too. But putting that all aside, Mr Smith wasn't telling the truth. I didn't know exactly how he wasn't telling the truth, but he wasn't, and Mr Potter, well, he was just not right, I felt. His presence, as another witness to the existence of Mr Phillips, was a bit too *convenient*, I felt.

Mr Andrews would have seen Phillips and this Potter bloke pass by from his seat in the quire. I could, probably, have gone back to the Whispering Gallery, leaned over and called down to him. But even if you're not religious, you don't shout out in a church; it just isn't done. And so although the thought of walking, even in a downward direction, on those bloody stairs again made me want to scream, I started to make my way back down them anyway, legs trembling as I did so. When I reached the quire, however, I did eventually, scream. Anyone would have done so in my position.

I didn't know how Mr Andrews had died. There was nothing to actually see about the body that could give me any clue. All I could make out was that there was blood. On the stall beside the body, it could have been leaking from Mr Andrews or there was a possibility it came from the body lying behind the chaplain, that of the unfortunate Mr Ronson. In spite of Mr Andrews's belief that he had to guard Ronson's body from some of his fellow Masons, it hadn't been moved so far. It was still there, with, I noticed, one of Mr Andrews's still warm as – I touched it – dead hands on its shoulder. He'd died very recently and, although blood was present, and in spite of the fears he'd talked to me about, I had to assume he'd done so naturally. He wasn't young, he wasn't right in the head, and a bloke he knew and trusted had died. We were all in the middle of a bloody furnace – his heart could very easily have given out. If I reckoned that the blood had come from Mr Ronson's body, it all made sense. But something in me, that bit that lives in fear and suspicion of everything and everyone, niggled away. What if what Mr Andrews had said about his Masonic 'brothers' was true? After all, if they had killed him because of what he knew about Mr Ronson's death, maybe they knew he'd been talking to me? Maybe I was next on their list for the 'chop'?

Although I was muttering to myself, telling myself

it was bloody stupid what I was doing, I moved the body to have a better look at it. Mr Andrews looked as if he were at peace and so, in spite of all the things he'd told me earlier about the Masons, I couldn't really believe he had been killed. I'd at least half convinced myself that he'd been an old man who was out of his mind.

I put my hands around his chest and began to push him a little way along the quire stall, away from the blood. Of course I couldn't see exactly what I was doing at that moment because I couldn't stand up, push and hold my torch all at the same time. But when I'd finished, I took my torch out of my pocket and shone it down. Mr Andrews had toppled over to one side, so that his behind was sticking up. Cassocks as worn by priests and other divines are usually black and the one that Mr Andrews wore was no exception. He was a thin man and the cassock would, as it had done in life, have hung very loosely on him had it not been stuck to him by all the blood. There wasn't just blood either; there were rips, great gashes in the cloth of the cassock, too. Strange though it was, given the almost peaceful look on his face, Mr Andrews appeared to have been violated, stabbed in his nether parts. Whether that had actually killed him, I couldn't know. But the poor old sod had been attacked up his backside and I had to stifle a scream once I realised this.

As soon as I was able, I ran towards the stairs down to the crypt – there wasn't, after all, anyone else about in the cathedral whom I could see. But once I was in that crowded half-asleep basement I made myself slow down before I found someone to tell. After all, given what was going on outside, people had enough to worry about. I looked for the Dean, but not finding him, I went over to the bloke who was currently on the book.

'I need somebody to help me,' I said. 'It's Mr Andrews.' I didn't know how else to put it. 'He's had an accident.'

The watchman, a short, very posh-sounding chap who was probably in his fifties, looked at me and then said, 'An accident? What sort of accident?'

He'd looked at me as if I was nothing. Some hysterical, wide-eyed brown bloke was probably what he saw.

I leaned in close to him, which was obviously

something he really didn't like, because he tried in vain to pull away from me. I held his head and whispered, 'He's dead.'

The bloke, a Mr Harris, I later discovered, looked across the top of his little round glasses and gave me a stare that told me he didn't believe what I was saying.

'I'm an undertaker by trade,' I continued. 'I know a dead body when I see one.'

He gulped. 'Well, then, we must deal with him, er . . .' he said.

'Yes, but quietly,' I said. 'These people down here . . .'

'Oh, quite so! Quite so!' He was white now, poor chap. 'How did he . . . ?'

'I don't rightly know.' I didn't want to get into that. I can't always be certain about everything I've seen and the nature of Mr Andrews's wounds were so peculiar that I didn't feel able to trust myself.

Mr Harris said he'd tell people that it wasn't safe to go into the cathedral for a little while and then he got two fellows to come with me. They'd been near to hand when I was telling the book man what had happened and they'd both volunteered to come.

As we walked back up into the cathedral it struck me how quiet it was now. The Dean had, it was said, ordered all the doors to be shut because of the storm outside giving those of us in the cathedral no option but to wait it out. We weren't locked in, but I did have a feeling of being trapped, and I was beginning to panic. By the time we entered the quire I had begun to shake.

'So where are we looking?' the taller of the two watchmen said.

'On the left,' I answered. 'In the front row of stalls.'

I heard him move over there and then stop.

'Nothing here.'

I'd had my torch pointed away from those stalls until now. I swung around and, standing next to the taller bloke, I looked and saw what he saw.

'Nothing?'

My heart began to pump hard now as I began to search through the stalls behind where I'd found Mr Andrews.

'Mr Ronson was here, too,' I muttered as I looked, amazed, at absolutely nothing human at all.

The shorter of the two blokes, who had been

looking on the other side of the quire, came over and said, 'Nothing over there.'

They both looked at me. 'Are you sure that you saw Mr Andrews?' the taller one said.

I scraped my hand along the quire stalls in front of me and then held my bloodied fingers up for them to see. 'Look!'

'Blood,' the shorter one said. He shrugged. 'Someone could have tripped and hurt themselves. Things happen in the dark.'

'There's a lot of it,' I said as I scraped even more up with my hands.

'If Mr Ronson was, as you say, put over here . . .'

'Yes, but where is he now?' I said. 'Where is he now?'

These blokes didn't believe me.

But then had I seen Mr Andrews, or had he and his grisly, strange wound just been inside my head? Something bloody had been laid on these stalls at some point because there was blood everywhere. These two blokes had seen it, so that, at least, wasn't my imagination. Mr Andrews could have been lying dead in the quire stalls and someone could have moved him. But why? Unless he hadn't been dead. He'd still been warm when I touched him. And then I remembered that George the choir boy had been looking for Mr Andrews. George would, possibly, know what was what. If George was all right himself, of course . . .

'Everyone who isn't in the crypt is up on the roof,' the taller bloke said. 'With that wind out there fires can spread from one building to the next in a heartbeat. We're still not out of the woods yet, not by a long chalk. The cathedral is completely surrounded.'

'I didn't see George down in the crypt,' I said. 'And he had been looking for Mr Andrews. He asked me about him. If we can find George, maybe . . .'

'You'll find that Mr Andrews was just asleep,' the shorter man said. 'As for Mr Ronson's body? I expect the Dean's had it moved. Mr Matthews wouldn't want it left out in an undignified fashion. That's what's happened, sure as eggs are eggs.' He smiled.

He was, I felt, humouring me in that way people who know me are inclined to do. But this man didn't know me! Was I so obviously round the twist to him?

'Mr . . .'

'Bolton,' he said.

'I'm not mad, you know,' I said.

'I didn't say that you were,' Mr Bolton replied. 'I wouldn't say anything like that, especially not to a chap I didn't know.'

They were all so posh, these architects! But then not just anyone can do fire-watching duty and good on 'em for it. I knew I was becoming silly with it all now. I muttered that I was sorry.

Mr Bolton's taller mate, who was called Mr Arnold, said, 'We'll go down and tell Mr Harris that everything's tickety-boo.'

'Yes, but it isn't,' I began and then I stopped myself, my words fading into just a load of muttering.

If nothing else we should get the coppers in to see to Mr Ronson! But then where his body was now, God alone only knew. All that stuff Mr Andrews had told me about the Masons had really unnerved me. It was tommyrot, of course, but with that howling wind moaning around the building whipping up flames that could kill us all in minutes outside, my nerves were stretched very tight. I kept telling myself this as the two blokes took me back down to the crypt once again.

I looked in every corner I knew underneath the cathedral but I didn't once find George, Mr Andrews, the Dean or even, as far as I could tell, Mr Phillips. I even asked around for the bloke with the mask, but no one seemed to have seen him except, of course, for Mr Smith and the Dean, who'd told me he'd seen him on the roof. Now joined by Mr Bolton and Mr Arnold, Mr Smith said, 'You seem to have a knack of missing Mr Phillips, don't you, Mr Hancock? Everyone else has seen him, everyone except you.'

Everyone except me had also *not* seen Mr Andrews sitting up dead in the quire stalls. I began to question myself seriously in my head until yet again, thinking about Mr Phillips and what Mr Smith had said about him, made me stop.

'Only you and the Dean have seen Mr Phillips,' I said to him. 'I haven't come across anyone else who has actually—'

'I've seen him several times myself,' Mr Arnold cut in sharply. 'As have you, I believe, haven't you, Cyril?'

Mr Bolton looked away when he agreed with what Mr Arnold had said. I didn't believe him, he looked far too shifty to me. Not that I could prove anything by this, and I was still the only person, as far as I knew, who had seen Mr Andrews dead.

'There you are,' Mr Smith said to me with a shrug. 'No mystery.' Then he smiled. 'The best of us get confused up there in the dark.' He looked upwards to the ceiling of the crypt. 'A lot of people say the cathedral is haunted, although I don't actually hold with that myself. But the dark does play tricks and the dark combined with the fear everyone is feeling is a powerful thing.'

I agreed with him because it was easy and I was exhausted. But I was very suspicious, as the dreams I had shortly afterwards when I lay down on the crypt floor for a kip made plain. I must have slept for about an hour. When I woke up with a gasp later on, there wasn't much moving about in the crypt. Only outside in that furious firestorm was there real movement.

Chapter Eight

One of the cathedral ladies saw me move and came over with a cup of tea. As she put it in my hands she said, 'You were making noises in your sleep. Are you all right?'

I wasn't, but I didn't tell her that. She seemed like a nice middle-aged lady, what would she want to know about my dreams of death? There'd been no blood in my nightmare this time, just a feeling of desertion, as if everyone close to me had suddenly died. Although the bombing had stopped, I wondered how things were back home. It seemed, just as people were saying, as if Hitler had been targeting the actual Square Mile as opposed to the Docks or anywhere else. So maybe, for once, bombing down our way had been light. Having said that it's well known that the

Luftwaffe often drop what's left of their loads just anywhere on their way back to the Channel. Bastards! And what of my old Auntie Annie up in Finsbury? Although not at the centre of the action as we were in St Paul's, she must have seen a fair old bit where she was – and Annie, like me, was no lover of air-raid shelters. I tried to imagine her sitting in her chair in her scullery, all disapproving and covered in dust. But at moments I could also see her dead, too. It wasn't a dream, it was just a picture in my head.

I stood up and lit a fag. Once I'd smoked it, I planned to go up into the cathedral and see what was happening. Milly or no Milly, I'm too restless a soul to sit about doing nothing. And if the kid was about and I could get her to come down to safety in the crypt, then so much the better. Maybe I'd even get to see Mr Andrews, if I was lucky. I literally shuddered at the thought of that. Mr Andrews was dead! People could say what they liked about his having been asleep, but I'm an undertaker, I know what a dead person looks like and he was as dead as it's possible to get when I found him. I looked over to where the women were and I saw Mrs Andrews, who managed a little smile in my direction. She obviously didn't know. As soon as I'd finished my fag, I went up above where I found that the door to the left of the Great West Door was open and crowded with blokes. Over the tops of their tin hats all I could see was flames of red and yellow moving as if they had muscles. I walked towards them across a floor that was still wet with Mr Ronson's blood. If he had, as Mr Andrews had claimed, been sacrificed in some way, then whatever he'd been sacrificed to had been given a lot of the red stuff to be getting on with.

As I got closer to the door, someone I didn't know turned and looked at me.

'You from Hitchcock's, are you?' he asked.

'No,' I said.

'They've all come up to see what's what,' the bloke said. 'Must be shocking to see your place of business burn to the ground.'

Some people were on the steps outside, some of them women who were crying. The textile wholesalers Hitchcock, Williams and Co. had had it. The Dean had given instructions that nobody should be going outside because of the fierceness of the storm, but people – mainly Hitchcock employees – were ignoring this, and Revd Matthews was himself nowhere to be found. I recognised a couple of people from the crypt including the young lad, Ted, and his girl Mabel, who had been crying. Going to work every day was something a lot of people had begun to take for granted just before this war started. The last twenty years haven't meant much in the way of money for ordinary working people, but just before the war things were, I felt, picking up. What must it be like to go to work and find that your company as well as your job just didn't exist any more? My apprentice Arthur, Doris, our office girl, and my old bearer Walter walk to our place every day over broken glass but, so far, there's always been a job at the end of it for them. There's always a chance that one day there won't be. There's a big chance of that.

'Do you know where the Dean is?' I asked the bloke who'd spoken to me earlier. He was a watchman, but one that I hadn't come across before.

'Up on the roof, I think,' he said. 'I think he's just about up there all the time now that things are so bad. But I don't rightly know. When the All Clear went, some people thought that we were safe and sound and started out into the street. But as you can see . . .' He moved his hand out in front of him in a half-circle.

'The All Clear?' I hadn't heard it. I must have been asleep. 'When?'

He shrugged. 'Half an hour ago? An hour? I don't remember.' His smoke-blackened face had just a tinge of copper on the cheeks now, courtesy of Hitchcock, Williams and Co. 'It doesn't mean anything, anyway, not to us.'

I stared at him.

'The water's running out,' he said. 'Everything's ablaze: the Guildhall, Barts Hospital, City churches whose names I don't even know. The LFB can't get to everyone and, anyway, what can they do even if they do? They've been told to save this place at all costs.' And then he leaned in close to me and I could hear that his accent was almost exactly the same as mine. 'But what can they do, really? We're fucked,' he whispered.

Pulling back, I looked into eyes which were easily as dark as my own.

'Where are you from?' I asked.

He smiled. 'Your manor originally, or somewhere nearby.'

'But you're not—'

'I'm an architect, my name's Roger Garner and I live in Wood Green,' he said. But then he leaned in towards me again and said, 'But for them in the know, there's a little group of Spaniards at the top of Brick Lane. The name I was born with was Roger Garcia. My dad changed it, after the Spanish war . . . We're not Spaniards, well, a long time ago we . . .' He looked down at the yellow of the flames reflected in the marble beneath his feet. 'We were a long time ago, way back.'

I'd heard that there were Spaniards, from donkey's years ago, living somewhere in the Shoreditch area, but I'd never knowingly met one before. There'd been some bitterness towards the Spanish after their civil war. A lot of East Enders, commies mainly, lost their lives fighting for socialism out there. Then when General Franco and the fascists won, many people felt as if it had all been for nothing. We know now that the weapons Franco had were German and that Hitler was using the Spaniards to test them out for him. Some people don't like this too much. How Roger Garner knew I wasn't one of those people, I couldn't imagine. Maybe, seeing as how we had no water, it was by way of some sort of confession? After all, being a Spaniard, he would certainly be a Catholic and he'd made it very plain he felt we were doomed. But why he'd say such things to me, I didn't know. All I can say now is that even when people don't know what I do for a living they sometimes tell me personal things or secrets about themselves. There is something about an undertaker, even a barmy one, that almost draws such information out of people.

'Have you seen Mr Andrews?' I asked him after a reasonable amount of time had passed since his confession.

'No,' he said. 'There was a rumour that he was dead, though, but it was a load of tosh. Mrs Andrews was very chipper when I last saw her.'

She'd been fine when I'd seen her too.

'I think that all the cathedral staff must be up on the roof now,' Mr Garner said.

'Fighting the fires?'

'As best they can,' he answered. 'Mind you, come to think of it, the Dean and the other clericals have been up there for a very long time now.' He frowned. 'Other chaps have come and gone up and down to the roof, but I haven't seen Revd Matthews, Mr Andrews, or even that young choir boy, for probably the best part of an hour. Just the heat for that length of time could kill you!'

The stench from the fires was awful – a mixture of burning cloth, animal fat, wood smoke and tar. I started to cough, along with just about everyone else at that doorway. I went inside after a bit, unlike the rest of them. Out in the glare of the fires, they all continued to watch Hitchcock's burn while I disappeared into the darkness and on to the bloodied floor of St Paul's. If someone had indeed sacrificed Mr Ronson to something to save the cathedral, they hadn't done a very good job. According to Mr Garner the stores of water we had had were running low and even with the LFB doing everything they could to save the cathedral, how did we know they would continue to have any water themselves? As well as meeting Mr Garner, my brief trip outside the cathedral had shown me enough for me to realise that all the streets around us were on fire. We could all burn, or boil alive inside our gilded marble prison. It was a possibility.

I told myself very firmly that I still had Milly to find. I also told myself, with good reason, that the fact that no one seemed to be worried about where Mr Ronson's body had gone to was strange. It had completely disappeared and, whether anyone believed that Mr Andrews was alive or dead might be by the by, but that Mr Ronson had gone was a certainty and the fact that nobody seemed to care was frightening. Saying that the Dean had moved him 'somewhere' wasn't good enough.

I'd just distracted myself beforehand, afraid as much as anything of my own damaged mind. Now I decided that if something was going on, I was going to find out what it was. Although I knew that I could be burnt to a crisp at any minute, I didn't do what I did this time as a distraction. I did it because I, like Mr Garner, needed to find some sort of peace before I died.

* * *

I searched the quire stalls, the quire aisles and the north and south transepts. If someone had really hidden Mr Ronson's body, then it was unlikely that they'd do it anywhere as obvious as those places, but if I was going to explore the whole cathedral, then I had to do so properly. In the dark and with only that weak little torch to guide me, I had to look carefully into all the corners and crannies of the great cathedral to make sure that I didn't miss anything. Even then I couldn't be certain that what I was looking at wasn't anything sinister. Not that everything in that dark, threatening place wasn't sinister. The great columns on each side of the nave looked as if they disappeared up into smoke. It gave them, to my mind, a look of the gates of Hell of the religious instruction of my youth. In the quire my little torch would sometimes catch the edge of a glittering mosaic; a pointy-beaked peacock, open-mouthed fish and, far away, heavenly people. I would have prayed too if I could, I was so afraid. My mother, God bless her, would have told me to force myself had she been with me. Something was coming, because all the hairs on the back of my head were standing on end.

'Mr Hancock?'

I didn't recognise the voice. A figure in the middle of the nave was speaking to me. Small drips of water from the stirrup pumps up above pitter-pattered on to the top of my head.

'Mr Hancock?'

Were it a ghost from the Great War it would have called me 'Private' or just 'Hancock', but it addressed me as 'Mr', and so it must have been real.

'Yes?' I answered. 'What do you want?'

It began to move towards me. Quite tall, parts of it swished against the bloodied ground as it moved. It was literally trudging through Mr Ronson's offal.

'I don't want anything,' the voice said. 'I've come to tell you something.' And then, as if suddenly falling in as to what the problem was, he said, 'It's me, Mr Hancock, George.'

'Oh, blimey!'

I felt a fool. Of course it was George, George the choir boy in a long flapping rain mackintosh.

'Sorry, George,' I said as he got closer. 'I didn't recognise you. It's so dark in here and, I'll be honest, son, it's a little frightening, isn't it?'

'We could all die,' the lad said simply. But he didn't

sound what you'd call upset until he said, 'Not that any of that matters. The cathedral is in great peril and that is what we have to think about.'

He stopped then because he was crying. Even in the young, crying amongst men isn't looked well upon and I knew that I should tell him to 'buck up' or something at this point. But I didn't. It's not my way. Men cried in the Great War and their officers said stupid, useless things to try and make them stop. They did, generally, then some of them went off and shot themselves. I've seen it with my own eyes. I let George cry.

After about a minute, the lad appeared to pull himself together and he said, 'Mr Phillips says that if you'd like to wait in the quire stalls, he'll come and see you about that little girl.'

'You've seen him? Mr Phillips?' I asked.

'Of course,' George said. 'As everybody's told you, Mr Hancock, you keep missing him.'

'So where is he?'

'Up top,' George said as he looked up into the black smokiness of the dome. 'You don't need to go up there again and he'll be down in a minute, when his shift it over.'

He moved as if to go but, as he went to go past me, I grabbed hold of one of his arms. 'George,' I said, 'have you seen Mr Andrews?'

'Yes.' I couldn't see his face, not clearly, not through the thick, thick gloom. It had been George, I remembered, who had asked to see Mr Andrews shortly before I found what I knew deep down inside and, whatever others might say, was the chaplain's dead body.

'And the Dean?'

'Reverend Matthews? He's on the roof,' George said.

The Dean, like Mr Phillips, and like Mr Andrews, was recently always somewhere that I was not. In spite of, apparently, being just about to meet Phillips, I was beginning to worry about the Dean. Was he really just 'up top' all this time, or had he, too, gone the way of his seemingly unfortunate chaplain?

George tried to pull himself out of my grasp, but I hung on tightly because I still had something else to ask him and also because I was becoming alarmed by the boy's caginess.

'George,' I said, 'do you know what has happened to Mr Ronson's body?'

'Mr Andrews moved it,' he said.

'Yes, to the quire. But now it's gone.'

'I don't know anything about it.' His voice was barely a whisper. Underneath my fingers, his mackintosh-clad arm squirmed and twisted. 'I have to go.'

I didn't tell George that I thought he was lying because, if he was, then he was doing so reluctantly; I could hear both the fear and the embarrassment in his voice. At heart he was a good boy and that is something that I believe to this day. But I knew as he broke free and left me, that he wasn't telling me the truth. I also knew that there was no power on earth that was going to make me go and wait in those bloodied quire stalls for anyone.

I hid. I wanted to see whether anyone did, in fact, come to meet me in the quire, but I didn't want them to know that I was there. I wasn't thinking about Mr Andrews's Masonic theories at the time. I didn't know what was going on. But I was afraid. Crouching down at the end of the quire stalls nearest the high altar, I kept on looking around me to see if anyone was coming. I looked towards the door to the Whispering Gallery mostly. Time passes slowly like this and I was quite glad that I couldn't see my watch, though I would have been able to if I had got out my torch. To be truthful, after doing this once, it was too much trouble for me to be bothered to do it again.

'Up top' in the Whispering Gallery and beyond, I could hear the voices of the watchmen still shouting to each other to go here, there and everywhere to fight the flames. I imagined that Mr Phillips, if indeed he was actually real, would be coming down after the fifteen- or twenty-minute stint most of them did. When the shift changed I'd know, because men would start gathering in the cathedral to go up while others would begin the long climb down. I wouldn't be able to miss him easily.

Some blokes, some of the next shift, came up from the crypt and stood around the door to the top. I couldn't hear everything that they were saying, but I did manage to catch Mr Ronson's name a few times. The men seemed to be saying they were sorry he was dead but they didn't sound upset about it. As a nation, we tend to hide our feelings but there was something else in the words of these blokes that was something like disappointment.

'Mr Hancock, I am Harold Phillips; I understand you've been looking for me.'

Where he'd come from, I couldn't imagine. What was certain, though, was that there was no way on earth he could have come from above. I'd been watching in that direction for some time and I'd heard and seen nothing. Mr Phillips, if Phillips he was, had come from the direction of the high altar. I stood up quickly, while he stepped backwards, and I shone my torch into his face.

The mask was easy to see. They generally are, even if they've been made for a person who can pay a lot for them. However skilled the artist, you can't put back what isn't there completely. This mask was very rough and ready. Even by the weak light of my torch I could see that it didn't really fit. But because I didn't want to take the risk of embarrassing the poor bloke by staring, I looked away.

'I understand you brought a little girl in with you when you came on shift,' I said. 'Milly.'

'I've no idea what the child's name is,' he said. 'But

yes, I came in with a child. She was outside, just wandering. I was afraid for her.'

His voice was muffled slightly but because I wouldn't look up at his face I couldn't see whether this was because of the mask or not.

'Why?'

I would have thought that someone would've told him that Milly was missing by now, but obviously no one had. So I told him and he said, 'Oh, well, I haven't seen her since. We've been' – he wiped one of his hands across his forehead as if to illustrate the smut and grime on his face and therefore his involvement with the fire – 'run off our feet.'

I looked up just at the moment that the mask moved. What would have happened, had I not seen that, I really do not know. It came free from his face in a way I hadn't expected. Mr Phillips, so Mr Steadman had told me, had lost his nose and much of his mouth in the Great War. Mr Phillips, or whoever he was, saw the look on my face and then looked down at what he now had in his hand. He punched me so hard in the face that I lost consciousness.

Chapter Nine

I didn't know where I was when I first came round. When darkness is complete there's nothing to give you any clues. Sight was hopeless as a measure in this case and so it was, in a way, a good thing that some of my other senses started to take over. The fact that I felt wet was a starting point but it was the smell that really got to me. It was metallic and sadly very familiar. Either the blood was someone else's or it was my own. But then Mr Phillips, or whoever that fresh-faced nutter had been who had hit me, had thumped me really hard and had probably broken my poor old conk. It certainly felt painful enough to be broken.

I didn't even bother to look for my torch on the basis that he must have taken it off me. I wasn't wrong.

What he hadn't taken, however, was my box of matches. After digging around in my jacket pocket for a bit I found first my fags and then my matches. I lit a match and looked around. I was in what seemed to be a cupboard and I wasn't alone. Mr Andrews and what was left of Mr Ronson were in there with me. As the only one of us who could make any sort of sound, I let out what I hoped was a scream – who knew, maybe someone would come and rescue me – but what came out was a whimper. Christ, but my head hurt! The 'Mr Phillips' who had hit me and who was most certainly not that gentleman, had meant to do me some serious harm. In fact, why or how I was still alive I wasn't to know until later on. All I did know then was that there was someone running around the cathedral impersonating Mr Phillips. This badly masked man, God knew where he'd got his mask from, had known both where Mr Ronson's body was and the fact that Mr Andrews was really dead. My Swan Vesta went out just before it burnt my fingers and so I took out another match and lit it. As I moved my hand around to try and find out exactly where I was, I caught sight of poor old Mr Andrews's face which now had the appearance of being battered; his head was also at what I knew was not a natural angle. He'd been shoved in what was a narrow, very tall cupboard, without too much ceremony. Poor old sod, he'd been a bit mad with all his barmy ideas about the Masons – if indeed his ideas had been barmy, I was now thinking – but there'd been no harm in him. He may even have been right about why Mr Ronson had died and who had killed him. These were frightening thoughts although in a way they were also comforting for me. If I was in company with real, stone-cold corpses, then what was and had been happening wasn't just doing so in my head. I looked at the mess that was Mr Ronson and I thanked God that at least I was used to this sort of thing. On top of everything else that was happening to me, the last thing I needed was to be sick all over myself. After all, wherever I was now, I had to find some sort of way to get out.

My match went out and so I lit another and this time, instead of looking at the bodies flung in with me, I looked at the doors in front of me. About four feet up from where I was on the floor was a handle which was just above a keyhole. I'd have to stand up to get to it and so, once this next match had gone out, that was what I did. I had to push down on the floor and what I thought was a leg beside me to do so, but, as I've said before, squeamish is something I am not. Pushing up on knees that are quite stiff these days without climbing hundreds of stairs wasn't much fun, though. As I creaked my way upwards, I found myself swearing under my breath as the pain cut into my kneecaps. There isn't much, if anything really, to recommend getting old. Once I was up, I pushed down on the door handle which I knew before I even touched it wasn't going to let me out because the door was going to be locked. It was and, what was more, I could hear footsteps outside it. Was this a friend or a foe coming towards me now? I held my breath and waited. When the voices started, they whispered and maybe because of that, I didn't recognise either of them to begin with.

'Why did you put him in there?' one hissed. It sounded angry.

'He wasn't breathing,' the other voice said. 'He's dead.'

'Are you sure?' the first one asked.

There was a pause. They mean me, I thought, they're talking about me!

'I hit him and he stopped breathing,' the second man said. 'That's it.'

It had to be 'Mr Phillips' – he it had been who had hit me, after all. But that he'd hit me hard enough to stop my breathing was frightening to hear. He'd stopped it for so long, in fact, that he'd thought I was dead! Was I? I wanted to touch myself just to make sure that I wasn't, but they were close by and I really didn't dare do anything. If they found me alive, they probably would kill me.

'Well, that's it, then,' the first man said in what sounded like a very determined sort of way.

'What is?'

'The wog makes three deaths . . .'

'Four.'

There was silence and then the first man said, 'Yes, of course, I forgot.' It was spoken in a sad voice which, considering they were talking about at least one murder – my own death included – was strange to me. And who on earth was the *fourth* victim? 'Isn't that enough?'

'Mr Phillips' snapped. 'You know that it isn't!' he said. 'You know what still needs to be done! God Almighty, why did the bloody Jerries have to pick tonight!'

The first man sighed. 'Maybe it wasn't meant . . .'

'Wasn't meant?' 'Mr Phillips' said, obviously outraged. 'Wasn't bloody meant! What kind of talk is that?'

Nothing more was said then and the next thing that I heard was the sound of their footsteps as the two men walked away from wherever I was. They left me with a lot to think about, that was for sure! People had died, been killed, and more were about to follow if that last remark was to be believed. Why? Was it, as Mr Andrews had said, to do with some strange Masonic sacrifice? Were these men killing people to save the cathedral in some sort of magical way? If that was the aim of all this, it wasn't working very well. Maybe that was what the other fellow had meant about what they were doing not being 'meant'? Last time I'd looked the fires were still threatening St Paul's and, in the far, far distance I could, even in my cupboard, hear the sounds of desperate shouts from the watchmen in the galleries and on the roof. But then maybe that was why they, whoever they were, couldn't stop killing, because it just wasn't working. 'Phillips' had cursed the fact that the Jerries had come on this particular night. Their night of sacrifice? Who or what they were offering up these sacrifices to, I couldn't imagine. The Masons, as far as I knew, were a bit like a club – albeit one I couldn't join. Though they were a bit odd and concerned, so the Vatican had always maintained, with things of a supernatural kind, I'd never personally really believed that they involved themselves with devils. I didn't and don't believe that there are such things, not really. But what I've always known is that those who do believe can be dangerous. I wondered whether my old mate Revd Ernie Sutton was one of them. And anyway, what had 'Mr Phillips' meant about there having been four deaths? Whose was the fourth body, and where was it?

But I didn't have a chance to think about that any more because someone was putting a key into the lock in front of my face. I had thought the two men had gone away!

* * *

'You've got to go!'

It was George, the young choir boy, and he was pulling me out of that cupboard whether I wanted to come or not. He must have seen Mr Ronson and Mr Andrews in there with me and, in fact, I had seen him actually look down at them at one point, but he seemed neither upset by it nor surprised. He knew.

'George . . .'

He closed the door behind me and then leaned on it while he turned the key in the lock.

'Leave, Mr Hancock,' he said as he finished securing the door, 'leave right now!'

'What?' I was still pretty shaken up and my shoes were covered in someone else's blood.

'Leave the cathedral.' George put a hand on my shoulder. 'You've seen—'

'I've seen what, George?' I said. 'Dead bodies? You've seen them too, George, you . . . Bloody hell, you must have lied to me about seeing Mr Phillips! George . . .'

He let go of my shoulder as if it were on fire. 'Leave!'

'But the City's ablaze!' I said as I watched him disappear into the gloom.

'You're safer out there than you are in here,' he answered. 'Please go!'

I would have gone after him if I could have seen where he was going. But I couldn't. I was, it seemed, in that area behind the quire known as the quire aisle. The cupboard I'd been shoved into was not, I could see now, a permanent part of the cathedral. It was like a very large wardrobe and what it was supposed to be for, I didn't know. There'd been no robes or cassocks, or whatever, in there. Not that I could really know that for sure, I hadn't exactly looked beyond the dead bodies and I certainly wasn't going to try and have another butcher's in there, that was for sure!

Shadows of the flames outside, maybe by now even touching the side of the building, made weird patterns on the columns up to the ceiling. I couldn't go out there! Just the thought of it made my heart jump in my chest. I'd come into the cathedral to get away from the fire but now, by looking for Milly, I'd become part of something I couldn't even begin to understand. For the first time since I'd been hit I put a hand up to my nose and found a broken, bloodied mess. The bastard had snapped it! I've a big, what some would call a

Roman, nose and so I suppose it had made a decent target. That I'd stopped breathing when he hit me would have been worrying had I not been thinking about young George by that time. What exactly did he know about all this business and why was he in the cathedral anyway? Most kids of his age were evacuated and it was well known that the choir school of St Paul's had been temporarily moved down to somewhere in the West Country. I looked around for him again, but God knows where he'd gone. For now I had to think about what I was going to do next. If I took heed of George I'd take my chances out amongst the flames. If I stayed, however, I couldn't imagine that I'd be in any sort of danger if I was with other people. For a little while I was right.

'You have to keep your chin up, don't you?' Mr Webb said with a chuckle to his wife.

Poor but honest, she just smiled and then looked down at her painful-looking dry hands. My sister Nancy's are the same. Soap powder is so hard to come by now, women have taken to using Borax or even ammonia in order to get a lather going in the weekly wash.

'Course you do,' he said, answering his own question, as I imagined he often did. 'Can't let the Jerries get us down, can we?'

From over in one of the darker corners of the crypt, I heard the distinct sound of kissing; wet and long and, in its way, quite as patriotic as Mr Webb's sentiments. After all, if the nation is to carry on and have a future, people need to keep having kids.

The posh woman I'd seen when I had first come into the cathedral, plus the older Jewish woman, were lying side by side on blankets on the floor. They both looked at me, frowning, staring mostly at my nose, but neither of them said anything. Only the bloke on the book in the crypt had actually asked me what had happened. I'd gone up to him fully with the intention of telling him about Mr Andrews and Mr Ronson. But I couldn't, and when he asked about my poor old conk I mumbled something about having fallen over in the dark. Young George could be having a game with me about how much danger I was in in this place, but I doubted if that was the case. He had looked at me very seriously and, besides, how, if he didn't know what was happening, had he found me in that cupboard? How had he known that I was going to be there? Thinking about young George was, I now noticed, beginning to make me shiver. He'd set me up with that meeting with 'Phillips'. Had he known that violence towards me was possible even then? Had he only later got cold feet about that?

The kissing in the corner sounded as if it was getting even more passionate. In spite of myself I looked to where the sound was coming from and saw the briefest flash of a long, pale leg. At the top of the leg was a large, dark hand. Lucky blighter! I'd have given anything to have my Hannah with me at that moment. I took my eyes off the couple in the corner and began looking around the crypt at my fellow shelterers again. There were a lot more than there had been even since the last time I'd been down there. Not many people may live in the City but a lot of them do fire watching on the roofs of the businesses, churches and monuments. With the City on fire we were packed out. No 'Mr Phillips' and his mate, whoever he was, as yet, though. It would have to be someone, I felt, who had claimed to have seen Phillips earlier on. To anyone with half a brain the bloke with the dodgy mask could not in any way be Mr Phillips. But Mr Smith, Mr Bolton, Mr Arnold, young George and the Dean had seen him, or claimed to have done so. Surely the Dean couldn't be part of this . . . whatever it was, too? Surely if he had seen Mr Phillips, he couldn't have seen 'him' properly?

'What the hell are you doing here?'

I looked up to find George standing above me, his face red with what looked like anger.

'I told you to go!' he said as he first looked around and then dropped down beside me.

'I decided to stay,' I said calmly.

'They tried to kill you!' he whispered.

'Who did?' I said. 'Who tried to kill me? You know, don't you, George? You know exactly what's going on here.'

George looked away. 'You can't stay here . . .'

'Why not? Why can't I stay here?' I said angrily now.

'Because they're here!' he said.

I followed where he was looking, but I couldn't see anyone I recognised as having anything to do with 'Mr Phillips'.

'Who's here?' I asked. 'What—'

'Any one of them!' George leaned in towards me and whispered. 'It's not your fault, but you saw and heard things that you shouldn't have.'

'Things that I shouldn't have?'

'They're here!' he repeated as he looked around the crypt once again. But the place was full and so I couldn't possibly know who he meant.

'Where?' I asked him. 'Where are—'

'Everywhere!' He looked back at me, his eyes full of tears. 'If you're lucky, the fact that there are so many people here will save you,' he said. 'They have to get rid of you, they have no choice! You should be dead anyway. I saved you! You should have gone when I told you to! Now if you stay they'll kill you and if you go, well . . . If you try to leave now they will try to kill you.'

I attempted to grab hold of him to ask him more, but the boy was too quick for me, and as he stood up and moved away he just said, 'Sorry. I didn't mean to . . . It's all for the best, you know it is.' He shook his head. 'Sorry.'

I was frightened. Who wouldn't have been? Someone had tried to kill me and now, apparently, a lot more people had the idea I might be better off dead too. And if George was right I was well and truly trapped now. I'd thought about who might be after me before, but now the idea that maybe even more people were involved than I had at first thought crossed my mind. After all, if not all watchmen were Masons, then the opposite applied to those people not in the Watch. Some of them could be in the Brotherhood – if indeed it was the Brotherhood that was behind these deaths anyway. After all, Mr Andrews had been a Mason himself and he had not only been against this 'sacrifice', he had died, not of natural causes, himself.

''Ere, mate, got a fag, have you?'

A tap on my shoulder shocked me so much that it sent me flying across the floor like some sort of barmy scalded cat.

'Er . . .'

'Blimey,' the tin-hatted watchman said, 'I only asked!'

Chapter Ten

I moved quickly and quietly in and out of the sleeping and sometimes groaning bodies on the floor. I'd seen George leave and I'd decided to follow him. I couldn't stay in there, not with the kind of fear that bloody boy had left me with! I can't stand people looking at me at the best of times, but under these circumstances it was proving to be impossible. Not knowing who, if anyone, was going to murder me, was not something I could bear.

'George!'

I could see his long body with its long mac and cassock underneath swishing against the floor as I ran to try and get close to him. But as I began to run, he, first looking behind to see where I was, began to run too.

'George! Why are you running away?' I said as I

puffed and panted after him. And then I said, hoping against hope that it might actually shock him, 'What have you done?'

This made him stop. There were other blokes about but it was suddenly as if, to George at least, the two of us were all alone. His face, by the dim light from the little lamp underneath the dome, looked much older than his years. He said, 'I'm so, so sorry. I believed, still believe, it is for the best. But . . .' He paused, weeping a little now. 'I didn't even try to stop it. I didn't even try!'

'Stop what?'

He turned immediately and then ran full pelt for the door beside the Great West entrance. It was open and he shot through it like a rocket. I didn't even attempt to follow. He was outside, God knew where, and, besides, the world was melting out there. Whether I stayed or left made little difference as far as I could see. Whatever was going on in the cathedral, I had the feeling, at that moment, that soon none of it would matter. I might feel trapped but at least I wasn't burning – yet. It was the end and, although I fear death and the nothingness I can't help but feel that it will bring, I knew in those seconds that followed that I wouldn't be going into it on my own. Not if the fires took me and my whole world away with them – and they were the most powerful thing I could see then. Outside the door that George had shot through everything was as hot and red as a blast furnace. It took me a while to realise that there was a hand on my shoulder.

'Everything's not as it seems,' Mr Smith said.

He smiled, this bloke who was one of those who claimed to have seen Mr Phillips. I cringed away from him. 'Somebody tried to kill me!' I said. 'I don't care much about how it looks, Mr Smith. An explanation would be nice, if you have one!'

Whether he knew about 'Mr Phillips' and my brief sojourn into that cupboard with two corpses, I couldn't be sure. But he did seem to have some knowledge about what was going on. He said, 'If you come with me, I'll show you what's happening and I'll tell you why.'

'Mr Ronson is dead, as is Mr Andrews,' I said. 'Don't try to tell me otherwise, I've seen them. Some kind of ritual . . .'

'No, no, you're quite wrong there,' Mr Smith said.

'Quite wrong. Mr Ronson and Mr Andrews were accidents. No ritual was involved in their deaths, none at all.'

He said it all so calmly that for a moment I was too shocked to breathe.

'Accidents?' I murmured huskily. I moved closer to him now, my fear suddenly receding, and quickly, too, as my anger went on the increase. 'Accidents! Mr Andrews was stabbed! In his . . . up . . .' In spite of my lack of religion I couldn't bring myself to say either 'bum' or 'backside' in a church. '. . . his bottom,' I said. 'Mr Smith, watchmen are dying here, watchmen who are trying to defend this cathedral!'

People standing at the western doors were beginning to look and so Mr Smith took hold of my arm and pulled me to one side, into the gloom. There his manner changed completely and my fear began to return.

'Andrews and Ronson were enemies of the cathedral!' Mr Smith spat into my face. 'Enemies!'

They hadn't come across to me as enemies. Mr Andrews had been strange and maybe even a bit mad, but that he cared about the cathedral was something I had never doubted.

In spite of my rising fear, I said, 'I don't believe you.'

'Not everything is as it seems, as I've told you before,' he replied.

'Then why not tell Mr Andrews's wife, at least, that he's copped it? Why is it a secret? Why deny—'

'We have to get through this night!' he said. 'None of us reckoned on all this!' he swept a hand around and out towards the fires. 'It was not meant to be like this! But it is a fact, and we have to deal with it. Now, are you interested in saving this cathedral or not?'

'Of course I am!' I said. 'But I'm also interested in why someone I believe was pretending to be your Mr Phillips tried to kill me!'

He opened his mouth as if he were about to say something, but then he closed it again. For several seconds he looked up at me and then he said, 'I can't tell you about that. You just have to come with me and—'

'No.' I shook my head, I was furious. Who the hell did this bloke think he was, ordering me about? 'Forget it, mate. I've been told things by a lot of people and I don't know whom to believe. All I do know is that someone who calls himself Phillips tried to kill me. I'm not going along with anyone I don't trust and that includes you.'

Mr Smith put his hand into the pocket of his jacket and said, 'I mean you no harm, Mr Hancock. Not personally. All will, I promise, become clear.'

He had a gun in his hand now and it was pointed at my stomach. I sighed. I wasn't exactly afraid at that moment, and I don't say that because I want to seem heroic. I was so confused and tired by that time – not to mention sore around my nose, too – that I honestly couldn't even begin to care by then.

'Where do you want me to go?' I said.

Whatever was happening was happening 'up top', but then that had been, I imagined by then, inevitable. Just my luck. My lungs already felt bunged up and scorched, why shouldn't they have to endure more climbing up in front of a geezer with a pistol? My poor legs, stiff as coffins the both of them, were so weak by this time that the bugger had the inconvenience of having to wait for me to move as he pushed me forward with his gun.

The noise at the top, in the Whispering Gallery, was

enormous. Shouting, buckets clanging, the mechanical sound of stirrup pumps, water . . . men trying to save the cathedral from the fires.

'Everyone's trying to save the cathedral,' I called back to Mr Smith. 'I'd help myself if you'd take that gun away from my back. You could do worse than getting a bucket of water yourself.'

'You don't understand and shouldn't try,' Mr Smith said. 'Not yet.'

I'd thought about running up the stairs and away from him but now I could hear that he wasn't even out of breath I decided against it. My legs felt as heavy as granite and although my breathing wasn't so bad, I knew it wasn't going to stay that way. By the time we got to the Whispering Gallery I'd be speechless. Not that I'd probably ask any of the blokes up there to help me even if I could speak. Who in all of this great big cathedral could I trust? I didn't know who were the villains and who were not. I didn't know why Mr Smith felt the need to put a gun to my back.

I plodded onwards and upwards. Getting short of breath now, I said, 'Mr Andrews . . . he, er, he . . . talked about a sacrifice. Mr Ronson—'

'Ronson was going to go to Andrews with his suspicions. He couldn't do that! Andrews was an enemy, a fool . . .'

'So you killed him?' I stopped and turned around to look at him. He was one step below me, his face shadowed by his tin hat and covered in darkness, I couldn't see any of his features.

'No,' he said. '*I* didn't.' But he didn't even start to explain and just pushed me. 'Move along.'

'What about young George?' I said. I didn't move. I had to catch my breath and I also had to decide whether I thought Mr Smith would really shoot me or not. If he did, were there enough like-minded watchmen who would cover up for him? How many deaths could be covered up even on a night like this? 'What's George got to do with all this?'

Mr Smith did not reply.

'Mr Smith?'

'Onwards and upwards, Mr Hancock,' Mr Smith said as he moved up on to the step I was standing on. The gun went from being pointed towards the middle of my body to being aimed at my head. Whatever he was doing, he wasn't joking, this character.

I thought about trying to get the gun off him. I *thought* about it. But seeing as much death as I do makes you cautious in the end. Before this war began I would have said that I was, if anything, careless about my own life. I'm not married, I've no little'uns, and certainly, ever since I came back to this country in 1918, my future has not seemed a bright one. Things would improve if Hannah were to do me the honour of being my wife, but that will never happen. That aside, though, for some reason lately, I want to live. What for, I cannot say. I've helped a few people, I suppose, in the past few months which, perhaps, has made me feel more useful. But maybe I'm just more frightened than ever before. Maybe the bits of bodies the Heavy Lifting boys and the coppers have dragged out of the London mud for me to bury have terrified me. I'd be even madder than I already am if that hadn't happened. I walked 'onwards and upwards', getting ever closer to the voices in the Whispering Gallery.

When we got past the passageway and up to the top of the stairs and after Mr Smith had let me rest against the wall of the staircase for a bit, he told me we were to go on further, up beyond the Whispering Gallery.

God, outside again to the bloody Stone Gallery!

'What are you going to do?' I said as I listened to my heart smash against the side of my ribs. 'Throw me over the parapet?'

If a body fell through the flames from the Stone Gallery and into the burning streets below, who would know it wasn't an accident? Just like Mr Ronson's fall from the Whispering Gallery earlier, it was possible.

Again Mr Smith did not reply. I put my foot on the first of those crumbling stone steps up to the Stone Gallery.

There was nothing happening in the black winter skies over London. No Luftwaffe aircraft, no ack-ack guns, only search lights scanning through and across the tops of the flames. The City was in such a state now, the Luftwaffe could come back and finish it off whenever they wanted. We came out, Mr Smith and me, into such smoke that we both choked and coughed until we could hardly breathe. All through this the pressure of his gun, in my back again now, didn't slacken off once. I looked around me and saw several blokes I knew I'd seen before, but some looked away as soon as they caught my eye while others didn't seem to even register the fact that I was there. At least some of them must have seen Mr Smith's gun on account of his being far from secretive with it.

The Stone Gallery is another 119 stairs up from the Whispering Gallery, so I was exhausted. I'd been up and down to these galleries more times than I'd wanted to already; my knees were trembling, and my chest was literally on its last knockings. I couldn't go another step. But Mr Smith, I now discovered, had another surprise in store for me. Another 152 stairs up to what's called the Golden Gallery. This is also outside the cathedral, but much higher up underneath the ball and lantern. On this occasion the Golden Gallery was shrouded in thick smoke.

'I'm not going up there,' I gasped as Mr Smith pointed me towards the staircase that leads up into the Golden Gallery. 'I'd rather die!'

I heard him take the safety catch off and saw him point the weapon at my head.

'I don't care,' I said. 'I'll have a heart attack . . .'

'Which will be much quieter than if I shoot you.'

'Exactly,' I said, 'so bloody well just do it.'

But in spite of the fact that we were high up in the sky, there were still people about and I wasn't sure that Mr Smith wanted to attract their attention. He lowered the gun.

'Let me rest for a moment,' I said. 'Let me be.'

He gave me about five minutes, then we pushed on upwards.

Although the steps to the Golden Gallery are inside the cathedral, on that night it was like walking up into the clouds. To be honest I never really believed at that time that I'd ever be walking back down again – and in a way I was quite right in that.

Unlike on the Stone Gallery where there'd been a lot of people, there were only three Watchmen, apart from Mr Smith, up in the Golden Gallery. There was Mr Bolton, some other bloke I'd seen about but whose name I didn't know, and the 'Mr Phillips' who'd busted my nose up earlier. As he walked towards me, smiling, he held up something that I soon came to see was Mr Phillips's, or someone's, face mask. Like a lot of those things it was made of metal and, as he placed it down on the gallery floor behind him, it made a heavy, clunking sound. He didn't of course need it; he had, like everyone else up on the Golden Gallery, a perfectly normal face.

'You're not supposed to be here,' he said to me. Behind him I could just make out some other figures, a man in civvies and a woman. 'You stopped breathing. You were dead.'

I didn't want to think about that and so I ignored it.

'What's going on here?' I said. 'Where's Mr Phillips?'

Mr Smith put a hand on the so-called Mr Phillips's shoulder. 'Mr Phillips' said, 'Because of all these fires this has become far more complicated than it should. Took us by surprise, I can tell you. It's also far more urgent. *You* shouldn't be here at all,' he said to me. 'The cathedral should be quite free of people sheltering.'

'The young lad George let me in to the cathedral,' I said. 'Blame him! He's one of yours, whatever you are, isn't he? Let me in against Mr Andrews's wishes, George did. The late Mr Andrews knew something about young George, didn't he?'

'Mr Phillips' looked at me steadily. 'Maybe he did,' he said. 'He certainly knew about other things. But,

Mr Hancock, the chaplain is dead and so we'll never know now, will we?'

He was posh, like most of the watchmen. If he was a watchman. But if he was, why had he felt the need to impersonate another member of the company? Maybe I was thinking this through and maybe I wasn't, but the next voice that I heard wasn't posh and I recognised it.

'Mr Webb?'

He was standing behind the watchmen with someone else; I thought it was a woman at first. But it wasn't a woman, it was a girl, and she had long, blond hair right down to her waist.

'Milly?'

She only opened her eyes a crack when I spoke to her. Leaning up against Webb, she was half asleep by the look of her, poor kid.

'You've known where she was all the time!' I said to Webb. He had a proper self-satisfied expression on his face. Not that he was looking at me at all.

'She'll do a lot more good this way, won't she, Mr Rolls?' Webb said to 'Mr Phillips' with a look of near worship on his mug. So that was his name, Mr Rolls.

I'd heard it somewhere before but, at that moment, I couldn't remember where.

'Do more good in what way?' I asked. All their faces and, presumably, mine, too, were lit up red by the sea of flame down below in the streets. I felt my breathing coming short as a terrible thought developed in my mind. 'What are you doing to the poor kid?'

Men on the cathedral roofs below, real men, lifted buckets and fought with barely adequate hoses.

'Oh do shut up!' Mr Rolls exploded at me. Just like that. From being perfectly calm he went to completely berserk in a matter of seconds. Again he hit me, the swine, and again it was right on my poor old conk. I fell, as I had done the time before, but I didn't black out. As I lay on the ground I watched Milly laugh in a way that reminded me of the faces that poor half-dead opium addicts pull. I've buried a few in my time; I know that they exist and what they look like. This kid put me in the mind of such unfortunate folk. Now I remembered who Mr Rolls was.

'You work with Mr Phillips, don't you?' I said as I held a hand up to my nose. I was just covered with blood by this time. 'The real Mr Phillips.'

Mr Rolls raised one perfectly undamaged eyebrow and smiled. From where I lay on the ground I could see the great dome sweep down towards the street below. Both the dome and the City it rose above glowed red.

'We're saving the cathedral,' Mr Rolls said.

'Then why aren't you fighting the fires with the rest of the blokes!' I replied. 'What are you doing up here with a young kid full of drugs? What kind of men are you?'

Mr Webb leaned down and pulled me roughly to my feet. 'It's only a transaction, is all it is, mate,' he said. 'I told you the kid was no good. Her own father knows she's no good. It won't be no loss or nothing.'

No loss? What the bloody hell did that mean? But part of me did know. Part of me was coming to a truly horrifying conclusion.

Mr Rolls called over to Mr Bolton and the bloke I didn't recognise, 'Go down and make sure no one else comes up. When we're ready I'll call you to come and assist.'

They walked towards the stairs that lead down to the Stone Gallery and then disappeared below. This left Mr Rolls, Mr Smith, Mr Webb, Milly and myself. I still had that blessed gun at my back, courtesy of Mr Smith. I wondered how many more weapons were going to come out during this shift of the St Paul's Fire Watch. Not that these men could possibly be what I would consider proper watchmen. Webb wasn't a watchman at all and it was doubtful that Mr Rolls was. If he had been a real watchman, why would he have disguised himself as Mr Phillips? How, I wondered briefly and with terror gripping my mind, had he got hold of what could only be Mr Phillips's face mask? Mr Andrews's mad words about the Freemasons came back to haunt me. I knew what they were about to do to Milly. She was, after all, only a child, and Mr Andrews had told me that when churches were built in the old days, the gift of a child to . . . whatever, was preferable to that of an adult. He'd told me to look after her for a very good reason.

'If you've already sacrificed Mr Ronson and Mr Andrews to whatever you sacrifice to . . . the Beast—' I began. I was cut off by the sound of Mr Rolls's laughter. 'You're Masons, aren't you, you—'

'The Beast? What Beast, Mr Hancock? Do you even know what you're talking about?'

They all looked at me as if I'd gone mad.

Suddenly even breathing the word sacrifice sounded stupid. Mr Andrews had been a strange old man with some barmy ideas, why had I listened to him? Of course they hadn't brought the kid up to the Golden Gallery to kill or 'sacrifice' her, that was ridiculous! Mr Ronson had fallen from the Whispering Gallery in a very regrettable accident and Mr Andrews I couldn't exactly account for, but this could all just be about child prostitution, couldn't it? Horrible as that whole subject is, I tried at that moment to convince myself that was indeed the truth of the matter.

'George Chivers, Milly's dad, and me have been mates for years,' Mr Webb's cracked, coarse voice cut across my thoughts. 'Architect, he used to be, just like these nice gentlemen here.'

'He sold his own daughter to be used by these men!' I said. 'All of them!'

'George Chivers?' Mr Webb smiled, his false teeth clacking apart as he did so. 'Nah! George C is far too pissed to think of anything except his booze and his bed. His liver's gone. George ain't moved from his place for years. It's me what keeps George going, me what teaches his kids what they need to know out on the streets, with blokes.'

I looked down into his face and saw something that was evil. I've seen it many times before, I know what it looks like. He was a pimp! He had sex with his mates' poor little kids, put them out on the streets to do what they did with other men, and he had to take his cut of the money gained from that too, oh yes indeed he did! His poor, tired but honest wife probably didn't know anything about it – or rather, I hoped that she didn't. Not that I thought that much about her now, because I was so angry that all I wanted to do was hit her husband.

'You . . .'

'George Chivers's old mates, Mr Rolls and Mr Bolton and all of them, at first contacted him, of course, but then when he told me about it, I took it over for him,' Mr Webb continued. 'George couldn't work it out properly, didn't understand. He thought it was just the usual with the kiddie. But it's such a big idea this. Most people don't really get it, do they, Mr Rolls? A very special job. So I did it, for a commission of course.'

'A rather large fee as I recall,' Mr Rolls said. 'Mr Smith, you and I must change now for the ceremony. Mr Webb, if you would kindly cover this Israelite with Mr Smith's revolver. We will deal with him in due course.'

Deal with me? I imagined this was a terminal thing of some sort. They had, after all, tried to kill me before. Why they didn't do it at that moment I still don't know. Maybe the ceremony they had planned included the presence of some poor schmuck from outside?

'Certainly chief,' Mr Webb said. 'You get changed.'

Changed? Changed into what? And what was this 'ceremony' Rolls talked about? I couldn't see that these men had anything like bags full of robes or whatever such people wore with them. And now I was a Jew to these people, was I? He'd said it with such contempt, the word 'Israelite', I wondered if these men were less Masons and more Nazis! Mr Rolls turned around to pick up a box I'd not noticed before which was behind him on the floor. At the same moment, Mr Smith began to pass the revolver across, behind my back, to Mr Webb. Milly, slumped against the railings looking out across the burning city, was on

Mr Smith's other side. If I was going to try and do anything, now was probably the only time I'd have the opportunity of doing so. The moment when Smith's hand let go and Webb's hand took control of the weapon was possibly the only chance I was ever going to get. As I felt Smith's arm stretch behind me, I pushed myself away from Webb and twisted round quickly. I didn't get the gun. It fell on to the floor with a metallic clatter and I lost sight of it.

'Bloody hell!'

I was hit again, although whether it was by Smith or Webb, I couldn't tell. The three of us, all bent to the floor now, pushed and clawed at each other, looking for the weapon that would give either them or me control over the situation. What was going on or about to happen on the Golden Gallery was no longer my concern. I just wanted to get away from there, preferably with young Milly, her foul mouth and all, in tow.

'What the hell are you doing?' I heard Mr Rolls yell. 'Grab hold of him, for God's sake!'

I pushed Mr Webb away from me with my left shoulder. I heard him grunt as he slammed into the railings around the gallery. A fist, Mr Smith's, it must have been, came up from low down and punched me yet again in the face. This time, however, it wasn't my nose that caught it, but my cheekbone. I was, I imagined, going to end up looking like an old boxer after all this punishment. If, that was, I ended up anywhere.

'I'll have you over the fucking side, you ugly wog!' I heard Webb mutter through breathless gasps. I saved my own insults in order to hang on to my breath. I wasn't strong. I'd been up so many stairs in the past few hours the muscles in my legs were strained to breaking point. As for my breath, well, that was coming hard again now, very hard. Where the hell was that blasted revolver?

'This what you're looking for?'

We all stopped at once, Webb, Smith and me, as soon as we heard her voice. I looked over my shoulder and saw Milly, smiling, standing beside Mr Rolls. She had the pistol we'd all been looking for aimed at his head.

Chapter Eleven

Webb was the first one to speak.

'Milly, doll, don't—'

'Don't what, Charlie?' she said with a laugh in her voice. She put one of her small fingers on the trigger.

Mr Rolls, whose handsome face was now visibly pale even through the red and gold lights from the fires down below, looked across at us and said, 'Smith, I thought you drugged the bloody child!'

'I did!' Mr Smith replied. 'As God is my witness! A pipe of opium, as I told you, a—'

'Why don't you tell them, Charlie?' the girl said to Webb. There was a look in her eyes I hadn't seen just minutes earlier. It was the kind of sobriety a person doesn't associate with people who use drugs like opium. Webb, I noticed, couldn't meet this new, sober gaze.

Still looking at Webb, Milly said, 'Cat got your tongue, Charlie?' She laughed. 'As Charlie well knows, one pipe ain't going to do for me,' she said. 'Been smoking four years now. He's been giving it to me! I can sober up from it just like that, these days!' She snapped her fingers up at Mr Rolls's face. 'I'm a clever girl, I am!'

'Mil—'

'And thank you for it, Charlie! Thank you for that opium!' Milly said. 'Because if I hadn't had it, I'd've not been able to do the blokes what I've done and that includes you too, Charlie! But now—'

'Put the gun down, Milly love; I swear we'll just go on home now and—'

'I thought I just come here for the usual. Do a few blokes and get a few bob,' Milly said. 'It was a laugh when I first got here. I ran about having a right old time! Doing it in a church? What a hoot!' The wind was whipping through her hair now as tendrils of air from the storm around the cathedral reached up towards the golden ball and cross at its apex. Small she may have been, but Milly Chivers's face was as old and as hard as stone. 'But Charlie, this time nobody wanted to fuck me, did they?'

Webb didn't answer, neither did anyone else. Maybe Mr Andrews hadn't been wrong after all. Webb had implied that Milly had been sold to Rolls and the others. But if she wasn't sold for sex, then what these blokes purchased the girl for had to be what I had feared the most.

'I knew you and these blokes were going to do me in,' Milly said.

'Milly!'

'You,' she looked directly at me as she spoke, 'get over here.'

In order to emphasise her point and probably to stop Smith or Webb from trying to block my path, she pressed the pistol hard against Mr Rolls's neck. I stumbled forwards.

'Mr . . .'

'Hancock,' I said as I stood beside her panting from the fear, the wind and the heat all around me. On the floor behind Mr Rolls I could now see what was in the box he had only just opened. It was a jacket with some ribbons laid across it. If this was what he had planned to wear for some sort of devilish ceremony, then I wasn't very impressed. They were so very ordinary.

'Mr Hancock, I think I'm right in thinking that you ain't with this lot,' Milly said.

'Yes. Milly, I tried to help you, earlier.'

She completely ignored this. 'You know what to do with a gun?'

'Yes,' I said.

'Take it,' she said as she pulled me towards her. 'Hold it on him.' She pushed it still further into Mr Rolls's neck as she slipped her small hand from under mine. 'We're getting out of here, Mr Hancock.'

She sounded so confident and also so much older than any ten year old I'd ever met before, that for a while, I was lost in admiration for her. I didn't ask her how we were going to get out and maybe I should have, but then even if I'd done so, I doubt whether I could have prevented what happened next.

'If either of you move, Mr Hancock'll kill your mate,' she said to Webb and Smith as they stood seemingly quite calmly in front of her. Mr Smith did as he was told. Mr Webb did not.

Moving towards her, he said, 'Babe—'

'Don't you "babe" me!'

I thought she just punched him. She was small, and so what she did didn't look all that much to me. It was only when Webb first gasped and then folded over under her blow that I knew something had to be wrong. His hands flew to his guts and he made a sort of gurgling sound in his throat.

Smith, who was now attempting to hold up the falling Webb, said, 'She's stabbed him!'

I felt Mr Rolls's body flinch and tense up underneath the pistol and I said to him, 'Don't do anything! Don't do *anything*!'

Now I was truly lost. I'd come to save a little girl from something horrible, and now she'd stabbed a man. Not a nice man, admittedly, but a man she was standing over and smiling at now, as he bled down his trousers and on to the ancient stone floor.

'He's dying!' Mr Smith was down on the floor with Webb, now looking up at the girl with absolute terror on his face. 'What—'

'You always told me and Rita to carry blades, didn't you, Charlie?' Milly said, ignoring Smith completely.

'To protect ourselves? Well, now I have protected myself, so there!'

'Milly,' I said.

'The only way we're going to get out of here is to get rid of all of these,' she said as she looked around at the three men who had been our captors. Then before I could answer her or plead with her to stop what she was doing, she took hold of the box of clothes on the ground and smacked Mr Smith around the side of the head with it. With a grunt, he fell unconscious across Webb's now gasping body. Milly was terrifying me.

'I am not killing this bloke!' I said as I nevertheless still held the gun up to Mr Rolls's head. I had killed far too many people in the First Lot. One is too many, and I had stabbed, shot and beaten far more than just one to death back then. Their faces, as well as their blood and guts, are very central to my waking and sleeping nightmares. I wasn't killing again, not that night, not ever.

Milly shrugged. She looked down at Smith and said, 'I haven't killed him. He'll be all right in an hour or two.' Then she pointed to Rolls. 'He tried to kill you,' she said. 'He'd kill you now if he could.'

'I know,' I said. 'But I'm not killing him, I'm—'

'Milly! Love . . .' Webb was coughing up blood now and, although I knew that he was a goner, I had to say something about getting him to a doctor.

The girl looked at me with both coldness and what looked like pity. 'He's dying,' she said simply. 'He's got TB anyway. There ain't no point.'

For the first time in a long while, Mr Rolls spoke, 'She's a demon! Hancock, for God's sake, you have the gun! Shoot her for—'

'If you shoot me, you'll be doing exactly what he and them other nuts have wanted all the time!' Milly said. I was breathing hard now and couldn't speak but she must have been able to tell from the look on my face that I wasn't going to do her any harm.

Milly put something, I imagine the knife she'd stabbed Webb with, in her pocket and began to rummage through Mr Rolls's clothes box. She nodded her head towards Rolls and then said to me, 'There's some stuff in here we can tie him up with.'

At the bottom of the stairs up to the Stone Gallery, there were men both Milly and I knew, waiting for some sort of signal from Mr Rolls. I didn't know exactly what that was about. I had an idea based largely upon what Mr Andrews had told me earlier. But Milly, so she claimed, knew.

About halfway down from the Golden Gallery to the Stone Gallery, I tapped Milly on the shoulder and said that she and I needed to talk. It was pitch-black on that staircase, with only the light from a little torch Milly had with her to light our way. She sat down on one stair and I followed suit, a few steps above her. As I looked down at her face, I was struck by how old she looked for her age, and it wasn't just her behaviour that made her seem like an adult.

'Mr Rolls worked with my dad, years ago before I was born,' Milly said. 'Mr Phillips did too, but he ain't here. I think he's part of this, what's going on here, but I ain't seen him tonight.'

'What is going on here?'

I was in a stairwell with a child who had hit one man hard enough to knock him out and all but killed another!

'You have to know drinkers and drug takers to understand it all,' Milly said. 'But the short of it is that Mr Rolls knew my dad had fell on hard times and he knew that he had little 'uns. He asked my dad if he could buy one of us. Dad must've thought it was for the usual reason, I know I did. So he told Mr Rolls to speak to Charlie. Charlie's looked after business for Dad for years, just like he did with Mum.'

'Charlie was your mum's pimp?'

'Charlie and that sad thing of a wife. Yes, they pimped for Mum and for me and me sister Rita, too.'

The Webbs had to have money. Men pay more than the going rate for youngsters. And yet the Webbs and their kids had looked so poor!

'As I say, I thought this job was just the same as usual,' Milly said with that cringe-making adult knowingness in her voice. 'I thought it was funny Mr Rolls should be pretending to be Mr Phillips; men do all sorts to make themselves excited and so I didn't think anything about it. I did think it was funny being brought into the cathedral. I had a right good game of it at first as you know, running about. Truth was the size of the raid took them all by surprise. They had duties to do and couldn't deal with me as they'd wanted straight away. I thought it was peculiar but I didn't think that the Watch blokes were like . . . you know, bad blokes . . .' She looked down at her hands. 'But then they're not. Mr Rolls ain't in the Watch at all and them as are with him are, I think, only in it for what they want to do tonight.'

'Which is what?'

'To kill me,' Milly said simply. 'They've got some sort of idea that killing me will save the cathedral.' Of course she, a child, had been the sacrifice all along. Her eyes filled with tears now and suddenly she looked a lot younger. 'Charlie sold me to them so that they could kill me! He told them I was ten. He tells all the blokes I go with I'm ten; I thought nothing of it. I run around the cathedral for a laugh, yes, but also so that by playing like a kid they'd be bound to believe his story!'

'You're not ten?'

She looked at me as if I was mad. 'I may be small, but I don't think you're daft enough to think that I'm ten, Mr Hancock!'

I had at first, but now that I'd actually been with her for a while, I knew that she just couldn't possibly be that young.

'I'm sixteen,' Milly said. And then, seeing that I

wanted to ask her something else, she added, 'And yes, I do take opium sometimes, but it does knock me out and so I didn't smoke it tonight. I knew something was wrong. I tapped the opium pipe they give me out on the floor of one of them other galleries.'

She started to stand up.

'How did you know that something was wrong?' I asked. Prostitutes live in such strange and at times very fanciful, as well as a brutal worlds that I find it hard to know how they separate the lies that they're always told by blokes from reality.

Milly looked down at me with an almost pitying eye. 'Same as when you fell in, I should think,' she said. 'When they started killing people. Mr Rolls hadn't seen my dad for years and years. He ain't got no idea how old I really am. I saw him push that bloke off the Whispering Gallery. I knew that weren't no joke, whatever silly old childish cobblers they told me about it. By the time they dressed me up as a bloke so they could get me up in the Galleries without no one knowing, I was bloody terrified, I can tell you.' She pulled a face. 'Called me "Mr Potter" they did! Bloody hell!'

I'd felt in some way that 'Potter' wasn't right. Now

I knew why. I was just rising to my feet myself when a voice boomed up from way down below. 'Mr Rolls!' it said. 'Mr Rolls, are you ready yet?'

For a couple of seconds, Milly and I just looked at each other. I shrugged, not knowing what to do while she waved her hands at me as if urging me to say something. I knew I didn't sound a bit like Mr Rolls, but in the end I just called down anyway. 'Not yet!'

There was a very short pause before the reply came, 'Okey dokey!'

I looked at Milly and she at me and neither of us knew what to do next. Milly seemed to think that the majority of the watchmen were decent blokes not involved in any of this sacrifice nonsense. But Mr Andrews had trusted no one, apart from Mr Ronson and, later on, me. There was of course the Dean, too, if we could just get to him. But how we were going to do that and who we might or might not be able to trust, I didn't know. There was also the danger that remained, that the whole place could burn to the ground any moment, too. I said to Milly, 'We're just going to have to go down there and see what we find. We don't have a choice.'

She didn't say anything, but began walking down the stairs. I followed. My legs were so stiff now it was like walking on stilts. But that really wasn't the worst of it. What was really bad was what was going on in my head. The ghosts from the past were being joined by the ghosts from the present, the ones from this night of fire and wind and terrible strange death. I had come to the cathedral to shelter from the terror in the streets and yet what I had found inside had been almost worse. As both the Dean and Mr Andrews had said, the enemy didn't have just one form on this terrible night, it had two – one without and one within. And now Milly, the girl I'd set about to 'save' in some way, had in all probability killed a man. Could I have stopped her from doing that? I wondered.

When we got to the bottom of the staircase there was not a soul to be seen. There were no bombs, incendiary or otherwise, falling any more but the flames from the streets down below were still threatening the cathedral. The wind, if not as high as it had been, was still up and, besides, we'd both heard someone call up to Mr Rolls only moments before. I couldn't believe that the Stone Gallery could be deserted and as I felt a hand fall on to my shoulder, I knew that it wasn't.

Mr Bolton said, 'What are you doing down here?'

I still had Mr Smith's gun in my pocket. I put my hand on it before I turned to Mr Bolton and said, 'There's been a bit of a change of plan.'

'Oh.' He was so intent upon looking at Milly that he didn't see me take the gun out and point it at him for a couple of seconds. When he did see it, however, he immediately put his hands up to his shoulders as his mouth dropped open in shock.

'Milly and myself are leaving,' I said.

The girl, looking around nervously, said to him, 'You alone?'

'Yes . . .'

'You had some other fella with you earlier,' I said. 'Where's he gone?'

'Down.' He pointed towards the floor.

'If you're lying . . .'

'I swear . . .' He waved his upheld hands wildly. He was very scared and could be telling the truth even though I doubted it at the time. I pushed him against the side of the cathedral wall.

'Mr Hancock!'

I had the gun at his throat and so I couldn't turn around easily. 'Milly?'

'Mr Hancock, some other geezer!'

Still I couldn't turn. But when I heard the voice of the 'other geezer' I thought that maybe everything was going to be all right after all.

'Mr Hancock?' It was Mr Steadman. Although he was Mr Rolls's business partner, my earlier conversation with him had given me the impression that he was probably not part of this plot to 'save' the cathedral.

'What's going on?' Mr Steadman asked. 'Why have you got a gun?'

None of us, except perhaps Mr Bolton, saw the other chap arrive. He must have come on tip-toe. Up behind Mr Steadman, he hit him so hard on the back of the head, I could have sworn that I heard his skull crack. Keeping the gun as close to Bolton's head as I could, I turned, and as I did so, Milly ran towards me and clung on to my side. The 'other bloke', the one who had been with Mr Bolton earlier, stood before us. He had a truncheon, like a copper's, in his hand. He held it high, threateningly, as he stepped over Mr Steadman's body. I didn't know at the time whether the poor bloke was alive or dead.

'Give me the gun!' the bloke said. 'Give me the girl and the gun and you can just walk out of here!'

'I'll go with the girl *and* the gun, if it's all the same to you,' I said. 'Mr Bolton can come along with us too.'

'No!' Bolton was so afraid he was almost weeping.

'How did you get away from Rolls and Smith?' the bloke continued. And then suddenly losing control he shouted, 'God Almighty, do you know what you've done!'

I couldn't actually see where the entrance to the staircase down to the Whispering Gallery was, but I knew that if I just kept on moving around the circular core of the cathedral I'd get to it eventually.

Mr Bolton, trembling as I moved him along with me, said, 'Fred, don't bother about me, please! Just go up to Mr Rolls and—'

'The cathedral is going to die because of you!' Fred spat vindictively out at me. 'If not today then sometime soon!'

Shuffling along the wall with Bolton under one arm

and Milly clinging to the other, I said, 'You know something, Fred? Blood doesn't do anything. Spilling it only makes whoever does it a beast. I know.'

'Do you? You're not one of the Brotherhood, so what do you know? The great architects of the past, Wren included, always consecrated their buildings with the sacrifice, a child . . .'

'I don't believe that,' I said. 'Christopher Wren was a genius, a modern man, so I've always been told. He would never have done something so primitive.' Mrs Andrews had made a point of saying that Wren was a good man. 'Never!'

'Blood will purify! Blood will purify!' The bloke looked mad, all the veins on the side of his neck were standing out. 'Hitler will destroy us unless we make a gesture, a sacrifice!'

How had this group of men come to this conclusion? I wasn't to find out for a while. What I had to do at that time was to get Milly and myself to someone not involved in all this who would believe us.

'Mr Hancock!' Milly nudged me and then tilted her head towards the left. 'Stairs!'

So now we had to go down. Stiff legs or no stiff legs,

I had to take Bolton with us, and I had to keep him, if I could, for as long as it took to find someone I could trust. But I wasn't going to take Fred. I didn't want him to follow us, either.

I paused just before the stairwell. 'Fred,' I said, 'Mr Smith and Mr Rolls could probably do with some attention.'

'Don't tell him that!' Milly said. 'Don't tell him anything!'

I didn't mention Webb. I assumed he had to be dead by that time. As we disappeared down the stairs towards the Whispering Gallery, Fred ran off in the opposite direction, towards the staircase going further up. I jammed the pistol into Mr Bolton's back and then whispered to Milly, 'Now we've got to run for it.' I pushed Bolton and urged him to move as fast as he could. Behind us the night sky was drowning in smoke and breathing was hard and tasted of death. As I thundered down the stairs after Mr Bolton I screamed just a little at every painful step. I wasn't walking down those stairs, I was flying.

Chapter Twelve

We made it down to the cathedral floor without any further incident. Men were going about their business on the Whispering Gallery, but no one I recognised, and consequently no one I felt I could trust. I needed to find the Dean or Mrs Andrews or, now I came to think about it, Mr Garner. If he was a Catholic, then he couldn't be a Mason, good or bad. But the church was empty and Milly and myself had only a sobbing Mr Bolton and the lamp underneath the dome for company. Those moments standing at the bottom of the Whispering Gallery stairs in silence, watching the smoke from the fires outside leak into the cathedral and swirl around the quire stalls, were amongst the most terrifying of my entire life. It was so desolate, so old and dark, so much the house of a doomed but jealous God. As superstitious thoughts began to crowd out my reason I began to wonder whether these renegade Masons might have something after all. Not that I wanted to hurt anyone. I just felt that something in that place was reaching out, needing something . . .

But fortunately I didn't have too much time to consider such barmy notions because now I could clearly hear angry voices on the stairs behind us.

'They're coming,' Milly said. 'They must've untied Rolls. Because *you* told them!'

Ignoring her criticism I said, 'We need to get down to the crypt. At the very least Mr Andrews's wife is down there.'

Holding tight on to Bolton, I ran with Milly at my back in the direction of the stairs down to the crypt. We were just running around the edge of the quire stalls when Bolton said, 'There are brothers down there too, you know! In the crypt! How will you know whom to trust?'

But I ignored him. If we didn't go down to the crypt, what were we to do? It wasn't as if we could exactly go outside. And then the noises that had come from the Whispering Gallery stairs burst out into the body of the cathedral.

'Where the hell are they?'

Milly said, 'We've got to get out of here!'

'Don't be stupid!' I replied. Yes, there were people outside the cathedral but most of them were either hanging on for dear life to fire hoses or they were screaming. I could hear them. As the sound of feet running across marble began I looked up to see whether there was anyone in the Whispering Gallery. There were a lot of blokes up there now but they were all doing something other than looking downwards. Those men were really saving the cathedral.

'You've had it!' Bolton smirked.

Whether I'd have hit him if he hadn't said what he did, I don't know. But I gave him such a clump across the top of his bonce that I knocked him out cold. I feared I may have killed him. Not that even that made me stop at the time. As Bolton fell I took hold of Milly's hand and said, 'Run!'

'Where to?'

Dark figures were hurling themselves across the

marble floor at us. There was only one realistic direction to go. 'Out!' I said.

Running, Milly answered, 'I told you that!'

The nearest way out was the smaller door to the south of the Great West door. It's almost impossible to describe the pain in my legs by this time, but suffice it to say that if we hadn't been being pursued by men who wanted us dead, I would have sat down, rolled myself a fag, and probably would never have shifted again. In fact, I was running so fast that when we did get to the door, I slammed straight into it with my shoulder.

'Ow! Bloody—'

'Get it open!' Milly said as I turned the handle backwards and forwards, all to no avail.

'It's stuck!' I said. 'Or locked or . . .'

At some time during the night the Dean had ordered everyone to keep away from the doors. Maybe he'd actually had some of them locked. The sound of running feet behind us was getting louder.

'It's locked!' I cried, sweating now with the effort of trying to move the thing. 'Christ!'

I saw Milly's head turn this way and that through

the gloom and then suddenly she took hold of my arm and said, 'This way!'

I couldn't see where she was taking me, only that it was back into the cathedral. Pulling me towards the right she said, 'Here!'

Stumbling after her through the smoked-filled gloom, I felt her push against something and pull me across what I quickly saw was a threshold. Together we both ran to push the huge wooden door we'd just stumbled through closed behind us. Even as we did this we felt the dull thud of at least one body that wanted to follow us smash against the door. But how were we going to keep the blessed thing closed?

'Does this have a lock or . . .' I was looking but I couldn't see anything.

'Push it! Harder!' Milly screamed.

There was grunting and groaning from outside and I struggled to push my weight against it.

'Push!'

'I am!' I shouted.

Milly was between me and the door, which seemed like a rather awkward and silly place to be until I saw what she was doing.

'Push harder!'

There was a bolt, a huge great black metal thing, and Milly was trying to push it home. I knew I couldn't press myself any harder against that door and so after telling Milly what I was about to do, I took my shoulder away from the door for just a second and then threw myself back at it with all of my strength. For one breathless split second, our pursuers were half inside but then, as I smashed myself back, they fell away from the door and Milly pushed the bolt home in one easy movement. As soon as this was done, we both dropped to the floor behind the door and, dripping with sweat, listened to the low moans of fury from the men outside.

Where we were was in a hallway. I don't know what I'd thought the place the door led to was going to be like, but I'm pretty certain I hadn't reckoned it was a hallway, especially not one with a staircase. I could have been forgiven for having a little moan about yet another bloody staircase, especially another spiral one, but this was very different from those others I'd staggered up and down before. Even in the semi-darkness I could see that it was beautiful. Although it was a spiral, this staircase was wide, and it hugged the walls of some sort of cylinder. A tower, lined with pale stone stairs, winding up to high above our heads, each graceful step balanced as if almost by magic just lightly on the back of the one below. There was a rail, too, a delicate iron affair that could just occasionally be seen in detail as it passed below one of the windows right up high in what I could only think had to be the southernmost of the two towers at the front of the building. It was, I knew, square from the outside, so this curving interior was a surprise.

Milly got to her feet before I did and flashed her small torch around to illuminate the place. As well as going up, the staircase also went down for a few steps. These led to a door which Milly tried to open and when she failed, she said, 'Locked.'

'Shine your torch up,' I said to the girl. Milly did as I asked and we saw, not right at the top of the tower, but a fair way up where the staircase ended, another, much larger door. Painfully, I got to my feet. 'We'd better see where that goes.'

'But where are we?' Milly asked.

'I think we're in one of the towers,' I said.

'So we don't know where that door leads to, do we?'

'No.' I began to walk slowly upwards. Not that these stairs were anything like as difficult as those leading up to the galleries. Shallow and smooth, these were a doddle.

Milly behind me said, 'Mr Hancock, these stairs could lead us in to trouble!'

I stopped, turned and looked down at her. She was so bloody tiny, no wonder it was so easy to believe she was only ten years old. 'Milly,' I said because now I had to say something, 'you have just, I think, killed a bloke. We're in trouble whatever way we look at it!'

I could see her face go red, even in the semi-darkness. 'That were self defence, that!' Milly said. 'They was gonna kill me!'

'I know that Mr Webb was coming towards you, but,' I replied as calmly as I could. If I hadn't been so sure that the men up in the Golden Gallery were set on killing Milly and probably me too, I would have handed the girl over to someone. She hadn't shown a shred of pity or remorse since she'd stabbed Webb, not one. 'But you didn't need to actually kill . . .'

'They was gonna throw me over the side!' Milly said as she stepped up on to the same stair as me and looked hard into my eyes. 'You know that? Some fucking ceremony that included them cutting my throat and then throwing me into the fires in the street! Webb would've watched! Call that doing *nothing*, do you? What was I supposed to do?'

'Milly, you're not in the least bit upset, as far as I can tell,' I said.

'Your face hurt, does it?' If she thought that changing the subject like this was going to make me blind to how she was behaving, then Milly Chivers was very much mistaken!

'We're not talking about my face,' I said. 'Now . . .'

'Cause I bet that it ain't,' Milly said. 'You've had your nose busted right up and a cheekbone, by the looks of it, too, but I don't s'ppose you can feel a thing.'

I made myself ready to protest, to say that what she was talking about was quite untrue. But it wasn't.

I sighed. 'No,' I said. 'No, I can't feel anything. In situations like this, in danger, your body doesn't let you feel too much. There isn't time.'

I knew men in the trenches who managed to stagger about on broken legs, they were that pumped up with fear and trembling. It's a well-known thing.

'But—'

'Well, it's the same with me,' Milly said. 'I'm in danger, so I can't feel.' And then I saw, or thought that I saw, just the tiniest bit of dampness in the corner of one of Milly's eyes. 'Can't afford to feel.'

'Milly . . .'

She shoved me with her tiny fingers just below my chest. 'Come on,' she said, 'we need to find out where these stairs go to.'

I turned and we trudged on upwards. As we got closer to the door, the well in the centre of the staircase became darker and more menacing. Just before we got to the top, we heard the sound of voices down below as, I imagined, our pursuers tried the door we'd bolted once again.

The door at the top of the staircase was actually a double one surrounded by a huge and ornate wooden frame. Curved like the wall they were set into, these doors were panelled and made of the same heavy, dark wood as their frame. I took hold of the handle on the left-hand side, but neither it nor the door moved. I looked down at Milly who was now chewing nervously on her bottom lip. There were definitely people down below trying to get in to wherever it was we were. Both

Milly and myself knew it. We also knew that neither of us had a clue as to where this new door was going to lead. I pushed on the right-hand door with my shoulder, not knowing whether I'd find people or fire or even the outside of the cathedral beyond it. It gave underneath my weight and Milly smiled. I put my head around the door and for a moment I saw absolutely nothing. I could hear voices, a way away admittedly, but I couldn't see anything. For a moment I thought about just shutting the door and not even bothering to move forward, but then I looked down at Milly's hopeful face and I said, 'I don't know where this is, I can't see anything.'

Impatient with me, she put her torch in my hand and said, 'Use this!'

I put the torch on and saw what looked like another corridor with various doors leading out from it. To our left, on what had to be the western end of the cathedral, was something large, a window, covered over completely with blackout curtains. So dark and funereal was it that for a moment it quite put me in mind of my shop back home in West Ham. Maybe it was this familiarity that made me move forward and pull Milly after me into wherever it was we were.

* * *

Public buildings, like hospitals, town halls and churches, always have hidden areas that the public do not ever actually see. Places like store cupboards, cellars and dumb waiters are kept out of view. For someone in my job, however, that isn't always the case. In fact, more often than not, the hidden places are areas with which we have a lot of contact. After all, when a person goes and sees his doctor at the hospital, the last thing he wants to be confronted with is said physician's dead body being stretchered down the main staircase towards him. No. While a kindly nurse tells the patient that Dr So and So isn't on duty today and so he's seeing Dr Such and Such instead, I'm carrying So and So down some hidden back stairs, past a laundry chute and into the cellar. This place, wherever Milly and I were now, was just one of those areas.

'What's this all used for?' Milly said as she followed where I was shining the torch with her eyes.

'I don't know.'

The corridor we were on continued down some steps in front of us and then up another small flight. To my right, on the same wall as the entrance door, was another small door which could, I reckoned, possibly lead up to whatever was in the top of the tower; bells or a clock. Also to my right, but on the opposite wall, was a doorway almost exactly the same in appearance as the one we'd just come through. The corridor between the two large doorways led off to the right into some shadowy place that my little torch could only very barely make out.

Almost before I'd noticed, Milly ran down the steps in front of me and then up the other little flight opposite. I could hear thumping noises from the stairwell behind me. They sounded ominously like Mr Rolls and his mates trying to get in to find us. I followed Milly without speaking, first down and then up the few stairs that led to where she was standing. Looking right as I got to the top of the steps I saw first blackness then, as my eyes adjusted to the conditions in the cathedral, I saw the little splash of red light from the lamp directly underneath the dome.

'Blimey!'

We were on a balcony at the far western end of the cathedral directly, as far as I could tell, over the Great West Door. I felt a bit sick at the thought of where we were until I found the wrought-iron fence in front of us and put both my hands on it. Milly, watching the blokes moving around on the Whispering Gallery way, way in front, if not that far above us, stood in silence. I was I admit, impressed myself. But then I began to hear other noises, from directly down beneath where I was standing. Familiar voices.

'Get it open!' I heard Mr Rolls says angrily.

'It's bolted from the inside!' I think it was Mr Smith who replied.

I leaned very carefully and quietly over the fence and made out, if not actual features, the movement of bodies down near to where we'd entered the tower. I thought I was at least very hard to see, but I'd not taken into account the fact that Mr Rolls and all his blokes had torches too. Suddenly a light was shining right into my face and there was a shout of what sounded like triumph from below.

'What's up?' It was one of the blokes up in the Whispering Gallery.

From down below, Mr Smith answered his question. 'Murderer!' he yelled. 'Up in the Triforium! A murderous girl and a madman!'

From the Whispering Gallery came, 'Murder?'

'Yes!' The voice of Rolls was loud, clear and very distinctive. 'Gentlemen, we have traitors in our midst!' he said. 'It's Phillips here. A madman and a girl who seek to destroy our beloved cathedral are trying to get away. One poor man has already met his maker because of them and in front of my eyes, too! Stabbed!'

'Oi!' I put a hand over Milly's mouth and then whispered for her to be quiet. Yes, they knew where we were, but I wanted to hear what else they were saying. I also wanted to know when they were coming.

It was then that, unwittingly, Mr Smith said something to the men in the Whispering Gallery that gave me some hope. 'And they killed Mr Ronson!' he said. 'Pushed him to his death on the cathedral floor!'

'Crikey!' came a voice from the Whispering Gallery, followed by 'Good Lord!', 'What say?' and 'Bloody hell!' Other voices joined in too, all shocked and horrified at what had apparently been done by Milly and myself. They couldn't all, I reckoned, be putting on a show for Mr Rolls and his mates. If I was right then, unlike poor old Mr Andrews, I reckoned on very few of the actual watchmen being involved in this murderous attempt to save St Paul's. We could actually be up against a very few, maybe even only five or six men at the most.

I yelled out, 'That's not Mr Phillips! That's a man called Rolls who isn't even a watchman at all!'

'Don't listen to him!' Mr Smith shouted. 'Just . . . Anyone who can get down here, please help us get this door open!'

'They'll kill again!' Rolls said.

I didn't even get a chance to draw breath before the sound of men running to get off the Whispering Gallery thundered in my ears. Below I saw one of the dark shapes by the door break away from the others and move away somewhere I couldn't see in the darkness. I suspected it was Mr Rolls. I didn't know whether he'd picked Mr Phillips's mask up from the Golden Gallery floor and put it back on again or not. But if he hadn't, then that could explain why, if the figure was Rolls, he was hiding himself away from all the other blokes now. All I could do was tell them, yell out and hope they might believe me. I took a deep breath.

'Mr Hancock, don't say a word!' a familiar voice said to me. 'Run!'

Chapter Thirteen

'George?' I thought he'd left the building.

But he was standing behind Milly and myself and, as the girl held her torch up towards his face, I could see that he had been crying.

'The men won't believe *you*,' George said. 'You've got to get away from here! You've got to run!'

'Run? Where?'

'I don't know!' George pulled his fingers through his hair and began to cry. 'I thought it would be all right! I thought . . . Mr Smith and Mr Bolton said that Mr Andrews was stupid!'

From way down below came the sound of men hammering on the door to the tower.

'You, George,' I said, 'you were part of this . . .'

'I didn't think that anyone would die!' George

sobbed. 'But then there was Mr Ronson and Mr Andrews. Mr Andrews died trying to stop them taking Mr Ronson's body. He died! I saw! It was terrible! And then, then you almost died, Mr Hancock . . .'

I felt my anger flare up inside me like a bomb blast. 'And Milly!' I added. 'Milly here!' I tipped my head at her and then I looked at his face.

Nothing.

He was looking at her as I spoke and yet there was nothing at all that spoke to me of any compassion for her on his fresh young face. He was one of those people who thinks that women and girls like Milly are scum. I hated such people.

'You knew, didn't you?' I said as I moved in closer to the boy. 'You knew that Mr Rolls and his mates were going to kill this little girl!'

'No! No! Yes!' he whimpered. I looked down below again at the men still gathering to try and open the thick ancient door. George, still crying, was now bent almost double in front of me.

I looked at him again and said, 'What happened to Mr Phillips, George? The real Mr Phillips?'

He shook his head as if just by doing that he could sufficiently answer my question.

'Answer me!' I said. 'What happened . . .'

'Mr Phillips pulled out of this! Mr Rolls took his place tonight!'

'How do you know all of this, George?'

There was a pause, just a short one. But George stopped crying then. 'My father was a Mason,' he said. 'He died.' He didn't say how or when, but then he looked up at me. 'Mr Rolls was his friend. He said that I could join the Craft and save the cathedral. He said my father would have done so. He said that was what my father had wanted!'

'And you . . .'

'Mr Hancock, I have done such terrible things! I watched, I *watched* Mr Andrews die!' He put his hands up to his mouth and I think he said, 'How can I atone?' But it was very quick and as soon as he'd said it he reeled away back to where he'd come from, across the balcony towards the north. I didn't attempt to follow him. At the time and in spite of his youth, I felt badly disposed towards George. I don't always have a lot of time for all the Commies we have in the East End;

they can, to be honest, be a bit much. But people like George make people like me think about class and the way it works in England. George could cry over the death of two middle-class men, but the life of a kid like Milly quite clearly meant nothing to him. People like her mean nothing to far too many people. I hope that if we do ever come through this war and conquer Hitler, things like Class will change.

'What are we going to do now, Mr Hancock?' Milly said after a pause. 'Shall we follow that boy?'

'No,' I said.

'But . . .' Milly must have taken notice of the blank look on my face because she went silent herself now.

I sat down. Right there on that balcony, with the whole dark cathedral spreading out in front of me. I didn't have a clue. At that moment all I could imagine was giving in to the men who were pursuing us and, once we were caught, trying to persuade those not involved with Rolls and company to take our side. As a plan it was well nigh useless. Even with Rolls hiding down in the cathedral, Smith and his other cronies could easily get to us first and kill us before any of the other blokes arrived. We still had the gun, of course, but what did that matter with so many men pursuing us now? Gun or no gun, they would overwhelm us. It wouldn't be difficult.

'Get up!'

I thought it was them at first until I realised that it was in fact Milly. She pulled at the shoulders of my jacket and said it again, 'Get up!'

'Milly, what's the point? They—'

'That boy, that kid in a dress,' she said referring to George, 'he went this way.' She pointed to our left, towards the entrance to the northern of the two church towers. 'We're following him,' Milly said. 'We ain't dying, not in here. We ain't doing what *they* want.'

And then with a remarkable amount of strength for such a little girl she pulled me to my feet.

Mr Smith, Mr Bolton and whoever else was down below and involved with them, used the fair few blokes who came to help from the Whispering Gallery, to push the tower door open. They then told those watchmen to get back to their duties, which they did. Those blokes, the real watchmen, they only helped out because they truly believed they were doing some good by helping Smith and Bolton to find us. Those men worked that night like I've never seen civilians work before. But now the 'bad men' were coming up behind us and so we ran into the northern tower and found out that the door to the stairwell over it was closed. I discovered the little door that led out on to a place I'd never seen before and one that I will now never forget.

This balcony is so easily overlooked. It runs, although it isn't connected to it, from the balcony at the western end of the cathedral along both sides of the nave and around the bottom of the dome. I thought that it finished right at the back of the church behind the high altar. I was to be proved wrong on that count, however. The balcony is below the Whispering Gallery, although probably only by about fifty stairs. There are actually several small doors into this place, the same as the one that I found, from the area I later learned was called the Triforium. It's a cross between a museum, with rooms for books and old exhibits and what have you, and a storage area for brooms and spare electrical wire and things of that nature. The door, a nondescript and small thing, opened easily and as we heard the sound of Mr Smith and his men thundering up the stairs, I pulled Milly in behind me.

'Where are—'

I slapped a hand roughly over her mouth. We could be seen from almost everywhere in the cathedral! We could also probably be heard. I had to assume that the men who were following us knew about this place and so, still with my hand over Milly's mouth, I looked around for somewhere we might be able to hide.

'Close the door quietly behind you and don't make a sound,' I whispered into Milly's ear. 'Not a murmur.'

She looked very serious, but she did as she was told and, as she pulled the door shut behind us, she cringed just ever so slightly at the soft clicking noise that it made. There was no way that I could see to lock the door – I didn't want to use my torch in case someone saw the light and spotted us – and so I had to think about how we might be able to hide on this balcony. It had probably been built so that workmen could maintain the upper part of the cathedral; Sir Christopher Wren was a man who thought of everything. I imagined it was still being used for such purposes now. But, like the rest of the place, it was dark and there was little I could see. As well as the men's voices behind us somewhere in the triforium I also knew that Mr Rolls was down in the cathedral somewhere, maybe he was even watching us right at that moment.

There was something else too. The balcony we were on, although surrounded by a rail, was narrow. And, although actually seeing the floor below us wasn't really possible, I knew it was there, far, far below us and that was good, or bad, enough for me. Where we'd come out was about halfway along the nave. I looked back towards the balcony at the western end, the one we'd just come from, and then to the east, towards the dome. There were no hiding places here. There were a few boxes, what could have been radiators, but that was about it. As soon as Smith and his men walked on to this thing, they'd see us. If we moved to get around into the dome or up towards the high altar, they would hear us. And anyway, I was scared. My poor old knees were tensing up again as my fear of heights took over once more.

A loud bang up in the dome made me almost jump out of my skin. This was followed by a voice which shouted, 'Up on the roof! The flames are gaining on us! Everybody up on the roof!'

There was a thunder of boots. I moved and, pulling Milly after me, shuffled towards the dome. It was just before we reached the terrifying corner where the nave fans out into the dome that my foot caught on something. I bent down to find out what it was. It was a blanket and it smelt of damp. As well as boots and voices up in the dome, I could also hear boots and voices in the triforium. I pulled Milly down with me and drew the blanket over us as quietly as I could. All I could hope was that Smith and his men didn't look under the blanket. If they didn't then, provided we could stay where we were until after they'd gone, we stood a chance of slipping back down to the cathedral floor and, hopefully, outside the building. Although I feared what might be out there almost as much as I dreaded the mad Masons inside. By the sound of it, almost everyone was fighting the fires up on the roof now. Everything around the cathedral was on fire. Ludgate Hill, Hitchcock, Williams and Co., Paternoster Row. The world was burning, or at least my world was. I looked at Milly as best I could through the darkness underneath the blanket and I wondered what sort of world she and all the other youngsters were going to inherit at the end of all this. We're not just in a war, we're also in the middle of something catastrophic in people's minds, too. It was mostly just old soldiers who went doolally after the First Lot. But it'll be civilians too, this time. They've seen too much, especially in London. Mr Rolls, Mr Smith and all the other blokes whose beliefs had twisted in this terrible war, wanted to do their awful deeds for very good reasons. They wanted to save the cathedral, to stop that evil maniac Hitler from destroying it. But the war had driven them mad. I knew that and to a large part I was actually sorry for them, even then.

It must have been about five minutes before the door on to our balcony opened and we heard the sound of footsteps. No words were spoken, but we knew it was them. Who else could it be? Milly gripped my hand tightly and I, I must admit, shut my eyes.

I've no idea how long it took for them to scan along the balcony and look behind radiators or whatever it was they did. I think at some point one or more of the men got close to where we were, but maybe the deep darkness on that part of the balcony together with its height put them off. But I heard the door open again and I assumed that they were filing through so I opened my eyes at that moment. Unfortunately, Milly, younger and much more impatient than I was took all this as a signal that she could move. Milly sat up and found herself staring, if at some distance, into a face.

'Mr Bolton . . . Lads . . .' It was Mr Smith's voice. Neither Milly nor I could see his face. But as we both got to our feet we could see that a little bunch of blokes were looking at us. We were at the corner of the balcony where it continues around into the dome. I looked behind me and saw that there was a small fence of iron between these two parts. We'd have to get ourselves over that if we wanted to continue running from these men.

'We can still use her!' a voice from down below in the cathedral boomed. It belonged to Mr Rolls, the madman in charge of this madness!

We had no choice. I picked Milly up and lifted her over the fence, hoping against hope that the floor over there was strong enough to support her. Not everything in buildings as old as St Paul's is always looked after. But Milly didn't come to any harm over there and so as soon as she was over, I followed. As Mr Smith and what turned out to be Mr Bolton, Mr Arnold and some other bloke came towards me, I swung one of my legs over the fence and staggered on to the balcony around the base of the dome. Milly, who was already running ahead of me said, 'You've got a gun! Use it!'

It was in my pocket. I put my hand in to get a hold of it, but I was shaking now and so I lost my grasp on the gun which clattered to the floor beside me.

'You can't escape, and even if you could, nobody would ever believe you!' Mr Smith said as he struggled to swing his short legs over the fence. As I bent down to pick up the gun I began to feel dizzy and felt as if I might fall.

'Come on!' I heard Milly squeal. 'Leave it! Come on!'

But I didn't want Smith and his blokes to get the gun! He was halfway over when I kicked it through the railings. It hit the marble floor down below with a crack. I heard a voice from down there, it was Rolls, say something, but I couldn't say what it was because by that time I was running. I followed Milly around the left-hand side of the dome, trying all the time as I did so not to look at the little red lamp down on the cathedral floor below. We were fortunately well ahead of Mr Smith and the others when I discovered that my assumption that this balcony stretched all the way around the cathedral was incorrect.

'We'll have to climb!' Milly said as she pointed to the top of the massive archway which marked the end of the balcony on the eastern side of the dome. Shaking like someone with St Vitus's dance, I pulled my torch out of my pocket and shone it in front of me. What I saw was so frightening that even when I recall it now I can feel myself begin to sweat. There was indeed a huge archway in front of us. Rising up from the end of the balcony it stretched over a great big space of nothing before it joined up with another balcony which this time really did lead up to the high altar. The arch wasn't, however, just suspended in mid air, it was attached to the marble wall behind it. It was in effect a ledge, albeit one with no railings to protect whoever might be bonkers enough to climb it. Above the ledge, however, there were railings which protected a sort of open chamber high up on the side of the dome. If Milly and myself were to climb this thing, we had two choices, we could just go straight over the arch, risking falling as we crawled down the steep opposite side, or we could climb up to the top of the thing and then try to scramble into the chamber. I went first. Knowing that I had first Milly and then the Masonic nutters behind me would, I hoped, make me hurry up.

Chapter Fourteen

Everybody says that if you're climbing something right up high you should never ever look down at the ground. I didn't, not once. I went forward on all fours and, when I heard the men running along the balcony towards us, I scampered up to the top of the archway calling out to Milly as I did so.

'Use your hands!' I said as I felt her very tentative steps behind me.

'Mr Hancock, I am so scared!' I heard her say in a voice so plaintive and so unlike her it almost made me cry.

'It's all right, love!' I said. 'Look, there's a ledge up here, you can get a hold under the railings and pull yourself up.'

At the top of the archway there was indeed a ledge

underneath the railings that protected that chamber. Smith was just putting his feet on to the end of the archway now and so I knew that I was going to have to try and pull myself up and somehow scramble into that chamber soon. I put my hands as far up the wrought-iron work as I could and then I pulled. I'm not a heavy bloke, but I am strong. That said, I couldn't even begin to haul myself up towards that chamber. I pushed down with my feet and pulled with all my strength, but I just couldn't get any purchase. Smith, though moving much more slowly than either Milly or myself, was gaining on us.

'Mr Hancock!'

Smith's fingers were touching Milly's heels. I pulled yet again and this time I felt some movement upwards. But I knew that it wasn't going to be anything like enough.

'Mr Smith!' I'd only just recently heard that voice; it was young George. 'Leave them alone! Stop it!'

I don't know whether Smith turned around to look at George or not. The boy was obviously way back along the balcony, having just come in as we all had, via the triforium. I just pulled on the railings and then took the next step of letting go with one hand and then grabbing higher up to pull myself forwards.

'It's wrong!' George said. 'I've come back because you must be stopped. It's wrong to kill Mr Hancock, he's entirely innocent.'

'Boy, you don't know anything about wrong or right!' Mr Smith replied. 'Is this cathedral still in danger?'

I managed to get one elbow hooked over the top of the railings. Below me on the archway, all other movement had ceased.

'George, are there fires still raging all around this building?'

'Well, yes they . . .'

'Then the cathedral is still at risk,' Mr Smith said. 'We have to make sacrifice, George. We all agreed, you included.'

'I know, but I was wrong. You killed Mr Andrews! I . . .' George began to sob.

With a massive effort, more of will than of physical strength, I pulled my poor old body over the top of the railings and into the shallow chamber beyond. I didn't even catch my breath before I leaned back over the railings and held my hands out to Milly. 'Come on!'

Still on all fours, she looked up at me with fear in her eyes.

'Your poor dead father would be ashamed of you, George Watkins!' Mr Smith said. 'He knew what had to be done! He was a brother, unafraid of the dark, willing to protect what is good, whatever the cost!'

'He was a real man,' another new and yet familiar voice agreed.

Milly managed to lift one small hand off the top of the archway while I strained to reach down towards her.

'Love!' I hissed. 'Just a little bit further!'

'George?' It was Mr Rolls. I didn't know exactly where he was but I knew he had to be behind us.

I took hold of Milly's wrist with the tips of my fingers.

'George, unlike Mr Smith, I think you should stop worrying about what your father might have thought about you,' Mr Rolls said. 'That ghastly old skeleton, Andrews, was obviously closer to your heart than your dear papa. I was wrong about you, George and I apologise.'

And then there was a cracking sound followed by a low, painful-sounding groan.

'Get the girl, Mr Smith,' I heard Mr Rolls say. 'Don't worry about the man. There's still time to save this place if we're quick.'

I heard George scream out, 'I'm dying!' And I looked around. The boy, who Mr Rolls had shot, was just a pile of dark agony at the other end of the balcony. The bastard had to have picked up the gun I'd kicked over the side!

Mr Smith made a grab for Milly's legs and, as she pulled them towards her body and out of his grasp, I felt her slip.

'Mr Hancock!'

I had the flimsiest grasp on her wrist but somehow I managed to dig my fingers into her flesh. As her legs swung out into space I heard her scream. My arm jolted with the weight of her and my shoulder swivelled and ground in its socket. Christ, it hurt!

I had to look down so that I could lean over and try to grab her wrist with both of my hands. She was so precarious. Just hanging out into nothing, her face turned up towards mine, its eyes pleading with me to save her. I worked my free hand down the arm that already had her and when I found her fingers once again I pulled.

'To blazes with this!' I heard Rolls say and then there was another gunshot.

One of the other blokes said, 'Mr Rolls! The ceremony!'

'To blazes with that too!' he said and then he shot again. At Milly.

I didn't feel her go limp, but she was completely still and silent when, with one huge last effort, I pulled her up and then over the railings. At that point I couldn't be certain whether she was alive or dead.

When I placed her down on the floor and she didn't fall over, I knew that Milly was alive. Killer she might be, but she was also a little girl to me and when I saw that she was all right I hugged her to my chest and kissed her hair as if she were my own dear daughter. Shaking now with shock, Milly began to shiver and so I took off my jacket, placed it around her shoulders and then sat her at the back of the chamber. High up in the vaulted ceiling behind us I could see a window which was not covered by any blackout curtains. It was completely red with flames. A horrible blood-curdling groan rippled along the balcony towards us as that poor lad George began to die.

'You bastards!' I yelled as I ran back towards the railings once again. God, it was hot up there, as if we were cooking in a great dark stove – which in a way we were. 'Hasn't your God or whatever it is you think you're killing for, got enough blood yet?'

Just below, on the top of the archway, I could see Mr Smith pulling himself up against the railings. I could push him off to his death without too much effort and I knew that I really should do so. But I also knew that I really didn't want to. I pleaded with him, 'Mr Smith,' I said, 'you're a watchman first and foremost, aren't you? You're a man of honour! The Watch *is* honourable! Don't do what Mr Rolls wants you to do! It's wrong!'

'In Solomon's Temple in Jerusalem, the floors were red with the blood of sacrifice . . .'

'Of animals, yes!' I said, hoping to goodness that my recollection of the little bit of Old Testament knowledge I had was correct. 'Not people!'

I looked into Mr Smith's eyes and I think that he was about to reply in some way. I hoped that maybe something I'd said might have made him think twice about what he was doing. I don't think he was a wholly bad man. He was a proper watchman after all. But what happened next came from outside our little drama up on that balcony.

'Rolls!' The voice came from the floor of the cathedral.

I could see a couple of blokes down below us, but I couldn't make out who they were. I did get the name of one, however, when I heard Mr Smith murmur, 'Steadman.'

Suddenly I felt some hope! 'Mr Steadman!' I shouted. 'It's Hancock! Are you all right?'

A torch beam hit me square in the face and made me blink. 'Hancock, thank God! I've a pretty sore head, but I'm alive!' Mr Steadman said. 'Are *you* all right? And the girl?'

'We—'

'Gordon, this doesn't concern you,' I heard Mr Rolls say with contempt in his voice.

'I'm in the Craft too, Eric,' Mr Steadman responded. 'I won't have what I love perverted by you!'

'I will save St Paul's Cathedral,' Mr Rolls said.

'Why?' Mr Steadman replied. I heard the sound of men's feet running across the marble below. 'You've never cared about the place! You never came on watch with Harold Phillips or me! You just have this, this interest in sacrifice! You just want to kill and then be thanked for it! No, you just want to kill, don't you? Like your idol, the Beast. Sidney Ronson never trusted you, he knew which way you were going!'

'We've locked the door, Gordon,' I heard Mr Rolls say slowly. 'The men you've sent to stop us, can't get in.'

'But the tower door is open,' I said. I called down to Mr Steadman, 'Rolls had to break the door in to get to us!'

Rolls laughed. 'We locked the door at the top of the stairs,' he said. 'Even if you do manage to push Mr Smith to his death, others, including me, will come to take his place, Mr Hancock. I will have that girl and I will kill her in the way prescribed in ancient rite.'

'You'll never get out of here alive, Rolls!' Mr Steadman said.

'You can't kill me!' I heard Rolls say. 'None of you can kill me! The whole nation, the Empire itself, will thank me! Hitler will never ever tangle with the Brotherhood again, not when he sees our power!'

One of the worst things in the world is a man with a mission. Anyone who thinks he's special, that his ideas are better than anyone else's, is dangerous. Just look at Hitler. Too many people had already died this night because of this bloke's obsession with offering blood in exchange for the safety of the cathedral. Not that Mr Rolls's 'mission' was about that really at all. As he'd said himself, he wanted glory both personally and for the 'brotherhood' or, rather, his version of it.

'Eric, the real heroes are up on the roof!' Mr Steadman said. 'The Dean and the other chaps, the watchmen who come here night in and night out are beating back the flames. We're not out of the woods yet, but as long as the bombers don't come back and as long as the LFB continue to protect the cathedral, I think we'll survive. The cathedral doesn't need blood, Eric! The cathedral doesn't need you at all!'

If what he was saying was true then maybe those of us who remained weren't all going to roast to death!

'Eric,' Mr Steadman said, 'you need to stop this now. It's wrong.'

I looked down at Mr Smith and I know that I saw desperation in his eyes. I said, 'Look, mate, whatever you blokes think you're going to do here tonight, it's not going to happen. People know. It's not just poor old Mr Andrews's ramblings any more. And George is dead! A young lad . . .'

'We planned it for months!' Mr Smith said. He sobbed. 'Why such a big raid tonight! Why not a normal, quiet Sunday . . .'

I felt like saying something about how even Hitler was against such a bunch of lunatics, but I didn't. He'd completely ignored what I'd said about George. Like Rolls, he just cared about this big plan they all had for the 'good' of the cathedral. Something very cold entered my mind then. It was a small, icy voice which told me I should just push Mr Smith off the archway and have done with it. He would have done that to me had he been in my position, I was pretty sure. And besides, if I killed him, maybe Bolton and the other blokes with Rolls would be too frightened to volunteer to take his place. Voices and faces from the First Lot jockeyed for position in my mind. I didn't know any of them. I don't usually. There's just mud and guts and faces are incidental, because out there in the trenches you always tried not to look anyone else in the face. At the end we were all too ashamed to do that. If you look at someone, then they can see you too. I looked away from Mr Smith. Then the lights all came on and for just a moment I thought I'd gone blind.

We all live in darkness these days. Our eyes are so unused to light that when we do see it, it hurts and makes us squint. Londoners have become moles.

'I can see you now, Eric,' I heard Mr Steadman say.

'I can see you too,' Mr Rolls replied. 'And I have a gun.'

Mr Steadman, or one of the few watchmen with him, had put on all the lights in the cathedral nave. Huge chandeliers fitted with electric bulbs. I had crawled around in the gloom for so long that I felt it was almost as if someone had just let the sun in. I heard someone say, 'The blackout! What about the blackout?'

But no one answered that question. The blackout for the time being was irrelevant. What was important was that what had become a sort of a battle up in the ceiling of the cathedral, finished. But in order to join battle, we all needed light.

Milly, who had been at the back of the chamber, came forward to stand next to me. 'Gold!' she said as she took one of my arms in hers. 'Look!'

The gold leaf on the mosaics and statues in the nave and around the dome can't be seen until the lights are switched on. A cathedral, even a great one, could be almost anywhere in the dark. But with the lights on everything changes. Halos of saints glowed with a pale yellow light, the Madonna and her Son re-enacted the agony of the crucifixion against a gilded mosaic sky. Up in the ceiling Latin words snaked around the curves of archways, and even these were made of gold. This was London's treasure house. Not the King's, not even the church's, but all of ours, us Londoners, for us to see any time that we liked. St Paul's wasn't going to fall, I remember thinking then, because it just couldn't. Hitler wasn't going to finish it off, and neither were Mr Rolls and his twisted band of followers. I looked along the balcony to where Rolls was standing and I saw a large dark heap at his feet. George. God Almighty what had that poor boy done?

Whatever it was, he'd paid for it with his life. Now there was just Rolls, his men and that gun. I heard and saw him take the safety catch off the weapon as a couple of men of the St Paul's Watch stepped on to the balcony and began to move towards him.

'You think you're the only one who can get through a door, Eric?' Mr Steadman shouted up from the cathedral floor. Now that I could see him properly I could see the damage one of Rolls's blokes had done when he hit him. Mr Steadman had a great big shiner round his right eye. 'Some of those same good watchmen you persuaded to break a door down for you, destroyed a lock for me once I told them the truth. Only your pitiful men really believe you now. Give up. It's over. You can't hope to get away now.'

Mr Bolton, Mr Arnold and the others on the balcony around the dome looked at each other and then, as a body, they seemed to slump. I suppose it is in the nature of followers to give up without a fight when the odds are overwhelming. They can, after all, always find someone else to follow, given time. But leaders are different. Leaders don't have anywhere left to go.

Mr Rolls put the pistol up to his own right temple.

Chapter Fifteen

'If I wasn't a Christian man, I'd tell you to pull that trigger,' Mr Steadman said into the silence that had now enveloped the inside of the cathedral. Outside, where the voices of the men fighting the fires were coming from, I fancied that perhaps the sky was not quite so red any more.

'I will pull it unless you come up here and face me, Gordon!'

I looked down at Mr Steadman and for a moment I wondered whether he would do this or not. He wasn't armed as far as I could tell. Unless I was very much mistaken there was only one gun in the building and that was the one that Mr Rolls was holding up to his own head. Mr Steadman began to walk towards the south tower stairs. Everyone waited for him to appear on the balcony. Only Mr Smith, who was now shivering on top of the archway below, didn't look in Mr Rolls's direction. Mr Smith looked up at me.

'I think my legs are going to sleep,' he said. 'I'm freezing! I don't know if I can stand like this any more.'

I heard Milly say, 'Well, that's hard Cheddar, ain't it!'

'Hancock, pull me in with you!' Mr Smith said. I heard a door open and close back along the balcony and I watched to see what Mr Rolls would do.

'I'm going to fall!' Smith said. 'My back, it . . .'

I ignored him. I did so deliberately. I didn't want him anywhere near Milly and myself because he was one of 'them', one of Rolls's men, and I couldn't trust him. I didn't want to.

'Mr Hancock!'

But we were all looking at Rolls and Steadman now.

'Give me the gun, Eric,' Mr Steadman said.

'You know that my brothers here will continue the work to protect this place,' Rolls said. But the blokes on the balcony in the dome looked even more downcast now. 'Without the protection of the ancient rites, London is dead!'

'Mr Hancock, I am, I was a watchman . . .' It was

honest and true and for the first time I felt actual sympathy for him. I looked down at Mr Smith.

I don't know for sure whether I tried to catch him as he fell towards the cathedral floor. I like to think that I did, but the reality is probably that by ignoring him earlier I had condemned Mr Smith to death. His legs went, then his back, and finally his cold, clawed fingers gave way and he flew with a speed I hope I never have to see again towards the marble floor below. The only good thing about it was that for a moment, Mr Smith's fall distracted Mr Rolls. As he looked over his shoulder he lowered his arm and, in that moment, Mr Steadman reached forward to grab the gun in his hand.

The struggle, from a distance, looked small and insignificant, like two blokes just simply pushing and joshing one another. You see servicemen doing this to each other sometimes when they meet on the street. It is, or can be, a form of affection amongst young men. But Mr Rolls and Mr Steadman were neither in the services nor young, and the weapon that was somewhere between them was very far from being a joke. I was, I admit, still consumed by what had just happened to Mr Smith and so although I watched what began to unfold over on the balcony my mind was not really there. I did see that the men with Mr Steadman began to move away from him, but I didn't, as Milly obviously did, sense that I was in any danger myself.

'Get back, Mr Hancock!' I heard her say as she pulled hard on the sleeve of my shirt.

'What?'

She yanked me away from the rail and backwards towards the rear of the chamber. 'You don't want to get shot, do you?'

I didn't know! I'd killed again! After all those many years following the Great War, I had done it yet again! I stood against that back wall panting while Milly very tentatively strained around me to see what was happening on the balcony. I didn't look. I was lost inside my own head. I could have saved Mr Smith! He would have gladly killed me given the chance, but that wasn't the point! I had known how dangerous his situation was and I had done nothing. Nothing!

The sound of one single gunshot was what finally brought me back to myself.

* * *

'God Almighty!' I heard someone say.

'Gordon! Gordon, are you—'

'I'm all right,' I heard Mr Steadman say.

This time I moved forward to look of my own volition. Mr Steadman and Mr Rolls were both still standing. Mr Steadman, however, was now the one who had the gun.

'It really is over, Eric,' he said.

Mr Rolls said nothing. He just put his head down and I think that he began to cry. Where the bullet had gone I couldn't see, but it hadn't hurt anybody. Down below in the cathedral I heard footsteps. It was one of Mr Steadman's men going to look at Mr Smith. It was more than I could do. I just stood sideways on, my eyes fixed on the two figures of Mr Rolls and Mr Steadman as well as the crumpled heap that had been young George. How could so many people have died for something I was still completely failing to understand? And what was I going to do about Milly? She smiled at me and I smiled back but I knew just as well as she did, that Milly had killed. She'd done it defending herself it was true, but she'd also done it with a cold precision that made me shudder. 'How are we going to get down from here?' Milly asked.

I didn't have a clue. I couldn't see any obvious way down apart from the very precarious way we'd come up. And now, with all the lights on in the cathedral, that route looked even more frightening than it had done in the dark.

'Well?' Milly asked again, impatiently.

'We'll just have to wait and see what happens,' I said. 'Mr Steadman and his men know we're here. We'll just have to wait for them to come and help us.'

But Milly was obviously very agitated. I wondered uncharitably whether this was because she wanted to get away and disappear. But then she said, 'I'm frightened up here.' And that made me feel rotten. The poor kid had been through so much, not just in the cathedral, but all through her life. Besides, if she did want to get away, wasn't that understandable?

We watched as Rolls and his men went meekly now down with Mr Steadman and his blokes. The fight, or so it seemed, had gone out of them all.

'We'll come and get you and the girl in a minute, Mr

Hancock,' Mr Steadman said as he pushed Rolls through the little door into the triforium.

Only three or four minutes passed at the very most. At the time, I don't remember hearing or seeing anything more until Mr Rolls and two of his blokes appeared down in the cathedral in front of the Great West door.

'Oi!' the chap who had been first looking at, and then covering up, Mr Smith's body shouted at them. 'Oi, you!'

But when he saw what Mr Rolls had in his hand, he hit the deck smartish. Somehow, Rolls had managed to get the gun from Mr Steadman and he and his men were disappearing through the Great Door and into what remained of that frightening flame-coloured night.

I turned to Milly and said, 'If Mr Rolls and his men are out and about, I have to find out what's happened to Mr Steadman!'

As I swung one very shaky leg over the side of the railings and back on to the top of that blasted archway again I told Milly to stay put. 'I'll get someone to you,' I said as I began to shuffle very slowly and nervously down the slope. I didn't want to be swinging about above the marble cathedral floor. But then I found something that meant it wasn't half as bad as I thought it was going to be. I discovered that if I hung on to the railings as I went down, when they eventually ran out, I could hang on to the marble lip from the floor of the chamber. It hung out from the wall just far enough for me to firstly get hold of it and then hang on to it as I lowered myself back on to the balcony. Had I been a short man, that wouldn't have been possible. But luckily I'm tall and so, for once, I was actually all right with being up high.

I was running along the balcony back to the door to the triforium when I heard a shuffling sound behind me. I turned and saw that Milly had one leg over the side of the railings.

'Milly!' I said. 'You stay put! I'll—'

'I'm frightened!' she shouted.

I walked back a little way towards her and said, 'Now look, you get back behind those railings, Milly. You'll fall!'

'Well, come and get me then!' she demanded.

Milly didn't need to be in the trouble she was in and

could very easily get herself out of it. She was safe enough where she was. I really had other things to do. Mr Steadman and his men could be injured or worse. I turned on my heel, yelling back at her as I went, ‘No! Rolls has got away and anything could be happening! Get back behind those bloody railings . . .’

‘No!’

I lost control. ‘Well, bleeding well drop, then!’ I yelled. It wasn’t that I didn’t care about Milly – I’d almost bloody died because of her – but I couldn’t let her put me off doing this, I just couldn’t. And besides, if I knew Milly at all, I had a good idea that she’d do pretty much anything to preserve herself.

‘Mr Hancock! Please!’

I ran on until I came to the door and I ducked down and went through it. At first I saw no one and then I heard a groan. There was an open door opposite me which led into some sort of storeroom. The groan had come from there. At the same time as I went in, the bloke who Mr Rolls had threatened to shoot downstairs arrived.

‘What’s going on?’ he said as he came panting up behind me.

'I don't know,' I replied.

'Oh, Lord!' The words were thick and sounded painful and they came from behind a very large wooden crate. The other bloke, a Mr Caldwell, and myself went to have a look. Mr Steadman was lying on the floor, holding on to the side of his head, wincing.

I bent down to take a look at him and, to be honest, I couldn't see that much was wrong. Or rather I couldn't see that his head was any more damaged than it had been before. 'What happened?' I asked him.

'I don't rightly know,' Mr Steadman said. 'We, Mr Neeson and Mr Harris . . . Where . . .'

'Over here, Mr Steadman,' another voice said from way over the other side of the room, underneath a window. Mr Caldwell went running over to the two men there.

I sat with Mr Steadman for a while, waiting for him to come back to himself as it were. From what he, Mr Neeson and Mr Harris had to say, it seemed that Mr Rolls and his men had jumped them, even though Mr Steadman had been in possession of the only gun in the place, as far as I knew. But I had my doubts. It had taken me quite a while to get to Mr Steadman and his compatriots after I'd left Milly. If none of them were badly hurt, which they weren't, why had they lain around for so long? Why had they, as I saw it, waited for me to come and find them?

'Someone should go after Mr Rolls and his men,' I said after a while.

Mr Steadman smiled weakly. 'Yes, but out into the—' He stopped, his eyes apparently, caught by something out in the triforium. 'Something moved!'

I looked over my shoulder but I didn't see anything. I thought he was making it up for some reason. I was getting the impression that Mr Steadman was not everything he wanted me to think that he was. I was both right and wrong about that, and about what he had just seen as well.

'When I saw the cathedral door open and Mr Rolls go out, I got the impression that the fires outside had died down a bit,' Mr Caldwell said. 'We could go out and try to follow them.'

'We could.'

But no one moved. I looked around the space between the packing crates at the groggy men on the floor and I made up my own mind. I stood up. 'Well, I'm going to have a butcher's outside anyway,' I said. I then added, forcefully, 'Rolls shouldn't get away, Mr Steadman. He killed George and he tried to kill a lot of other people too, including a young girl. It isn't right that he should be able to walk away from that!'

Mr Steadman lowered his head. I thought he might try to stop me, but he let me go. I had it in mind that because all of these men were Masons they exercised some sort of protection over each other. Again, I was both right and wrong about this.

I walked out of the storeroom and made a brief detour back on to the balcony once again. If I were to go gallivanting about looking for Rolls and company I'd have to at the very least tell Milly what I was doing.

As I walked out on to the balcony I saw a large group of men walk on to the Whispering Gallery. Smoke-smutted and, in some cases, soaked in water, they had to have just come down from the rooftops above. Clearly exhausted, they nevertheless looked cheerful, even from a distance. As they sat down and lit fags for each other, some of them even smiled. I heard the word 'control' from someone which I hoped meant that the fires might be being beaten back from the cathedral at long last. But any good humour that I might have been put into was soon to end as I looked into the chamber where I'd been not so many minutes before and found that it was empty. Milly was nowhere to be seen.

Very few things in this life are clear-cut. I'm a grown man, and I know that there are shades of right and wrong. That said, I like to know who my enemy is. I like to feel some sort of certainty about how many people I might be up against in any situation. In the First Lot it was everyone except my own mates. But here . . . Here there were killers on all sides, none of whom I came close to even partly understanding.

'Mr Hancock?' Mr Steadman had come on to the balcony and was standing beside me.

I turned to him and said, 'Milly's gone.'

'Has she?'

'Bloody kid! She must have climbed down all on her own!'

'How enterprising of her!'

He was so calm and I was so bloody agitated. God

knows I'd come to at least respect the girl, but the fact remained that she had killed Mr Webb up on the Golden Gallery. She had done that and I had seen her do it.

'Perhaps it is for the best,' Mr Steadman said quietly. 'Maybe the fact that Rolls has gone is for the best too!'

I looked at him and then down at the body of poor young George the chorister which lay at the far end of the balcony, dripping blood on to the marble floor below.

'For the best?' I said. 'How can the fact that someone who's murdered others being loose on the streets be for the best?'

Mr Steadman didn't answer me and for probably the best part of ten minutes, we stood together silently side by side on that balcony. From the Whispering Gallery the sounds of relief and even a little bit of joy, increased as we stood there. I hardly even registered the moment when Mr Steadman finally left.

'The Dean's just come down,' I remember him saying later. 'I'd better go and tell him something.'

Tell him what? I thought afterwards. Tell him *what*?

But he told him something, because when a group of coppers turned up later, Revd Matthews, amongst others, spoke to them. That was quite a bit later, however, and when I finally came down from the roof.

When I found out that Milly had gone and I'd had that short and to me frightening little conversation with Mr Steadman, I took off. I never thought that I would willingly go up into those high galleries of the cathedral again, but I did. Slowly this time, I climbed the stairs first to the Whispering Gallery and then up the even narrower flight to the Stone Gallery. I could have gone further and perhaps been even more private than I was, but the voices of the blokes from the LFB who were still filming up there were somehow comforting. I didn't go near them and they didn't go near me, but together we watched the fires burn and we watched the fires recede. Even before the first pale wash of daylight began to push its way almost painfully through the smoke, it was obvious that the fires were slowly coming under control. We were safe. But at what a cost. I walked around that gallery as many as half a dozen times; I looked and I listened to what people said and I felt nothing but desolation.

At first sight, what was out there was unrecognisable. Like a bonfire with bits of wood and old crates and half-burnt Guys sticking out of it. But then as dawn crept slowly up, I swear even the light was frightened to move too quickly that morning, for what had happened became horribly revealed. Someone in the film crew gasped. I heard someone else say, 'Christ, look at St Bride's!' He pointed to something still burning with a frightening ferocity. And yet in spite of the fact that the nave was indeed on fire, the spire was still standing. I later learned that St Bride's spire was the tallest that Wren ever built. That it stands still is testimony to the resilience of this city. Not that I felt that at the time. Up on the Stone Gallery watching dawn break, all I could see or feel were the skeletons that surrounded me. Skeletons of the Guildhall, London Bridge Station, Ludgate Hill, Paternoster Row, Fleet Street. I also felt the press of ghosts upon me, too, even out in the smoke-soaked air as I was then. Mr Andrews, Mr Ronson, young George, Mr Smith – even the horrible Mr Webb. I'd have had every one of them back, however awful. But they were gone and they weren't coming back, and at the time I didn't have any sort of idea what justice their families might be able to expect. Mr Steadman was organising some sort of cover up. I knew it. He'd let Rolls and his men go, just like that! Well, he was a Mason, too, even if he did disagree with Mr Rolls and his followers. There was, I was sure, some sort of rule in Masonry that meant you couldn't tell on another brother Mason. If *I* spoke, alone, who would listen? And what about Mr Phillips, the real Mr Phillips, what had happened to him?

I sat down on the stone floor of the gallery and I watched some old office building or such-like on Ludgate Hill burn to the ground. Although the fire-storm had been somehow brought under control by the firemen some hours before, this building still burned with a speed and ferocity that was terrifying. The roof had gone long before, but as I sat there I watched its guts disappear into red and yellow and listened as floors and ceilings, furniture and fittings collapsed in on themselves and became charcoal and liquid and dust. Finally the walls buckled and with a horrifying screaming sound, like a woman in pain, the outer walls first cracked and then separated. Then with a sigh, the whole thing crashed to the ground and I cried inside for yet another part of my present that had disappeared for ever. I'd never known that office building, I'd barely known Mr Andrews, Mr Webb, Mr Smith, George and Mr Ronson, but I mourned their passing just as surely as I'd mourned that of my old mates who'd died on the Somme. Directly or indirectly war had killed every one of them.

Chapter Sixteen

The crypt had almost emptied of visitors by the time I got there. The first-aid ladies were still making tea, but Mrs Andrews was not with them. She was sitting on her own over by Lord Nelson's tomb. When she saw me, she smiled. It made me wonder if she knew about her husband or whether in fact all of the past ten or so hours had just been an illusion. If they had, then in so many ways it would have been a relief. Everyone would still be alive, although I would be completely confirmed as a total madman. But I am not and have only ever briefly been a *total* madman. Mrs Andrews called me over.

'Sit down, Mr Hancock,' she said as she patted a wooden chair beside her. She smiled.

'Mrs Andrews—'

'It's all right, Mr Hancock,' she said. 'I know.'

I said nothing.

'My husband is dead,' she continued. Her eyes didn't so much as moisten. She changed the subject immediately. 'I'm sorry that the little girl you were seeking finally eluded you. But she survived and that is the main thing, Mr Hancock. They did not manage to—'

'Why did they think that killing a little girl would save this place?' I said. 'It's bonkers!'

'Human sacrifice is as old as time,' Mrs Andrews said. She then fixed me with a hard gaze. 'It is very powerful. Men of the Enlightenment, however, men like Sir Christopher Wren, did not hold with it; they considered it barbarous.'

'It is!' I looked around now to see who if anyone, was listening to this strange conversation.

'Is it?' She smiled again. 'Tell me, Mr Hancock, if you could only save that which you hold dearest by sacrificing the life of an unknown child, would you do it?'

Of course I went to say 'no', but then I stopped.

'Masonic history, like the history of this country, is

littered with violent and uncivilised acts,' Mrs Andrews said. 'We must oppose them. But we must also understand them too. These are desperate times, Mr Hancock. What the men who killed my husband did they did with the welfare of the greatest symbol this city has firmly in their minds.'

'Mrs Andrews,' I said, 'they killed Mr Ronson, too, and George the chorister.'

She put one of her thin, wrinkled hands up to my cheek. 'Mr Steadman, it would seem, knows the whole story,' she said. 'Go and speak to him.'

I stood up and, as I did so, I told Mrs Andrews that I was sorry for her loss.

'My husband knew as soon as he went against those people that he would die,' she said. 'He also knew that by opposing them he would be putting the cathedral in danger.'

'You mean that he believed that the sacrifice would actually save the cathedral?'

'Oh, yes,' she said. 'Yes, he did.'

I was stunned and she could see it.

'Mr Hancock, there are some things in life that are very wicked that can produce great good.'

'But . . .'

She raised a finger up to me and said, 'Which is precisely why those things must never be done. To give in defiles both oneself and that thing one is seeking to protect. You, Mr Hancock, whatever questions you may now have in your mind, would never kill a child to save even your own family. My husband knew that, he saw that immediately in you.'

I didn't say anything about what I knew had been Mr Andrews's main reason for talking to me about this sacrifice business, that I was a Catholic. And now I came to think about it not only was I a Catholic, but I was a complete outsider too. I couldn't possibly have been connected to what he suspected was about to happen in the cathedral. According to Mr Andrews, he and Mr Ronson had somehow known what some of their brothers had planned to do to save the cathedral. But how had they known it was going to be this particular night? Had they known that when the night started, or had that only become apparent to Mr Andrews after Mr Ronson's death?

I had a lot of questions, far too many for a grieving widow to provide answers for. I went up into the cathedral which was where I saw Mr Steadman, the Dean and a load of other watchmen talking to the coppers.

I had thought I might just move closer to the group and try to listen in to what they were saying. But Mr Steadman saw me and he came over immediately.

He smiled. 'I've finished telling the sergeant and his men what happened here,' he said. 'Those people sheltering in the crypt aren't required to talk to them. They, and you, saw nothing and so there's nothing for you to tell.'

I went from being half dead with tiredness to being incensed with anger in less than a second. 'But I *was* there!' I said, 'I—'

Mr Steadman grabbed my arm in a claw-like grip and began to frog-march me towards the Great West door. 'Let's go and have a smoke, shall we?'

He was covering it all up! I went with him, I didn't have a great deal of choice, but I was fuming. Crimes had been committed, men had been killed, I had almost met my maker myself! And now, just because they were all Masons together, it was being covered over. Mr Steadman pulled me towards the Great West door, opened it, and then pushed me outside. He followed directly after me, but I didn't notice that at the time. As soon as I was outside, everything except the scene that I was looking at temporarily disappeared from my mind. It wasn't dawn any more, it was daylight. With the exception of the smoke that still lay thick across the ground and sometimes in the air, everything could be seen clearly now. I looked down where Ludgate Hill had once been and I didn't recognise anything. There were shapes, no buildings. Where the sewers had ruptured there was a smell the like of which I knew from down our way, but for which familiarity did not bring any ease. Mixed with it there was also a sweetish odour which could have come from the stocks of incense in all the burnt-out City churches. It could also have been the smell of human bodies singeing and then cooking in the terrible heat. From where I stood it was as if only St Paul's had survived, only St Paul's existed.

'We took some casualties last night,' Mr Steadman said after I'd had a little bit of time to take in the scene around me. 'But then we were bound to, given the ferocity of last night's raid.'

As I looked into the street, small figures, people, scrambled up and down great piles of smoking rubble. They, like the scene in front of me, were uniformly grey in colour.

'Mr Ronson's accident was unfortunate, Mr Andrews and young George—'

'Were murdered,' I cut in. 'As well you know!'

Mr Steadman offered me a fag, which I refused in favour of one of my own cigarettes. I wanted nothing from him except words.

'Mr Hancock,' he said slowly, 'anyone who has been murdered will be avenged. Anyone who has been executed, however—'

I didn't know one from the other and I said, 'You call what happened to Mr Andrews an execution?'

'Mr Andrews unfortunately perished alongside the young chorister and a rather brave local man called Webb,' Mr Steadman said. 'They were fighting the fires outside the cathedral. Against the Dean's advice they went outside, you see.'

I was struck dumb. Mr Steadman had fought against

Rolls and Smith and the others, but now he was protecting them! How powerful those Masonic brotherhoods had to be!

'All but Webb's body, so far, have been retrieved. Very badly burnt they are of course.'

'What have you . . . What are you doing?' I raised my hands to take hold of Mr Steadman by his collar and to shake some sense into him. But he caught my hands mid flight and thrust his face into mine.

'We can't tell people what happened here last night!' he hissed. 'The Dean's distraught about the casualties as it is! Do you think—'

'The Dean didn't know?'

'Of course not!' He pulled me even closer towards him, so close I could smell his rank, exhausted breath. 'Mr Andrews, Mr Ronson and myself knew. Neeson and Harris I had to draft in last night because if I hadn't we'd have all had it!'

'But the girl . . .'

'Rolls began talking about blood sacrifice back in September when all this bloody bombing began,' Mr Steadman said as he loosened his grasp upon me a little. 'He's always been a bit odd, mixed with some unsavoury types. Rolls and Phillips and their little cabal, they talked about protecting all treasured buildings in this way, as if it were a sort of practical method like boarding a structure up. Nobody else listened! Some even laughed! That isn't, after all Masonry, that is pure, pagan superstition.'

'But—'

'But I attend the same Lodge as Phillips and Rolls and so I kept an eye out. Not that I knew it was going to take place last night. I didn't even know that a child was going to be involved!'

'But Mr Andrews did,' I said, 'or rather I think that he suspected it. At first he thought that Mr Ronson was the sacrifice. I know that. But he mentioned a child, or rather the tradition of using a child. The last thing he said to me was something about finding and taking care of Milly.'

I was stumbling over my thoughts and rambling. Mr Steadman sighed and then let go of me completely. He pushed his tin hat back slowly from his bruised and battered face which was almost indescribably sad. 'Gerald Andrews never trusted me,' he said. 'It was I who first told him about Rolls and Phillips, but because I was in business partnership with them, Gerald was suspicious of me. Sidney Ronson told him about them independently of myself. I told Gerald more because I felt that what Rolls was going on about was unsavoury. Poor Sidney, of course, understood far better than I the earnestness of his intentions.'

'You all went to the same Masonic Lodge.'

'Everyone, except Gerald Andrews, but including young George Watkins's late father. Poor George desperately wanted to follow his father.'

'And Mr Rolls . . . ?'

'Mr Rolls is the Grand Master of our Lodge,' Mr Steadman said.

I felt a shiver run down my spine. Had Mr Steadman let Rolls go because he was, effectively, his Masonic boss?

'No watchman worth his salt just falls off the Whispering Gallery,' Mr Steadman said. 'I knew Sid Ronson was watching Rolls and Phillips and so when he fell I knew it could have been them. But I still couldn't quite believe it. I'd never taken what Rolls and Phillips said as seriously as Gerald and Sidney had. Eric Rolls was, is, our Grand Master; I thought that he was just playing around with ancient ideas. Intellectual discourse. I never thought they'd actually do it.'

But *they* hadn't. As far as I was aware Mr Rolls had only masqueraded as Mr Phillips because he wasn't a real watchman. He'd become Phillips to get inside the cathedral. But why, when Phillips could so easily have done that himself had Rolls dressed up for the part?

A bus pulled in to a place that had once had a bus stop and people actually got out. There were no cars on Ludgate Hill that morning, no driver – myself included – would have even attempted it. But this one London bus just drove up, let some passengers off and moved on again as if nothing had happened.

'I have to go back to my office soon,' Mr Steadman said. 'Before our typist arrives, if she arrives.'

I was shocked by this sudden jump into something as ordinary as this bloke's job. 'What?' I said. 'What are you—'

'I have to get to my office, if it still exists, and cover up Phillips's body before our typist gets the fright of her life,' Mr Steadman said. Then, seeing the confusion on my face, he continued, 'I think that Rolls killed Phillips because I don't believe that Harold Phillips would or could actually go through with such a thing. Harold, I think, loved the cathedral too much to actually sully it if push came to shove. He was a most dedicated watchman.'

'Dedicated enough to disobey his boss?' I said.

'I believe so, yes,' Mr Steadman said. 'Harold's interest in ancient ritual was academic rather than practical.'

Mr Andrews had said as much to me many hours before. He had even become indignant at the idea of Harold Phillips being involved in such a thing.

'If they'd done it together, then Phillips would have smuggled Rolls in somehow, probably with the help of George Watkins. It's my belief,' Mr Steadman said, 'that Harold is lying dead on his office floor. He always used to stay at the office when he was on Watch duty, which he should have been on last night. I need to get over there.'

I caught hold of the sleeve of his jacket as he moved. 'So you can get rid of Mr Phillips?' I said. 'Cover up for your Grand Master yet again?'

Mr Steadman put his fag out on the ground in front of him and said, 'No, Mr Hancock, so that I can tell the police and make sure that Eric Rolls hangs.'

'But he's your Grand Master!' I said, being all bitterly theatrical as I did so. 'You let him and his mates go only a few hours ago!'

'I did that for the sake of the Dean and the cathedral,' Mr Steadman said. 'That such filthy outrages should take place here . . . No one needs to know that! I let him get away for all the reasons I have said and yes, also for Masonry, too. Masons are not like Rolls, Rolls is aberrant.' He looked as if he was about to cry for a moment and then he gathered himself. 'Neeson and Harris are coming with me,' he said. 'You can come too if you want, if you don't believe me. But I warn you, Mr Hancock, Rolls could very well be there before us.'

'Why is that?'

'Because in this madness he can't have got far and there's money in the safe at the office. He'll run now, he'll have to, but he'll need that money and I don't think he'll want to go to his bank. It may even no longer exist.'

And then he took a very familiar-looking pistol out of his pocket.

'I thought that Rolls took that away from you,' I said. 'You told me he had.'

'I lied,' he answered.

I looked into his eyes and said, 'I should just go in there and tell the coppers the truth as I see it now, shouldn't I?'

'You can.'

'Mr Rolls will still be arrested, everyone will know what a bastard Mr Webb was, and no one will ever trust anyone who's in the Masons again.'

Mr Steadman stood aside in order to let me pass. I had just pulled the Great West door a little further open when Mr Steadman said, 'Just remember that we run this country. Consider this in the light of the fact that you are a wog, Mr Hancock.'

When I was a child there were no grades of truth that I knew of. You were either telling the truth or you were lying, and if it was the latter, then, as often as not, your dad would at some point give you a clip round the ear hole. To the extent that we're supposed to guard our tongues in public places and with people that we don't know intimately, everyone these days conceals some things – that's war for you. But what I'd become involved with was something both sacrilegious, to established faiths, and also at the same time something very firmly at the centre of power. Whether Mr Churchill himself is a Mason, I don't know but at least some of those around him have to be. And as Mr Steadman had known as soon as he took me outside the cathedral to talk to me, getting a wog to shut up and toe the line doesn't take too much effort and no courage at all. I think I ended up hating Steadman almost as much as Rolls in the end.

I wanted to go home and I could have very easily done just that. The Duchess and the girls had to be worried about me, not to mention poor old Annie whose place I'd left to go out into the incendiary fires. They'd all be wondering what had become of me. But I'd made up my mind to go with Mr Steadman. Mr Neeson and Mr Harris had finished their long shift in the cathedral now and were leaving with us. We all set off for Holborn together in silence. The offices of Phillips, Steadman and Rolls were opposite Holborn underground station. It was where, many years before, George Chivers, Milly's father had come to work. There was no one involved in this, I realised as I trudged over crumbling heaps of bricks, who was not connected with the others in some way. Only the watchmen and the firemen who had actually saved the cathedral, the Dean and myself were outside this 'charmed' circle of connections. In spite of the fires still burning all around us, it was cold that morning and so I pulled my jacket hard around my body and wondered where on earth young Milly might be. I'd briefly given her my jacket when she was cold up in that chamber in the cathedral roof. I promised myself that as soon as I could, whether the kid was ever brought to justice for what she'd done or not, I'd go and see her and tell her what I thought. I'd also try to help her, if I could. After all, what her father and Webb had done to her wasn't her fault.

I don't know exactly how long that resentful trudge over rubble to Holborn took. We had to divert a lot; sometimes because of still-burning fires, sometimes because there was water from a burst main gushing out into the streets, and sometimes we were just told not to go a certain way by policemen or wardens. Buildings not actually collapsed would need just the very smallest nudge or vibration to make them do so. Even now that the raid was over and many of the fires out, the City was still a very dangerous place to be. None of us were youngsters either. Messrs Steadman, Neeson, Harris and myself were all of an age. We all laboured to get to Holborn and by the time we got there, we were all sweating.

The offices of Phillips, Steadman and Rolls were a bit rough around the edges with rubble piled up against some of the windows and the walls, but they were still standing. Mr Steadman and the other blokes set about looking round the outside of the place while I reassured a copper who came across the road towards us that we had a right to go into the building. Looters come in all shapes and sizes, including that of middle-aged men. After a brief chat with Mr Steadman and a butcher's at his office keys, the copper left.

Mr Steadman put his key in the front door lock and let us all inside. There had not been, I noticed, any rubble piled up against the front entrance door.

Chapter Seventeen

It's my belief that when Hitler is defeated and peace finally comes, London will change tremendously. The way the centre is laid out is still the way a medieval city would have been arranged. A lot of the buildings are either ancient or, like the offices of Phillips, Steadman and Rolls, Victorian. It was a tall, thin building, with five storeys including the basement. Where we came in on the ground floor there was really quite a neat office with a new-looking desk and typewriter as well as a fireplace that had the look of something fashionable too. The typist, who to everyone's relief hadn't turned up for work, sat here. But as we mounted the dark and creaking staircase up to the architects' offices and the storerooms, things became older, more worn-looking and haphazard. Great big drawing boards, some with plans actually perched on them, sometimes several boards to one room, stood where they would most easily catch the light. The windows, though dirty and now criss-crossed with tape, were large and must once have provided good views down into what used to be a lively street. I took a brief look out now and saw the half-wrecked underground station with ghostly-looking figures skirting carefully around it. The copper who had spoken to me earlier was on the other side of the road again, but he was looking up at the architects' office. At least there was someone to shout to should the worst, whatever that might be, happen. As it was the silence that had come upon all of us as we entered the offices was bearing heavily down on me at least. When we mounted the stairs up to the top floor, I was almost glad when Mr Steadman turned around and said, 'Phillips's office is up here.'

That Phillips's body might also be present in it was of concern to me, of course it was, but I didn't fear it as I think Mr Neeson and Mr Harris might have. Harris went very pale at the mere mention of Mr Phillips. We followed on after Mr Steadman and stood behind him when he stopped in the open doorway into Mr Phillips's office. For a second or two we all caught our breath and then Mr Steadman said, irritably, as if he were talking about an unwelcome guest, 'He's here.'

'Mr . . .'

Steadman stood to one side so that we could see into the room. Mr Harris almost immediately looked away. On the floor was the figure of a tallish man, lying face down in a large smudge of drying blood. How he'd died, I couldn't see but I assumed that violence of some sort had been involved.

Mr Steadman took his tin hat off and then wiped a hand across his brow. 'We'd best report this to the police,' he said. 'Poor Harold.'

Mr Neeson began, 'Mr Steadman, shouldn't we er, someone, I think, has cleared a path into the building. Shouldn't we look for—'

'Yes, you're right, I think someone else has been here, too. We should look for Rolls,' Mr Steadman said. 'Let me check the safe.'

He'd said that Rolls would need to come back for cash. He walked around Mr Phillips's body and towards a door at the rear of the office. He opened it to reveal a very small room with a large safe at the back of it. The door of the safe was wide open. Neeson and Harris followed Steadman and I heard him say to them that they should go up on the roof. There was apparently, some sort of platform or balcony up there. I bent down to look at the dead body in front of me as the three other men walked back towards the staircase once again. Even pressed against the lino on the floor, I could see that Mr Phillips's face was a poor, savaged thing. Without his mask he was almost unbearable to look upon. But I knew his type well, I knew and know men without faces. I know how bitter they are and the reasons for that bitterness that go far beyond just the way that they look. But the blokes I know are working class – poor and forgotten. How had a middle-class man like this, with a good wage, a profession and the best 'face' that money could buy, got mixed up with even the idea of human sacrifice? To be an architect he had to have been educated. How could he have given even the slightest heed to such nonsense? Blood is just blood as I know only too well; there's nothing special or magical about it. Gallons were 'sacrificed' during the Great War, gallons are spilt to this day, but nothing gets any better, no one is any more secure because of blood.

Although I did want to know how Mr Phillips had died, I didn't try to move him. That was for the police to do. I stood up and decided I'd go up on to the roof with the others. I doubted whether Mr Rolls was still in or around the building. As I went up the short staircase to the roof, I heard voices above me and they sounded very normal and conversational.

'Eric . . .' I heard Mr Steadman say. I felt my whole body go very cold. My head was just below the top of the stairs, which came directly out on to the roof as stairs on a ship do, and I could see the sky bearing down in shades of smoky grey on a scene I could not yet observe.

There was some sobbing which, to me, sounded like a girl.

Mr Rolls spoke next. 'If you hadn't come along when you did, Violet here would have been fine. She wasn't going upstairs. You would have found Phillips first, Gordon. Anyway, I thought you and I came to an agreement back in the cathedral. You put that gun down as I recall, Gordon, and let us go.'

'Arnold and Bolton were just idiots but I was always coming for you once you'd cleared the cathedral, Eric. I knew you'd come here, for money. Leave Violet alone,' Mr Steadman said, 'she's got nothing to do with this.'

'What is all this about?' I heard a young woman's voice say. 'Mr Steadman! I got into work and I was so proud of myself. I was so happy to see Mr Rolls was here!'

'I don't want to hurt Violet,' Mr Rolls said. 'But I do need some sort of way out of here.'

'There is no way out of here,' Mr Steadman said. 'Now we're away from the cathedral I'm going to turn you over to the police.'

'What for?'

'You know what for!' Mr Steadman said angrily. 'That, that in the—'

'Mr Phillips stabbed to death in his office?' Mr Rolls said with almost a laugh in his voice.

'Mr Phillips?' I heard the girl gasp. 'Is he, is he dead?'

'Eric . . .'

'Yes, I killed him,' Mr Rolls said. 'I'm so sorry about that, Violet, but Mr Phillips annoyed me intensely yesterday evening.'

I heard girlish sobs. I put my head just over the top of the stairs so that I could see. Steadman, Neeson and Harris were standing over on one side of the flat office roof while Mr Rolls, over the other side, was holding a knife up to the throat of a short, plump redhead. Mr Steadman was pointing a gun in the direction of Mr Rolls and, of course, the girl too.

'I suppose you killed Harold so that you could get into the cathedral?' Mr Steadman asked.

Rolls became animated now and I saw his face turn red. 'We planned it weeks ago! I knew that our old colleague George Chivers needed money and I'd heard that he, or rather his neighbour, Webb, put George's children to work on the streets. Chivers had not a clue about what was going on and, what was more, he didn't care,' he said. 'We had a victim whom no one would ever bother to trace, and we were both going to perform the ceremony up on the Golden Gallery. Then yesterday Harold showed his true colours and said he couldn't go through with it. All of a sudden he starts saying we should just forget all about it. I blame myself in a way. Harold was, I knew, basically of a tender-hearted type. I of course ordered him onwards, as his Grand Master! I told him to obey! But he wouldn't!' He took a deep breath and he shook his head as if he could barely understand this. 'Harold didn't think that I was serious! Can you believe he was humouring me? That was what he said, my interest in the occult was desperate and transitory and he was humouring me!'

'Eric,' Mr Steadman said, 'Harold did share some of your views, I know. He, like you, was much more interested in the esoteric side of Masonry than the rest of us. His interest was, however, intellectual. Eric, only madmen like Bolton would hold with all that nonsense put about by Crowley!'

'Nonsense!' He pulled the girl closer to him and as a consequence, she squeaked. 'Were you with him in Sicily? No you were not!'

'And neither were you, Eric!' Mr Steadman said. 'God, Crowley is a lunatic and a drug addict . . .'

'The Beast who, in his Abbey of Thelema in Sicily, opened up my mind!'

There was a pause then as Steadman looked at Rolls as if he'd just seen him for the first time. I didn't know what they were talking about at the time – except that Mr Andrews had talked about the Beast to me the night before. I had assumed it or he was the Devil. But was it this person, Crowley? Who was this Crowley, and what did an abbey in Sicily have to do with anything? Mr Harris and Mr Neeson looked about as confused as I must have.

'Gordon, I have seen what blood can do! It can make men powerful! The blood of a defiled child like Chivers's little girl could save this city! Good God, man, the Nazis are destroying the Brotherhood over on the continent! If we can save the great symbol of our city, if we can preserve our brother Wren's great Masonic masterpiece . . .'

'Eric, this isn't real!' Mr Steadman said. 'Wren never sacrificed anyone! What you tried to do, what you have done, is wicked!'

Again there was silence while Mr Rolls seemed to think about this. In the cathedral he had come across to me as a man obsessed but nevertheless in possession of his wits. Now he was a man breaking down and I honestly think that maybe he would have come quietly in the end, had he not seen me.

'Who's that?' he said as he spotted my head at the top of the stairs. 'Is that the dark fellow, that cockney you have with you?'

I climbed the rest of the stairs and showed myself. Rolls said to Steadman, 'He's not one of the Brotherhood. What's he doing here?'

'He's the only one, apart from Milly Chivers, who really knows now,' Mr Steadman said. 'What do you think he's doing here?'

'Well, I imagine,' Mr Rolls replied, 'that wanting to keep all of this quiet as you do, you plan to kill him.'

I took in a sharp breath and Mr Steadman said nothing to contradict Mr Rolls after that.

'Eric,' he said, 'you have to pay for what you've done here.'

'And you've got to redeem yourself as a brother and help your Grand Master,' Mr Rolls replied. He then looked at Mr Harris and Mr Neeson. 'And you two,' he said. 'The Craft comes before everything.'

Mr Steadman held the gun up and flicked off the safety catch. 'Eric . . .'

'You won't shoot Violet, will you, Gordon?' Rolls pulled the girl's neck upwards and pushed his knife into the flesh beneath her jaw.

'Don't kill me, Mr Rolls!' she said. 'Please don't!'

Mr Rolls laughed. 'Hey, Mr whatever your name is, on the stairs,' he said to me, 'move aside, will you? Violet and myself are coming down.'

Nobody said that I shouldn't and so I climbed out over the top step and on to the roof. Mr Rolls, with the terrified Violet in his grasp, was already moving. Maybe because the other men didn't say anything I thought that they weren't going to do anything either. So, if for no other reason than to save another girl from this madman, I decided to do something to him myself. I didn't know what. As he shuffled and pushed the girl towards the stairs my breathing became heavy as I made myself ready for him.

Rolls was careful, I'll give him that. As he started to descend he turned so that the girl Violet was facing outwards towards Mr Steadman and the others. It would have been very difficult and very risky to try and shoot him. But there wasn't anything he could do about me. That stairwell was open on all four sides and although he watched me all the time as he went down, when his head was only just above the top of the hole I moved very quickly around to the back of his head. I saw Mr Neeson gasp and Mr Steadman begin to run forward. But I had my right leg back by this time and before anyone could do anything, I laid into Rolls's head with my steel-capped boot. I did it with all of my strength and with such violence that Rolls's hands jerked away from Violet's neck as if they'd had a current of electric run through them. The girl screamed because Rolls fell like a stone and she began to fall after him. As with so many things in life, I'd failed to think through what I did and so if Mr Steadman hadn't been there to catch her, Violet would have fallen down the stairs too. But, unlike myself, who just flailed around trying to grab the girl, Mr Steadman pulled her firmly towards himself and then hugged her to his chest. I looked down the stairwell to where Mr Rolls lay motionless on the landing. I feared he was dead, that I had killed him, and so I was immediately sick over the side of the building. Mr

Neeson and Mr Harris thundered down the stairs to check on him.

'Well, he's still breathing, amazingly,' I heard one of them say eventually.

'I'll come down,' Mr Steadman replied. I then saw him pat the girl on the head and say, 'All right here for a bit, Violet?'

Her chubby cheeks wobbled with barely suppressed sobs. 'Y-yes, Mr S-Steadman.'

'Brave girl,' he said. And then as he walked towards the stairwell he looked into my grey, sick-splattered face and smiled. 'That was bloody brilliant, Hancock.'

I didn't say anything. I was shaking by that time and it was a bad bout. The stuttering when the bombs fall I'm used to, but the shaking only takes me over when the fear has actually passed and my body goes into a kind of shock. When I used to come home on leave during the First Lot, sometimes I'd shake the whole time until I went back to the front. When I finally came home for good it went on for months. It comes back sometimes now and this time I was grateful for help from Violet when we were told we could come down the stairs. Mr Neeson had got the copper from over by Holborn underground station and he was taking down particulars.

'You're trembling like a leaf!' the girl said as she held on to my arm. 'You poor man!'

All I could do was smile.

The copper, once we were all back inside the building, said, 'You'll all have to come down the station, you know. Once I've called an ambulance for this fellow.'

We all looked down at Mr Rolls who was now making groaning noises. In spite of everything he'd done, I was glad he was alive.

Chapter Eighteen

I thought that Violet and myself would be questioned. We were taken with the other men down to Snow Hill Police Station. We walked, as I remember, through all the rubble and the mud and dust. Soot and paper flew about and got caught in our eyelashes and eyebrows. Sometimes even a tiny piece of paper could have a number or a word on it that hinted at where it might have come from. Maybe from a book-keeper's office, or from a receipt book of one of the jewellers at Hatton Garden. All of this debris irritated Violet, who was very careful about her make-up now that she'd recovered from her recent ordeal.

'Get away, filthy thing!' she said as she batted a puff of dust and a fragment of paper away from her face. Still shaking, I didn't care. The bloody *Atlas of the*

World could stick to my face and it wouldn't bother me.

Snow Hill had been bombed earlier in the year and so the place was in a bit of a state. Violet and I sat out in a grim and filthy corridor while Mr Steadman and the other two men went into a room with two coppers. Later on those two coppers came out and two blokes in plain clothes went in. No one spoke to us or even seemed to take any notice of the fact that we were there. After what had to be almost an hour, Violet said to me, 'You'd think they'd offer us a cup of tea, wouldn't you? After what we've been through!'

And then she began to cry. I put one of my hands on hers and then, when she'd recovered herself a little, I gave her a fag.

'Blimey, you're still shaking!' she said as she took it from me.

'Yes.'

'But what a shock!' Violet said, her big made-up eyes staring wildly. 'Mr Rolls killing Mr Phillips! I thought Mr Rolls was a nice man! Was he a friend of yours, Mr . . . ?'

'Hancock. No,' I said. 'I, er, I met Mr Steadman—'

'Oh, in the cathedral, wasn't it?' Violet said. 'Mr Phillips always went on Watch duty in St Paul's. He liked it. I wonder why he wasn't there last night? I wonder why Mr Rolls killed him?' She began to cry again. 'Why did Mr Rolls kill Mr Phillips?'

I patted her hand again and said, 'I don't know. But I expect it had something to do with money. Most things do.'

'Oh, what with the safe being open and—'

'I imagine so, yes,' I said.

What else could I say? Violet, as far as I could tell, knew nothing about what had happened up at the cathedral. From what I could gather, if we hadn't turned up when we did, Rolls would have just taken the money from the safe, said ta-ta to Violet and gone on his way with the girl none the wiser. But Violet was no fool. She dragged on her cigarette and said, 'What were they all talking about on the roof of the office? About blood and that?'

I said that I didn't know. Of course I knew more than Violet, but I still had a lot of questions that I was determined to ask Mr Steadman before the day was through. I, after all, knew all about what had happened inside the cathedral that previous, terrible night. If he was going to stop me from opening my mouth then he'd have to give me some answers and pretty quickly, too.

Not that I had any expectations that the police would disbelieve whatever Steadman, Neeson and Harris were telling them. I imagined that everyone inside that room was a member of the Brotherhood.

Violet was taken home to her parents' house in Streatham in a police car. I was offered a lift back to Plaistow myself but I swapped that for the use of the only telephone in the place for a moment and a cup of tea with Mr Steadman.

'If you want me to keep to your version of last night's story,' I said to him as we went into the room with the telephone, 'you'll have to tell me what exactly that is. Who is Crowley, for instance?'

Mr Steadman told me to make my call and then we'd talk. I just had to hope that our telephone at home was still working. I asked to be put through not really expecting anything to happen, who does these days? But then, as if by a miracle, I heard our office girl, Doris, on the line.

'Hancock—'

'Doris!' I cut in quickly before the line went. 'It's me, Mr Hancock!'

'Mr Hancock? Oh, God,' Doris said, 'we've all been going mad here! Mrs H has been in tears over you!'

'I'm fine, Doris,' I said. 'I'm in the City—'

'Mr H, the City's still burning!' Doris said. 'Here, Miss Nancy wants a word . . .'

'Doris . . .' I didn't want to get into any sort of long conversation, especially not with either of my sisters. They can be a bit on the hysterical side at the best of times!

'Frank?'

'Nan,' I said. 'Look, Nan, I'm all right. Tell the Duchess to stop crying. I'm still in the City but I'll be home as soon as I can.'

I heard my sister draw her breath in sharply as if in disapproval. 'You'll get here as fast as your legs will carry you!' Nancy said sternly. 'Mum'll have a conniption if she thinks you're still running around amongst the fires. You with Auntie Annie still, are you?'

'No, Nan, I left and then I had to do things and—'

'Do things?' I heard her splutter with disbelief. 'Blimey, do what?'

'Are the horses all right?' I asked.

'The horses? God help us, Frank!'

'Nan, without the horses we don't have a business!'

She sighed. 'The horses are fine, Frank. Now—'

'Nan—'

'Oh, just get home, Frank!' Nan said impatiently. 'Make sure that Annie's all right and then get home.'

And then she put the telephone down on me. My family were all right, and so was my business. That, at least, was a relief. Mr Steadman, smoking on the other side of the plain, grey room, didn't make any sort of comment. I sat where I was and continued to shake. After about five minutes a middle-aged copper with a huge walrus moustache came in and gave us both cups of tea in thick, white, cracked china. I stuck my face straight into my cup and found that thankfully, the tea was full of sugar or something very sweet at the very least.

Mr Steadman put his cup beside him for a bit to allow the tea to cool and then he said, 'Rolls, once the doctors patch him up, will be arrested for the murder of Mr Phillips. Last night he was interrupted whilst stealing money from our safe by Mr Phillips. Rolls killed Mr Phillips, and then took his place in the cathedral so that Mr Phillips wouldn't be missed. This morning, fearing that maybe someone might go in to our offices and find Mr Phillips's body, he decided it might be best to go back and conceal it himself. But Mr Norris, Mr Harris, you and myself were a bit worried about how strangely Mr 'Phillips' was behaving on Watch last night and so we followed him. We caught him on the roof with our typist. The police have no need to speak to Violet, she's been through enough.'

I put my tea down and lit up a fag. 'That's the story you've agreed on, is it?' I said.

'What do you mean?'

'Mr Steadman,' I said. 'I know that you want to protect St Paul's Cathedral. I know you don't want the most important place in London to be associated with anything bad . . .'

'I think you'll find that Mr Churchill is of that opinion too,' Mr Steadman said as he fixed me with a gaze that told me I was on very dangerous ground. Had he, I wondered, or those plain clothes coppers he'd been with, actually spoken to Winnie himself? I knew that Churchill had given orders that the cathedral was to be saved at ANY cost. I knew that but still I had to press on. I had to!

'Mr Steadman,' I said, 'I know it's not just the cathedral you and all these coppers are protecting. Coppers are in your brotherhood . . .'

'Mr Webb, George the chorister and Mr Andrews died, as I have said before, fighting the fires outside the cathedral.'

'Yes, their bodies are charred and—'

'Ronson, unfortunately, fell from the Whispering Gallery and poor Mr Smith perished whilst trying to reach what he thought might be a small fire on the balcony underneath the Whispering Gallery,' Steadman said. 'Given the ferocity of last night's attack our losses have been slight. Only Mr Rolls's crime is unnatural. He let his personal fear of what is happening to our city and his greed overwhelm him. He was never a watchman, nor showed any inclination to assist his fellow Londoners. When he thought that he had been caught out in the cathedral he even tried to create panic by shouting up to the watchmen in the Whispering Gallery that a murder had been committed by you, Mr Hancock. That did not, as we know, succeed. So then he wanted to get out of the city and he took money that wasn't his in order to do that.'

'Mr Rolls will say that he was trying to protect St Paul's, he will talk about blood . . .'

'Mr Rolls has gone mad,' Mr Steadman said. 'I imagine that his association with, amongst others, Aleister Crowley, has turned his mind.'

I still didn't know who this fellow Crowley was but I left it a few moments before I said, 'I want to know. All of it.'

Steadman breathed in slowly. 'Mr Hancock—'

'The truth!' I said angrily. 'Tell the "wog" the truth and then he'll never speak or even think of it again! I mean,' I added tightly, 'as you said yourself back at the cathedral, it isn't as if I could tell anyone, is it? Who would believe me?'

He said nothing and so I waited. Outside in the street I heard what sounded like a lot of stones tumbling down to the ground. This was followed by a great deal of shouting and the smell of brick dust in the air. I carried on waiting. Mr Steadman got his cigarettes out of his pocket and lit up.

He dragged on his fag several times before he eventually spoke. 'Mr Rolls,' he said, 'like a lot of Great War veterans, came home from the trenches to a world he could not understand. He didn't know how those around him could be so uninterested in his ghastly remembrances while the British public, or so he felt, preferred that he remain quiet about his terrible experiences on the Somme.'

I knew that this was true – it had been the same for me – and so I said nothing.

'Rolls, like his father before him, trained to be an architect and was proposed for membership of the Brotherhood. Until this morning I didn't know myself that Rolls had actually come into contact with Aleister Crowley. I knew that he espoused some of his ideas, it was what first caused myself and others to watch him. Apparently Rolls and Crowley met in Cefalu in Sicily. Crowley lived there in the early twenties and I know that Eric Rolls went on some sort of architectural tour of Italy at that time and so I suppose they must have met then. Maybe he was with Crowley when—' He just broke off, just like that.

'Who is Aleister Crowley?' I said.

The answer when it came would have been funny if what had happened with Mr Rolls hadn't been so serious.

'The Wickedest Man in the World and the Beast are just two of the names Crowley delights in,' Mr Steadman said. 'He's a Satanist. He's also a Freemason, or rather he was.'

So that was what Mr Andrews had meant by 'the Beast'. Not the Devil at all, but this person, Crowley.

'What, did the Brotherhood throw him out?'

'Crowley is entirely discredited as a Mason,' Mr Steadman said. 'I told Rolls that he was a madman, but he wouldn't listen! People will clutch at anything they think might save them in time of war and Rolls had already been convinced of Crowley's authenticity years ago. They all started to whisper!' He pulled a disgusted face.

'What do you mean?' I said. 'Who?'

'Rolls, Phillips, and then sometimes Smith, would

come to the office, and that awful Bolton, too. In Smith's defence, he was a dedicated watchman and I think that the notion of saving the cathedral at any cost was something that he was completely sincere about. But, with the exception of Harold Phillips, they were a group of misfits, really.'

'Mr Rolls was your Grand Master,' I said.

'Mr Rolls is *still* our Grand Master for the moment,' Steadman said. He then paused for a second. 'Mr Hancock, sometimes bad people get themselves into positions of power before you know what their true natures are. Mr Rolls has been our Grand Master for nearly ten years. It has only been since the bombing began back in August that he's been talking about Crowley. Maybe the bombing was what he'd been waiting for since he had that encounter with Crowley? Maybe he saw the benefit that Crowley's sacrifice brought? Perhaps it made his life back then in the twenties make some sort of sense? We live in a world in ruins, what do I or anyone else know?'

There was another pause but I said nothing and just waited for him to continue.

'Aleister Crowley performed a human sacrifice at

what he called his Abbey of Thelema in Sicily sometime in the early twenties,' Mr Steadman said. 'This was documented at the time and Crowley was subsequently expelled from the country. Why he was not prosecuted, I do not know. There is a tradition, in this country and many others, of human sacrifice. It is not such an *outré* idea as some people may believe.'

'Mr Andrews told me it was something to do with protecting buildings,' I said. 'In the old days. He said sometimes it would even be done to protect a church. But not St Paul's. Christopher Wren hadn't done that.'

'It is thought that some of the earlier members of the Brotherhood, my architectural ancestors, may have used blood in this way,' he said sadly. 'But not Wren. He was a true son of the Enlightenment. Crowley would have us all back in the Dark Ages! But then when people are in a lot of trouble and they try to find solutions to their problems, sometimes what they come across is evil. I've no doubt that Eric Rolls felt that what he was doing by following Crowley's path was for the best. I don't know, as yet, whether he was an actual disciple of the Wickedest Man in the World.'

'But Smith and Phillips and some others went along with that anyway, didn't they?'

He shrugged. 'Yes. Although Harold Phillips did quite clearly come to his senses in the end. Harold was a nice man, a very committed member of the Craft, and a very academic person. Theory and practice were very different animals to Harold. I also think he found it hard to oppose his Grand Master; he didn't like conflict. His face, or rather what had happened to it, made him timid much of the time. Eric Rolls knew that.' He frowned. 'What he also knew after the very first time he mentioned the name Crowley at one of our meetings was that support for that man's ideas was only shared by a few.'

'Mr Andrews said he didn't know how many people were involved,' I said. 'He didn't trust anyone.'

Mr Steadman shook his head helplessly. 'Andrews trusted few people anyway, it was his nature! And yet he trusted George Watkins.'

I suddenly felt very cold. I'd liked young George. He had tried to save Milly and myself and had died in the attempt.

'George's father died in a raid just after Rolls began

talking about Crowley. Martin Watkins was of the opinion that it was all a load of rot. But when he died, and once Rolls knew that George was a chorister at St Paul's, Rolls began to suck up to the boy, promised him his father's place in the Lodge. He also convinced George that his father had been in favour of the sacrifice.'

'It's all very clubby, isn't it?' I said. My voice was bitter but I didn't care. I wanted him to know how I felt.

'You've never joined anything, have you, Mr Hancock?' he said.

I stopped myself from saying the obvious which was that no club I could think of would ever have me.

'Part of the attraction of societies, secret or otherwise, is that one rarely has to go outside the society to get what one needs,' Mr Steadman explained. 'To have someone involved in the plot actually inside, as in part of the cathedral, like young George, could only be beneficial. Similarly with the victim. To go out and buy a child from strangers could possibly be dangerous. Poor Chivers's situation was well known, we'd all worked with him and we'd all heard the rumours about what had become of him and his family. They turned out to be true.'

'Except that Milly isn't really as young as they thought she was,' I said.

'Wasn't she?'

'She's sixteen.'

Mr Steadman looked amazed. 'Good Lord!'

'Mr Webb, who was her pimp, said she was younger than she really was to attract more, er, more customers.'

'George Chivers lost control of his entire life many years ago,' Mr Steadman said. 'We, his fellow architects, if no one else, should have cared for him. But when a fellow is given so totally to drink . . .' He put his hand in his pocket, took out his watch and looked at it. 'Mr Hancock, I will soon have to go.'

He didn't say where to and I didn't ask.

'So you're covering up the deaths of young George, Webb, Mr Andrews and Mr Smith in order to save the Dean and the cathedral – and of course your "Craft",' I said. He didn't answer. 'But what about Rolls's other followers,' I said, 'what about Bolton and Arnold and what about this Crowley bloke? Do they get away scot-free?'

Mr Steadman stood up. 'If we are to protect the reputation of the cathedral and the Watch . . .'

'And the Masons.'

'Well,' he put his head down for a moment, 'yes. Arnold and Bolton were just followers. They'll be frightened, miles away now. They didn't actually kill anyone. Rolls pushed Ronson from the Whispering Gallery and Smith killed Andrews. That was particularly vicious but then maybe Andrews fought or something, maybe . . . As for Crowley? He's a drug fiend, Mr Hancock. He is old and sick and he can never return to his beloved Abbey of Thelema in Sicily because Mussolini, as well as Hitler, abhors Masonry.'

'I thought you said that he wasn't a Mason now?' I said.

Mr Steadman smiled. 'I said that he had been discredited. I never said that he had been thrown out.'

'So once a Mason—'

'Mr Hancock,' he said as he walked towards the door of that bleak, cold room, 'Fascism is doomed because it seeks to destroy us. It was laudable, in a way, of Rolls and the others to want to save the cathedral. But as far as the War itself is concerned they didn't need, and don't need, to worry. As I have said to you before, *we* run this country. We also run many others, too. Rolls, I think, chose to sacrifice that girl just as Crowley did in Sicily back in the twenties, because he wanted to. There have always been sadists in our midst.'

'Mr Andrews was killed in a very sadistic way,' I said, still shuddering even then at the way in which the old cleric had died from a stab wound in his poor old backside. 'Is that part of Masonic ritual, a punishment?'

'I think that possibly Mr Andrews and Mr Smith got into a fight, don't you?' Mr Steadman said. 'How else could such an outrage happen?'

And then he left me. I was in no doubt at all that anything I might want to say to the police would be treated as entirely irrelevant.

Chapter Nineteen

I began what I truly believed was my journey home, but troubling thoughts I knew I couldn't really do anything about drew me back to the cathedral. It wasn't that I wanted to see anyone in particular in the great church or even that I wanted to look at places where certain things had happened. I think in reality I just wanted to know that the place was still there. Meeting the Dean on the stairs up to the Great West door was a thing I didn't either plan or expect. He walked over to me and, to my amazement, he remembered my name.

'Mr Hancock,' he said, 'what a night you shared with us, eh?'

I looked down for a moment before I answered him. Part of me at least didn't really know quite what to say.

The Dean, I had thought, had known, at least in part, what Mr Andrews had suspected. He had, after all, spoken to me about enemies both inside and outside the cathedral. 'I'm sorry about Mr Andrews,' I said.

Mr Matthews shook his head sadly. 'No one apart from the firemen were supposed to be fighting the flames outside the building,' he said. 'We lost more people than we should have, Mr Hancock, but thankfully fewer than we might have done. I understand from Mr Steadman that you found the little girl. That is a relief. I fully intended to put her into the care of someone responsible in the Watch myself. But you took care of her yourself, which is admirable.'

Milly. Where was she, I wondered? And what, assuming that she had made it back home through the flaming streets of the City, was she thinking about now? One thing I knew was that she wouldn't, in spite of having nearly been killed, go to the police. Mr Steadman and his cronies knew that they had Milly's unquestioning silence, no matter what. Working girls don't talk. Not usually. But then this wasn't usual because this could involve her own father selling her for slaughter. Mr Webb had said that Milly's father hadn't known what had been going on or rather that was the impression he had given me. But I wondered. I also, for my own satisfaction, had to see Milly again myself.

'Mr Matthews,' I said, 'one of the men who was killed with Mr Andrews was a Mr Webb. His wife—'

'Oh, yes.' Dean Matthews frowned. 'Poor woman. Our ladies are looking after Mrs Webb and her children in the crypt. She is really not strong enough to be left alone as yet.'

'No.' I really had to fight to hide my disgust. Webb's wife had known all about Milly and her sisters and what they did for her husband. But then that was going to make what I was about to do all the easier. I am not by nature a cruel man. I don't find it easy to make people cry.

'Mr Matthews,' I said, 'do you think it would be all right for me to go and see Mrs Webb? Offer my condolences?'

He smiled. 'I imagine so,' he said. 'But do be careful as you go, won't you?' He looked around at the mud-dust- and rubble-caked steps and his face dropped once again. 'We don't want any more casualties, do we?'

I began to walk towards the Great West door.

Just before I drew level with him, Mr Matthews said, 'But most of us didn't succumb to either the enemy without or the enemy within, did we?'

I moved myself closer to him very quickly now. Did he know? In spite of everything that Steadman had told me to the contrary, did the Dean really know what had happened on the night of 29 December 1940? Just the thought that he might, made me flush with anger. Could this man possibly be one of 'them'? Well, my mate Ernie Sutton was a Mason . . .

'The enemy within?' I said. 'What, with respect Mr Matthews, does that mean?'

He blinked. No doubt somewhat taken aback by the violence of my tone, the straightness of my face.

'Well, the structure of the cathedral, of course,' he said. I looked and looked again at his face for any signs of untruth or dissembling, but I couldn't find any. 'As I think I said to you many hours ago, Mr Hancock, we fight both the Nazis, the enemy without, and the fragile and combustible structure of the cathedral, the enemy within. Sir Christopher Wren did not intend his great building to be attacked in this fashion.'

I left a slightly offended Mr Matthews and went into the cathedral and down into the crypt. Of all the people I'd seen in the crypt the previous night, only the exhausted-looking Mrs Webb and her children remained. The kids, who were being given tea by the first-aid ladies, seemed calm enough but the woman, sitting on her own, over by what looked like a charred and headless torso, smoked with wildly shaking hands.

As I sat down next to her, Mrs Webb tipped her head at the torso and said, 'They say, these ladies here, that that was a statue from the old cathedral, the one what burnt down in the Great Fire of London. A saint, burnt and without its head.'

I looked at it. 'Tortured,' I said. 'It looks tortured.'

'Yes.'

I didn't look at her. I wasn't sorry for her loss. 'You and your husband tortured Milly Chivers and her sister, in a way,' I said, not able to keep back what I wanted to say any longer. 'Where does she live, Mrs Webb? Where is Milly now?'

There was a pause and she just managed to get out

'I . . .' before I said, 'And don't try to make anything up, Mrs Webb. If you do, I'll just go out and get the coppers right now.'

It was difficult to know how bad the building on Garlick Hill where the Chivers family lived really was. Although described to me as a Rookery, it wasn't the sort of place I'd envisaged such a crime-ridden relic of the past to look like. Rookeries to my way of thinking were great big wooden buildings, usually held up by rough timber piers, hanging over fathoms of thick London mud. I suppose that what I expected was something out of Dickens. What I found was a crumbling Edwardian building whose gutters had been blown off by the bombing and the pavements around which were covered with glass, plaster, broken stone and sewage. The smell was no worse than it was at home in the East End, although this being the City, and after the night of fire we'd all just had, smoke was uppermost amongst the terrible stinks that day. The spicy smell of burnt incense from all the churches, of fine old wood, polished and preserved by centuries of loving care, the dull crackly smell of paper and, of course, the overriding stench of cooked meat. As I went in to what was a dark, rubbish-covered hall, I found myself breathing very lightly in case I actually took in any ash from a burnt human body. I know that the Hindus cremate their dead and I understand all the arguments for it on the grounds of hygiene, but I can't bear it. To me, a burning human body will always bring to mind the Great War, now this war too.

Mrs Webb had described this building as 'flats', but it was more a rooming house, really. The Webbs, probably because of their business 'interests' in Milly and her family, had two rooms on the first floor; the Chivers family had only had one. I stood outside it for a second, trying to listen for any noises inside before I knocked. At first no one answered and there was no sound from inside. I knocked again. I was determined not to speak or shout. I didn't want Milly, should she be inside, to know it was me. If she knew that, she almost certainly wouldn't come to the door. I decided on one final try and knocked again. It was after that third time that I heard a cough from right behind the door. It was followed by a short, frightened gasp.

I left it a few seconds to see what might happen and

then I turned the door handle and pushed on the door with my shoulder. To my surprise it came open easily and let me in to a place that had a very different smell from that of the burning human body.

The room, which couldn't have been any more than ten feet by fifteen feet, smelt of sour bodies and booze. Not a decent beer smell, or even something sweet and alcoholic like sherry; it was the stench of cheap gin. At first I couldn't quite work out what I was looking at because of the rough piece of grey cloth that kept on flapping into my face. But then I saw that the room was divided in two by this thing. On one side was a single bed with a bloke laying flat out on top of it. He had a bottle in one hand and, strangely for a drunk, which he surely was, a book in the other. But then George Chivers had by all accounts been an educated man. He had been an architect. From the way his face looked, lined deeper than the bloody underground, that could have been fifteen, twenty or even more years ago. On the other side of the curtain was a rather tidier double bed with a washstand at the side of it. On the walls around the bed cigarette cards of film stars were pinned up in haphazard groups. A young girl in a dirty brassiere and knickers sat on this bed and beside her, much prettier than the girl and fully clothed, was Milly. She looked up at me with utter contempt on her face.

'What do you want?' she said. 'How did you get here?'

I nodded towards the other girl and said, 'Is that your sister? Is that—'

'Never mind who that is!' Milly said as she got off the bed and began to move towards me. 'What do you want, Mr Hancock? Do you want a hand-job, do you?'

'No! No!' I said and saw the other girl smirk as I did so. 'Milly, I . . . You can't live like this!'

The man on the bed turned over and snorted like a pig. I looked at him for a moment and, now I regarded him more closely, I saw that his features were fine, that he was not at all a bad-looking man. Or at least he hadn't been so once.

'Milly, this has to stop,' I said.

'Does it?' She gave me such a cynical look! But then I knew that I was not convinced I was right myself. People involved in that life, as I know only too well from Hannah, have rather different priorities. What they look upon as taking care of themselves, people like me see only as something wrong, something they should be saved from doing.

Although she was so much smaller than me, Milly hustled me out of that room and back into the hall with quite a bit of power behind her hands. As she shut the door behind me, she turned upon me angrily. 'You think that because you and me was pals for a bit last night, you can tell me what to do, do you?'

'Milly, those men . . .'

'Those men bought me from Webb, but now he's dead and the men are Gawd alone knows where!'

I bent down and I looked her in the eye. 'Milly, you killed Webb,' I said. 'You killed him!'

'So did you tell the coppers or didn't you?' she said as she faced me down, her arms folded defiantly over her chest.

I didn't answer. I didn't know what to say. I hadn't and wouldn't ever tell the police about what Milly had done. Even if I'd wanted to, the girl's very presence would give the lie to Mr Steadman's story and that, as I knew, was not something that was going to be at all easily challenged.

Milly sighed and then leaned against the smutted wall and lit up a fag. 'I don't know who them men were last night, Mr Hancock,' she said. 'They used to work with me dad, but that was before I was born and that's all I know. Dad, as far as I know, thought the blokes just wanted me for the usual. You know . . .' She briefly looked away. 'You can see how Dad is! He just sent them off to Webb and he arranged it all. As long as Dad's got a bottle, well, he don't care too much about who gives it to him or why.' She then looked me in the eyes with a pleading expression on her thin, pale face. 'But he's not bad! Dad's just, well . . . Dad would never have sold me to be murdered! I don't believe it! Not like that fucking Webb! Webb deserved to die! Webb . . . I hated him, and his missus, I . . .'

Her words fizzled out into a fit of childlike sobbing. I wanted to put my arm around her shoulders, to offer her some sort of comfort. But I knew that Milly would only associate that with what was done to her in the course of her 'business'. She could never, as Hannah always said of child prostitutes, have any sort of normal or even friendly relationship with a man. She was ruined.

'Milly,' I said after a short pause. 'There are people

who can help you. Even in wartime; you don't have to live like this.'

I was thinking of people like the Barnardo's organisation. I was even thinking that perhaps my own family could look after Milly – until I remembered how easy her killing of Webb had been. She was only a child, but how could I allow my mother and sisters to live with someone, even though a nipper, who could finish off a person as calmly as if she were wringing the neck of a chicken? I wondered whether Mr Webb had been Milly's first and only victim.

Once the sobbing had stopped, Milly dried her eyes. 'I couldn't leave Dad,' she said, 'or Rita. Who'd look after them?'

'You and Rita and all of your brothers and sisters could be taken care of . . .'

'Yeah, without Dad,' she said bitterly. And then she added, 'No. No, I couldn't do that. I could never leave him.'

'Milly, your father sold you!'

'My dad's a drinker who don't know what he's doing!' she replied. 'He's weak! He don't mean no harm! He never meant no harm to Mum!'

Webb had said that, in his opinion, George Chivers, albeit indirectly, had killed Milly's mother. The girl must have seen that flash through my mind.

'Dad never killed Mum,' she said sadly, as if she was so weary of answering that question. 'She just got wore out and died.'

I lit a fag up too now and leaned against the wall beside Milly. 'Don't you worry, Milly, about getting worn out and dying like your mum?'

'I dunno.' She shrugged. 'But without Webb about I stand more of a chance. More money for me and the others now anyway.'

'And Mrs Webb?'

'Rosina?' Milly laughed. 'On her own she's about as frightening as a bowl of cherries. Me and Rita can handle Rosina.' And then she frowned. 'Does Rosina know I killed her old man?' She didn't look scared about this at all, just curious.

'No one knows you killed Mr Webb except for Mr Rolls, who will eventually stand trial for Mr Phillips's death,' I said. 'And me, but for lots of reasons, I'm not saying anything.'

A voice from one of the other rooms down the hall rang out, 'Fuck off, you old bitch!'

Milly and I ignored it. Then she said, 'The only thing that Dad ever said to me about Mr Rolls was that he was a Mason. He said they was honourable men, that he'd wanted to be one himself one day. But then the drink took him.' She looked up at me. 'My dad would have been very powerful if he'd been one of them, wouldn't he? I'll never hear from anyone about what really happened in the cathedral, will I?'

'No.'

And then as the horror and the enormity of what had happened to both of us in St Paul's hit her she suddenly clung to my arm and said, 'Fucking hell, they wanted to kill us! They wanted to *kill* us! Why did they want to do that?'

I said that I didn't know. There was no point trying to explain it all to Milly. Rolls would certainly not go into what had happened in the cathedral, even at his trial. Even if he wanted to talk, he wouldn't be allowed to do so. Mr Steadman and probably many, many more men, would make certain of that.

I put my hand on Milly's shoulder and said, 'Who

can know what horrible, twisted habits and desires men have?'

She looked up at me and I saw in her eyes that she had a fair idea about a few of those.

'Milly,' I said, 'in your line of work you will meet blokes who want to do really bad things. You met some last night and I've no doubt that you'll meet more in the years to come. I know you say you have to do this . . .'

'When Dad needs drink he needs drink,' she said. 'He can't wait for us to get paid at the end of the week for doing our nice typing jobs! Me and Rita, we can make money just like that.' She clicked her fingers. 'And anyway, I've a habit of my own too.' She put her head down in what looked like shame.

Back in the cathedral she'd said she smoked opium. Rolls and Smith had given her some but not enough, apparently, to make her compliant with their wishes. Milly had to have a fairly big habit, I imagined. At that moment she looked very young for her age but with opium in her life, even without the odious Webb to feed it to her, she wouldn't look young for long. Milly would, if she needed to, I knew, find her own opium supplier pretty sharpish now.

I wanted to help her, I even left her one of my cards and told her to call me if she was ever in trouble. But I know that she won't. Milly loves her useless alcoholic father and she is herself addicted to a drug that will almost certainly kill her. I kissed her gently on the top of her head and then I left without once looking back at her. I heard her open the door back into her room and go inside. As she shut it behind her a bloke, her father, I imagine, said, 'Have you been working, Milly dear? How much did you get paid?'

So strange to hear a voice like that, smooth and educated, in a building that stank of stale booze, sewage and violent sex.

Chapter Twenty

I didn't know what to expect when I got back to Annie's place. I knew that where she was, just to the north in Finsbury, hadn't been as badly hit as the City, but the old girl could still very easily have bought it. Even the outskirts of the Square Mile are only thinly populated – Hitler knew what he was doing when he ordered the raid for a Sunday night – and there hadn't been many ordinary people, let alone any firemen, available for blazes outside the centre. All the firemen had had to work on the big things – or, to be more accurate, they'd had to concentrate their efforts on St Paul's Cathedral. But as I turned into Wilmington Square I was very quickly reassured that Annie was all right. Sitting on an old kitchen chair on the pavement, Annie was at the centre of a group of women, drinking tea from a very delicate china cup.

'Oh, there's my nephew!' I heard her call out. She waved a clawed, arthritic hand at me and I smiled and waved back at her. Two of the women with her turned round to look in my direction, one of them, wearing a tightly wrapped scarf around her head, puffed on what looked like a cigar. I later learned that it wasn't a cigar at all. This woman was very hard up and had actually taken to smoking dried leaves.

Annie's flat hadn't taken any damage during the course of the night and so when she'd finished talking to her neighbours, she took me inside to her kitchen and put the kettle on the range.

'Right firework display last night, wasn't it?' she said as she cleared a pile of tea towels from off her most comfortable chair and told me to sit down. She looked at me. 'Gawd blimey, your face is a bit of a mess, Frank!'

I didn't make any sort of comment.

Annie said, 'I sat in here and, I'll be honest with you, Frank, I prepared to meet my maker!'

Annie asked me what I'd done with myself all night long. I told her I'd been holed up in the cathedral crypt. I didn't give her any details about what had happened to me while I was there, but I did tell her how wonderful the St Paul's watchmen had been. Because they had. I was truly convinced by this time that the Dean had indeed had nothing to do with, or any knowledge of, Rolls and his sickening plans for the cathedral. Mr Matthews had simply led the watchmen magnificently, urging them and himself ever onwards to greater feats of endurance up in those hellish galleries on those awful burning rooftops. Mr Churchill, too, had played his part. The firemen had been told to save the cathedral on his orders and no one in their right mind ever disobeys Winnie.

As Annie sat down beside me to watch the kettle boil she said, 'So, I bet you met a few characters down in that crypt!'

I smiled and then for some reason I don't think I'll ever be able to fathom, I told Annie about Milly. Why I'd tell an old lady about a child prostitute was a mystery then and, although it is less of a mystery now, I still don't know exactly what started me off about it in the first place. I told her about how Milly's father had been an architect, how he'd turned to drink and how the girl and her sister basically supported him.

'She was, you know, sort of owned by another man,' I said referring to Webb. 'But he's out of the picture now.'

Annie looked at me very matter-of-factly and nodded. 'A pimp,' she said. 'Best off without him.'

I had resisted using the word pimp myself but Annie seemed to employ it without any embarrassment. I found myself, just for a moment, looking away.

'The girl's doing what she has to to keep her father,' Annie said. 'You might want to help her, Frank, but you can't. One way or another it'll all work out in the end whether you do anything or not.'

I looked back at her then and I know that I was frowning.

Annie smiled. 'Oh, you look so serious!' she said.

I almost felt that she was mocking me in a way. I wondered, in fact, whether she might know about Hannah and how I wanted to 'help' her, one way or another. But Annie didn't know. She did, however, have some experience in these matters that I had no idea about.

'Listen, Frank,' she said, 'I'll tell you something

now that you will find shocking. Just between you and me, it'll be. It's a secret, and it isn't known to your mother or your sisters. It wasn't even known by your father. Your grandfather, my brother, he knew. But then he had to because he was there when it happened.'

'When what happened?' I asked.

'When Herbert and Emily Hancock took me in,' Annie said. 'Your grandfather, Francis Hancock, who you was named for, was ten.' Seeing the look of confusion on my face Annie continued, 'Your great-grandparents were poor. They lived—'

'On Flower and Dean Street in Spitalfields,' I said. 'I remember.'

'Yes.' Annie smiled. 'And my mother lived in the flat beside them. My mother was a prostitute and she was mad, quite mad.' Annie's smile faded. 'Like you.'

I was shocked. I had lived all my life with the idea that Annie was my great-aunt. The story of how my great-grandfather had pulled his wife, his son Francis and daughter Annie out of the poverty of Flower and Dean Street was well known. Unlike most of the people in that area he'd succumbed to neither pimping nor robbery but had literally blasted his way out as a boxer. The money that Herbert made eventually allowed his son Francis to move to West Ham and start his own building company. He went into undertaking some years later, Hancock and Co. actually coming into being in 1885.

'Emily couldn't have any more children after she had Francis,' Annie said as she poured the water from the kettle on to the few leaves she'd sprinkled into her old brown teapot. 'The girl next door, my mother, didn't want a kid, it was bad for business.' What she said next she said very straight and without emotion. 'Herbert and Emily paid her some money and the girl – Lavinia, she was called – gave me to them.'

'Annie . . .'

She leaned forward and patted my hand. 'She wasn't a bad girl, Lavinia,' Annie said. 'I was only a baby when she sold me and I used to go and see her sometimes when I was older, when I heard her crying. She cried for the loss of me and for her other child, the one that had got her into trouble in the first place. I didn't know any of that at the time. All I knew was that the lady next door to us was pretty and well-spoken and very, very sad.'

'Annie,' I said, 'why are you telling me all this?'

Annie raised a finger up and said, 'Listen. When I've done you can have your tea and we'll never talk of this again. Now then . . . I was about eight when we moved out of Flower and Dean Street. Dad was becoming a bit famous in the East End and so we went to live over on the Mile End Road. I forgot about Lavinia. Then one day when I was sixteen, my dad took me over to the asylum at Claybury.'

I shivered at the sound of that name. How many times had I wondered when or if the nurses from Claybury would come for me with their straight-jackets and their cold baths and put me in that terrible cold hospital with all the other mad, staring lunatics?

'He didn't tell me why we were going,' Annie said. 'But once we were there we met this old man who was standing beside the bed of what looked to me like a little old lady. The bloke, who was very smart with a shiny black top hat and a cane, told Dad that his daughter was dying. He said that he'd have to make our meeting quick because someone like him couldn't possibly be seen in a place like Claybury. He stared at me long and hard and then he gave something in an envelope to my dad and then we left.' She took a deep breath in and then let it out with a sigh. 'The dying woman was Lavinia and the smart old man was her father. I don't know who the family are, but I do know that she was that man's only child and I was his only grandchild. What he gave my dad, your great-grandfather, was the keys to this house, for me. It was my inheritance.'

'Annie,' I said, 'I always, well, the girls and I always thought that well, maybe you were on the stage and—'

She laughed. 'I got this place from money showing my ankles to bankers? No, no, no,' she said. 'This house was given to me. Dad gave me the keys without a word when I was twenty-one and I rented out much of it to others then as I do now. I thought Dad had bought it for me and I couldn't understand why my brother Francis wasn't jealous!' She leaned forward towards me then. 'But Mum had died when I was eighteen and when Dad died four years afterwards, it was Francis who told me the truth. My blood's from the aristocracy, but my mother was mad. Francis told me Lavinia had her first baby because she let a man take advantage of her. I came along once she was on the streets. Whether she was born mad or became that way, I don't know. But what I do know is that old man, my grandfather, risked the world knowing his shame because he wanted to give me, his only living grandchild, something from him.'

'And Lavinia,' I said. 'Something from her too.'

Annie shrugged. 'I don't know about that,' she said. 'The poor thing looked all but dead by that time to me. But something like love was coming through. Maybe the old man feared I'd become mad like my mother and wanted to give me something so I wouldn't walk the streets raving. I loved your great-grandfather and grandmother, Frank, they were my mum and dad. But blood is very powerful and just as my grandfather wanted to give me something, so this little girl of yours wants to do whatever she can for her father.'

'He sells her!'

'My mother sold me! Herbert and Emily could've been anyone! Flower and Dean Street was known for its crime and its easy women in those days!' Annie poured tea into cups for us both and loaded them with sugar. She didn't have any milk that day. 'I know you say that this girl's father sold her for drink money, but even if he did do that, if she wants to stand by him, then that is what she wants to do. They're blood, Frank, and there is absolutely nothing anyone who isn't blood can do about that. She's gone back to him and you must leave it alone.' She shook her head. 'Blood is such a curse!'

We drank our tea in silence. I'd known as soon as I'd left Milly's terrible building that I would probably never see the girl again. Who was I, a lunatic, to interfere with anyone? The mad were, I knew, often made incapable of having children in places like Claybury and maybe that was fitting and right. Annie had never had any children and I thought that maybe that was because of her feelings about who her real mother had been.

'Yes,' Annie said simply, 'you're quite right there, Frank. What if I'd given birth to someone like Lavinia? What would I have told the baby's father? What would people who knew me as a Hancock think?

None of them were barmy! I couldn't embarrass my brother like that! Francis was a lovely man, he—'

'Granddad wouldn't have blamed you!' I said. 'God, Annie, is that why you never married? Is that why you live all on your own?'

She waited a moment before she nodded and then she said, 'Barmy in its own way, too, that is.' And then she smiled again. 'Maybe that's why I like you so much, Frank. With all your running about and your fears and your nightmares, you're sad like my mother and even though you're not my own blood, I feel a closeness with you I don't feel with anyone else. You, Frank,' she said finally, 'are the only person on this earth I am close enough to that I would die for.'

I drank my tea in silence, shaking. Just like Mr Steadman, Annie had entrusted me with a secret I could never tell anyone. I was well beyond exhausted and I think that if I hadn't got the point of what Annie was saying, I would have been angry. But my great-aunt, as well as my mother, my sisters, my nephew and my niece, even Hannah, loved me. What was more, they didn't have to spill anybody's blood in order to prove it. Not at that moment. What I had to understand, however, was the way that could change.

As I walked through the shattered streets of the City, beginning my long walk home from Annie's, I thought about what Mr Rolls, Mr Steadman, the Dean, Milly and everyone had been doing in St Paul's Cathedral only one night before. War makes desperate people of us all. The possibility of defeat and destruction of a place or a way of life that is loved is painful to think about. People over the ages have done whatever they felt they had to to protect their families and loved ones. Milly went out that night to earn some money for her father, the Dean risked his life on the roof of the cathedral not just once but many times, Mr Steadman fought against a man and a way of thinking he thought was wrong. And Mr Rolls and the men who followed him? In common with Mr Steadman, I can't put aside the notion that Mr Rolls might have enjoyed the killing that he took part in, but I can't prove that he did so, either. What I do know is that he tried to protect something very precious, St Paul's Cathedral, with something very powerful, blood. To him, I think, it was the most effective thing he could do. War pushes you into these corners! War makes you get things wrong because blood on its own isn't powerful at all, that's just a medieval story, that is. Blood is only strong because of what we do to preserve our own blood – whether it's the blood of our family, our loved ones, or the blood of our nation.

St Paul's Cathedral stands, if not whole, then at least proud and upright now. Blood didn't save it, water didn't save it, luck or prayer or the position of the stars in the sky didn't save it. St Paul's was saved by people.

Author's Note

St Paul's Cathedral

St Paul the Apostle (as well as, later on, St Thomas Becket) is the patron saint of the City of London. A St Paul's cathedral church has existed on the site of the current building since 604 when it was founded by the Roman saint, Mellitus. Its fortunes have always been very closely connected to the city it represents and there have been several St Paul's cathedrals on Ludgate Hill over the centuries. The most famous being, prior to the current incarnation, the medieval cathedral which was destroyed by the Great Fire of London in 1666.

The architect chosen to build a new cathedral for

London on the ashes of the old one was Sir Christopher Wren (1632–1723). A gifted draughtsman, Freemason and man of faith, he was a superstar of his time. Wren's aim was to build something that fulfilled his belief that 'architecture aims at eternity'. St Paul's should be, Wren thought, eternal. In fact, the story of the stone that Wren used as a marker point for the centre of the cathedral dome illustrates this belief.

During the building of the foundations for the current church, workmen found a broken gravestone bearing the inscription 'Resurgam'. This means 'I shall rise again' and it is therefore significant that Wren used this stone as the marker for the very apex of his dome, the closest point of his church to heaven.

St Paul's Watch was established in 1915 by Canon Alexander and Surveyor Mervyn Macartney. The idea was to recruit architects and other professionals to help protect St Paul's from Zeppelin attack during the First World War. In 1939, the Watch was re-formed by Dean Matthews to counter Hitler's nightly attacks on the capital. Two hundred and fifty architects, professionals and cathedral staff were involved, including the Poet Laureate, John Betjeman. During the course of the

Second World War, St Paul's suffered damage to the high altar and the north transept and, on the night of 29 December 1940, suffered bombardment by incendiary bombs. On that fateful night the then Prime Minister, Winston Churchill, phoned the city authorities and said that, 'at all costs St Paul's must be saved'. So powerful had the cathedral become as a symbol of beauty, national pride and resistance to oppression by Londoners of all races and religions, that it was absolutely essential that it survive.

Aleister Crowley
1875–1947

Aleister Crowley was born into a wealthy English family. His mother was a religious woman and belonged to a strict non-conformist Christian sect called the Plymouth Brethren. Aleister Crowley, however, was a rebellious child. When he was eleven, his mother caught him masturbating; he delighted in her disgust and in the name she called him, 'The Beast'. In years to come he would be known by this name as well as that of 'Beast 666' and 'The Wickedest Man in the World'.

In 1895, Crowley went to Cambridge University where, whilst still a student, he published several volumes of sex poetry. An increasing fascination with the occult led Crowley, three years later, to be initiated into a magical society called The Order of the Golden Dawn. He rose through its ranks quickly and was an acknowledged Freemason at that time too.

Inherited wealth allowed Crowley to travel and also to devote himself to the study of the extreme ends of occultism and conjuration that the Golden Dawn itself frowned upon. It was whilst on honeymoon with his wife, Rose Kelly, in Egypt that Crowley was 'contacted' by a spirit he called Aiwass. It was Aiwass who dictated to Crowley his *Book of Laws* from which Crowley's most famous saying, 'Do what thou wilt shall be the whole of the law' is taken. From this point on Crowley saw himself as a sort of evil messiah, ushering in a new post-Christian age of vice and depravity. This new 'religion' he called Thelema and, in 1920, he went to live in Cefalu in Sicily in order to found a 'Temple of Thelema'. There with his mistress

Leah Hirsig and an often-shifting band of followers, Crowley attempted to raise ancient gods, sacrificed animals and, possibly, human beings too, and had a huge amount of drug-addled sex. Vile rumours abounded which prompted Italy's then leader, Benito Mussolini – an avowed enemy of Freemasonry himself – to expel Crowley and his followers in 1923.

A heroin and cocaine addict for most of his adult life, Crowley died in Hastings in 1947. Whether he was indeed a very powerful magician or just a sex-obsessed charlatan is a question that still remains largely unanswered to this day.

Last Rights

Barbara Nadel

October 1940: The London borough of West Ham is suffering another night of horrific bombing and undertaker Francis Hancock is caught in the chaos. A man lurches towards him through the rubble screaming about being stabbed but there's no visible wound and Francis dismisses him as a madman . . . until the man's body turns up at his funeral parlour, two days later.

Suspecting foul play, Francis feels compelled to discover what really happened that night – but as he finds himself pitted against violent thugs, an impenetrable network of lies and his own fragile sanity, he realises that there are people who want the truth to stay dead and buried . . .

Praise for Barbara Nadel's novels:

'Unusual and very well-written' *Sunday Telegraph*

'Impeccable mystery plotting, exotic and atmospheric' *Guardian*

'Gripping and highly recommended' *Time Out*

'Intelligent and captivating' *The Sunday Times*

978 0 7553 2136 0

headline

After the Mourning

Barbara Nadel

It's the London Blitz of 1940, and undertaker Francis Hancock has seen the worst that humanity can do to itself. Why then does the murder of a young gypsy girl in Epping Forest move him so much?

Travellers, gypsies, the homeless, deserters and German spies inhabit this stretch of open ground that was once her home. Francis knows it's not wise to delve into this human melting pot, but he is drawn to the exotic customs of the gypsies, their music and magic.

But as he further investigates the slaughter of the girl, the death toll rises and Francis begins to uncover a much bigger conspiracy, at the heart of which lies something even the German *Führer* is prepared to kill for . . .

Praise for *Last Rights*, the first in the Francis Hancock series:

'A great depiction of the period and a touchingly involuntary new sleuth' *Guardian*

'A gripping and unusual detective story, vivid and poignant' *Literary Review*

'She confidently and convincingly paints a grim picture of a bombed-out east London . . . curious and memorable' *Time Out*

978 0 7553 2138 4

headline